No Time for Eulogy

Richard D. Thielmann

All rights reserved. No part of this book shall be reproduced or transmitted in any form or by any means, electronic, mechanical, magnetic, photographic including photocopying, recording or by any information storage and retrieval system, without prior written permission of the publisher. No patent liability is assumed with respect to the use of the information contained herein. Although every precaution has been taken in the preparation of this book, the publisher and author assume no responsibility for errors or omissions. Neither is any liability assumed for damages resulting from the use of the information contained herein.

Copyright © 2011 by Richard D. Thielmann

ISBN 978-0-7414-6933-5 Paperback
ISBN 978-0-7414-6934-2 eBook

Printed in the United States of America

This is a work of fiction. Names, characters, places, and incidents either are the product of the author's imagination or are used fictitiously. Any resemblance to actual events or locales or persons, living or dead, is entirely coincidental.

Published December 2011

INFINITY PUBLISHING
1094 New DeHaven Street, Suite 100
West Conshohocken, PA 19428-2713
Toll-free (877) BUY BOOK
Local Phone (610) 941-9999
Fax (610) 941-9959
Info@buybooksontheweb.com
www.buybooksontheweb.com

Other works by Richard D. Thielmann

A Matter of Revenge

The Price of Redemption

A Sense of Rage

A Pattern of Deceit

1.

Bad news comes like a slap in the face. It's an ugly intrusion that jars your psyche. When it is about someone else the shock wears off rather quickly and quiet relief sets in with the realization the unpleasant burden for dealing with the bad news rests elsewhere. You are merely a bystander splashed with the mud of its coincidental consequences. When it is your deal, however, you become knee-deep in the emotional muck.

This was the day Jack Phillips would get his slap and it would be very personal. The day was already lousy and it was only ten o'clock. With unresolved client problems, he paced his office as if each step might shake some resolution into his head. The parading he did around his office wasn't working and he finally resorted to the tried and true technique of staring out the window. That didn't help either, but he liked the view. It was westward ho; overlooking the scramble of buildings and the spread of urban Columbus sprawl. Way out there somewhere Jack knew there still had to be some farm land.

As he stared, his eyes glazed over and his thoughts slid away into some mental cavern that swallows up reality to provide a cavalcade of fantasy, or deeper yet, to melancholia. Sometimes out of such a brain pit comes a gem of an idea which solves a problem. Unfortunately sometimes there comes self doubt, self pity, or the replay of unpleasant memories. This time there would be no chance to find out which way it would go.

From the darkness of that near-trance Jack heard his office door open and close behind him. Figuring it was one of his partners who liked to bounce in unannounced; he didn't turn around, but waited to see which one and what would be said.

It always amazed him when they did that sort of thing, but they were younger and not as caught with convention – code for courtesy – and the courtesy that he might have liked.

He could have put a stop to them doing it, but then that would have changed the give and take dynamics on which their partnership had thrived. Whoever it was said nothing. Then a faint scent of her perfume, ever so lightly, let him know it was Janet.

Jack turned to see Janet Nelson agonize in a series of distorted facial expressions and suffer the discomfort of trying to get her legs positioned as she attempted to stay calm on the sofa near the far wall of his office. She was not doing very well with her efforts. She was a tall, relatively thin young woman with auburn hair and green eyes, and strikingly beautiful. Her awkward maneuvering on the sofa belied the athletic ability he knew she possessed. And she was a fabulous dancer.

Janet sighed, took in a huge gulp of air in order to balance herself, sniffed several times, and seemed to be settled. Jack could see how distraught she was. The sniffs were more than likely the result of crying. She had come into his office without warning, without saying a word, and had thrown herself on the sofa in a dramatic, demanding-attention action. Janet had his attention. She wanted it, she got it. As far as he was concerned, she deserved it.

They had worked together for more than ten years in the advertising business, a business that can be nasty at best and brutalizing at worst. The last five years they had been partners in their own ad agency along with Byron Adams. They had been successful in garnering several large regional companies as clients that wanted to go national with their advertising programs. Jack, Janet, and Byron were doing quite well financially. The fact that the three of them were doing well financially and professionally did not translate so nicely into doing well with their personal lives, especially Janet's.

Janet and Jack had never been lovers, but circumstances teetered on that aspect several times only to tip away from the kind of intimacy he thought she wanted. It's not easy defining and maintaining a relationship with a woman when there is no romantic intimacy. They had another kind of intimacy, however, that comes from long hours of closely working together. There were shared frustrations, self-confessed doubts, personal revelations, and the heady almost intoxicating euphoria of success. Those long hours together created a bond, a marriage of sorts that presumes something that may not really be there. Presumes mutual affection, Jack assessed. Respect and admiration are not affection. She had misread him, but maybe he gave the wrong signals. In any case, their relationship didn't go the way she wanted.

They remained friends, fortunately, very close friends, even after she married Ben Grossman. Jack figured marrying Ben was a reaction from not being able to nail him down. He thought that was what she wanted, but understood it might be his ego talking. In any case, Jack wasn't ready to get married. She might be the right person, but he wasn't ready. The subject of sex never had come up, but all the words and touches and life connections were there. It just did not seem right for him. He was confused about his feelings, not able to get past the remorse he felt for a failed marriage and disintegrated family. Jack assumed he was better off without the commitment. It was a moot point, certainly; she married someone else and, happily for Jack, remained his business partner. He recognized that Janet was superbly creative and very savvy about the advertising business.

Right now, by all accounts, her marriage to Ben was coming unglued; a free fall to disaster and that was taking a toll on her. She was not productive with either the running of the agency or in developing creative output for the clients. Her brain was stagnant, numbed by the turmoil of her dying relationship with Ben. Now, all of that emotion was in front of Jack.

"You look as if you slept in those clothes last night."

He said the words carefully, trying not to be unkind, but not ducking the reality. She looked like hell.

"I did."

"Ah, yes, the honesty. Why…why would that be necessary?"

She didn't answer, just looked at him. There was that plaintive, I'm-about-to-die look about her, that manipulative, helpless look of the lamb-to-slaughter, and then changing to the wry smile as if to suggest the irony of a film noir movie, as if to suggest that he must answer his own question.

"Hello," he spouted. "Don't look at me like that. We've been together too long for that kind of stuff. Are you dumping him or what? Don't play coy about it with me. We've got an agency to run, clients to serve, and a goddamn mountain of bills to be paid."

He knew he wasn't being very supportive, but that look she gave him made him lose his patience quicker than he would have liked. And he knew he should have been more comforting, put his arm around her shoulder or maybe even given her a hug. But he held back. Touching might be dangerous at this point, at least for him. She would like it, he figured.

"He has another woman. He wants to move to Las Vegas."

"You're kidding. Ben, Mr. Stable, Mr. Reliable, the man who treats you like the princess you feel you are."

She gave him a forlorn look. His sarcasm wasn't nice right now, but he couldn't resist the shot.

Jack wasn't surprised, really and did not want her to know that. Ben was a hustler, both in business and with women. Janet had been hustled. She was his wife at a certain point in time as he was passing through and it was convenient. Nothing in business or in personal relationships was permanent with Ben. Ben was the same kind of guy who sold patent medicine in the old West, sold swamp land in Florida, and never, but never considered settling for a life others would call normal. He was all for the abnormal, the transient, and the pursuit of his and only his happiness.

"How could I have been so stupid?"

She held her head with her hands as if cupping a wilted flower.

That question, along with a number of other questions women pose, should not, must not be answered.

He simply shook his head. His gesture conveyed everything required and he was off the hook. He wanted to be supportive, but did not want to be trapped into being the support system for the rejected woman. There was a balance he had to achieve. He had his own problems.

"I know things are bad for you, Janet, but we've got to get a new campaign together for Tilden Dairy. Two weeks is all we have. Milk is set, but there's a cheese unit that needs work…then yogurt has to be brought on line…

I know, I know."

"Home Grilled needs a menu work over and Bistro American has four new markets that have to have prep for new restaurant openings…for PR and ads."

"I know, I know."

"We have lots of work to do."

Jack wasn't unsympathetic, but there was so much to accomplish in a short time and he needed her to focus on the agency not on loser Ben. He knew she could do it; she just needed to get in gear. Besides, he did not want to get into the details of the failed marriage. Let her tell that stuff to one of her lady friends or her shrink.

"I know," she sighed.

"Listen, I realize this thing with Ben has you upset, but the best way to handle this in my opinion, and hey, I've known you for awhile and have some kind of idea what makes you tick…the best way would be to throw your creative energy into Phillips, Nelson, and Adams Advertising and forget what's-his-name. Right here with us is where your head should be."

She repeated the words *what's-his-name* and laughed. He knew he had her on the right track.

His phone rang and he looked at the panel that showed every light blinking. The agency seemed flooded with calls. Not usual, but maybe a good thing. This time it was not a good thing.

"Yes, Kari?"

"Your friend Mr. Parker is on the line."

Jack stared west again, out the window towards Dublin, taking time before he answered. Somehow, subconsciously resisting the call, wondering why; and why would Bill be calling him so early in the day. His calls usually came late in the day when he wanted Jack to meet him at some bar or club where he would regale him with the best investment there ever was.

Jack did not want to take this call right now and debated with himself in refusing it. On the other hand, it could be a way to break free of Janet. He was on guard when he pushed the button.

"Jack?"

"Yes."

"Damn, Jack, I'm real sorry…"

"About what?"

"Have you seen the news? On television…"

"No, what's going on?"

"It's about J.W. He's….oh, Lord. Jack…God I hate to be the one…"

"What about J.W.?"

Jack held the receiver so tightly his hand started to hurt.

"It's on the news…I thought…"

"What," Jack snapped.

"He's…"

He waited for Bill to say it, but he knew Bill could not and there was that shriek of awareness that raced through Jack's head screaming that his son was dead.

"J.W. is dead isn't he?" Jack whispered.

There it was. The bad news had arrived and it was more than a slap in the face.

"Yeah…sorry Jack, I'm damned sorry. Is there anything…"

It was blunt force trauma like someone had blindsided him with a baseball bat. He didn't wait for Bill to finish. He dropped the phone onto its cradle and used a remote to turn on the TV nestled into the side wall cabinet. There was a story in progress from LA and he muted the sound. The phone rang again.

"Yes."

"The phone lines are all for you Mr. Phillips…there's a reporter from the Dispatch and one from Fox News…and I think from some other friends. What do you want me to do?"

"Ned Curry one of them?

"Yes. Mr. Curry is holding."

"Put him through. Get rid of the others. Nicely, and politely. But get rid of them. Tell them I have left the office."

Sun played across the once farmland that was now a rambling metropolis. The river below glistened and the room was silent as Janet watched him and Jack wondered what the hell had happened. Ned Curry was one of his closest friends besides his partners. He and Ned were simpatico, always on the same page, pretty much the same outlook on life. It was easier talking with Ned than almost anyone else. He would know how Jack felt even if Jack didn't. Janet stood there and stared.

"Ned?"

"Have you…have you heard the news?"

Jack could hear how tentative he was asking the question and sympathized with his awkwardness.

"I did…sort of…no details. I cut off Bill Parker when he said J.W.'s death was on television. Shouldn't have done that to him, but the shock…I guess the shock made me react that way. Disbelief. What did they say?"

"Said he was found in Atlanta. That he committed suicide. No details. Said he was from Columbus. I think the press will be after you. Wanted to…to give you a heads up."

"Thanks, Ned. Appreciate it. I understand how tough it must have been to call me, but I…I appreciate it. I'll tell Bill that, too, when I get a chance."

"Don't worry about Parker," he said solemnly.

Jack's mind exploded with all the crazy thoughts and questions about his son. He was dead. As announced by television. Thanks, thanks a lot; we'll try to get through the rest of the day.

"What do you need me to do?" Ned asked.

"I don't know yet. Probably nothing. I'll get back with you…and thanks for the call."

After he hung up, he realized Janet was standing near him.

"Do you feel like crying?"

Yeah, Jack said to himself, he did, but somehow there were no tears, merely the agony that should lead to tears, all restrained, bottled-up, lying in wait like a preying tiger poised for an unsuspecting moment to pounce.

Here was the potential for touching again as roles reversed and she wanted to comfort him. He didn't let it happen, part of his steeling himself against the blow he had just received.

"Jack, I'm sorry." She breathed the words at him. "I'm so terribly sorry."

She made the move for him, the hug move, but he reached for the phone.

"Thanks. I know you care. Thanks."

Jack could not come up with J.W.'s phone number from memory. He flipped his planner to the phone number section and there it was: Home and Business. The cell phone number had a line through it. He had been instructed never to use it. He should have known the house number, but it had been three or four years since he had called it. That's how long it had been since he had spoken to or seen his son. Not by Jack's choice, rather by circumstances and his son's choice.

The number rang several times before the answering machine kicked in and the voice of Angelina spoke: "Hi, you've reached Angelina and Mario and Elena…we're not home now, so leave a message. Ciao."

Her Italian accent was unmistakable. There was no mention of J.W. as if he did not live there. No question about who ran that household.

"This is Jack. I heard about J.W. Please give me a call. I'm at the office right now. Let me know what I can do."

Maybe she was using the answering machine to screen her calls. Easier to deal with the press that way, but they'll be on her doorstep soon, if not already.

Janet put her arm around him before he could react. He had gotten away from her comforting once, not a second time. She squeezed slightly as she took his hand and kissed it and held it to her cheek. It was a sincere gesture and tears welled in her eyes.

"My problem doesn't mean beans," she sobbed. "Jack, I'm so sorry."

She let go of him and ran from his office. He was touched and he was relieved.

He had left the message on his son's answering machine, but he knew that was not the end of it. As much as Jack dreaded it he had to drive out to J.W.'s place and see if she were there. The thought of a confrontation with J.W.'s wife was not pleasant. Necessary maybe, but not what Jack wanted. He would have wanted that relationship to be smoother, more amiable, not the contest and harangue it had been.

Jack got his car from the parking garage the agency used and headed for his son's home. He wasn't sure exactly where he was going, but headed west, the address on a note card he programmed into his GPS.

J.W.'s house was out in the western burbs, Westchester Villas, where bastardized versions of Italian estates stood in princely rows. The development had all of the glitz, the false design, the incidence of copycatism, the pomposity, and many of the other characteristics of bombastic nouveau riche. There were the haughty airs, the poor landscaping, the tentative sense of accomplishment, and the genteel self-aggrandizement; this while many of these families struggled financially waiting to be transferred to the next corporate assignment or waiting to become partner or waiting for whatever future career nirvana they hoped would come along.

Jack was in a daze on this drive, lost in forced mental gymnastics trying to stave off the potential unpleasantness of what could and might confront him. J.W.'s death still had not sunk in with him. J.W.'s death was a news event on television, remote, disconnected, and apart from Jack.

Linking him to his son's suicide had not yet taken place. Jack knew the words, but he wasn't there yet with the reality.

It might have been a struggle to get to their house without the GPS. He had never been there before. The last time J. W. and he had been face-to-face was in the bar of the downtown Hyatt Hotel. He followed the directions of the flat, officious female voice, paid attention to the street names, and finally pulled up in front of this huge place. It was a place, not a house. Manicured lawn, fenced yard, lousy landscaping as previously noted, mandatory three-car garage, pots of flowers, and the overall feeling the entire setting was made out of plastic or the ceramic creation for a school project or Hollywood set. It was where the young successful Columbus new money lived. Hurray for their success, stylized and stilted as Jack thought it showed.

No one responded to the bell he heard ring inside. After a minute or so, he saw the curtains on one of the front windows flutter, a blurred, vaguely identifiable face quickly come and go, and then nothing. He rang again. The latch turned and Angelina pulled open the door.

"What you want?"

"I know about J.W.,"

He said the words calmly. He wasn't calm, but he knew he needed to hold his composure right there.

"I came to see if I could help…whatever you wanted me to do…"

"You can go away. Stay away. Why would you come here anyway? You never been here before. First time. Ridiculous."

"I wanted to offer my help…support…do what I could."

"Big deal."

"He was my son."

"I have no time for you. I go to the airport. There is no time for waste. I have to go."

"Going to Atlanta?"

"Yes. They call. Want me identify body. They already know who he is…enough to call me…tell me he is dead, but still they want me come and say is him. Stupid. They tell me…I ask…they tell me he shoot himself. He has all these guns, of course he shoot himself, he is crazy with these guns."

"Suicide? His gun?"

"His gun…how do I know? He is dead. There was gun right next to him. They say he shoot himself. What do I know. I go to Atlanta, I see him dead, I come back, I get Mario and Elena, and I go home. This is bullshit here…I go home to Italy."

There it was, brutally laid out. No remorse, no anguish, and no fear. Just a decision and a plan. Jack couldn't blame her really, she had no other family here in the U.S. And she had always hated this country. Everything in Italy was better; better wine, better stores, better lifestyle, and nicer people.

"What about the house? Your furniture and dishes? Everything…?"

Well, silly me, he thought, creating a problem where one did not exist. Here he was considering a practical detail. How dumb could he be?

"I tell lawyer what I want. He sends to me in Italy. He take care of everything. Take some time, but I wait. There is now the money for everything."

"Where are the children now?"

"With my friend, Julie Sorano. They okay. I have to go."

She slammed the door shut. As Jack walked to his car she backed out of the garage and raced down the drive and away, on to the airport.

He checked in with the office and before he could countermand the shift in contact he was connected to Byron Adams. Janet had gone directly from his office to Bryon's and told him what had happened.

Byron was partner number three, the quiet, back-room production guy who gets everything done that two crazies like Janet and Jack get started. He was the level-headed manager who leads the staff, pacifies the vendors, and makes sure everything gets done on time. He is by nature unruffled, genetically structured to be organized, and consistently, determinedly hardworking.

"I'm sorry...you must be devastated."

His voice was calm, as Jack would expect.

"I probably am, but I don't feel it yet, I'm sort of just numb."

"What do you want me to do?"

"I'm not sure. Hold down the fort. Projects need to get done. I know I should be involved, but...but I think..."

His brain was on a flyer. Some compulsion, some vision, some essence of something that said he should go to Atlanta. He did not know why, but he felt he had to go to Atlanta. He had to find out what this was all about with his son and the suicide. Suicide? It was hard for him to believe that J.W. had killed himself. Jack wondered what it might have been that was the motivation. Was it one issue or several issues? He had read about the circumstances of Ernest Hemmingway killing himself and he had thought, yeah, it made sense. Hemmingway was dying of cancer and he would decide when he went, not some goddamn disease. He remembered thinking how courageous that had been. Somehow he didn't see J.W. that way.

"...I think you guys need to go on without me. I'm heading for Atlanta. I'll stay in touch. I've got to find out what happened. Talk to you soon."

"Jack" Byron yelled into the phone.

"Yes."

"I…I wish I could do something for you…"

"You can. Keep things moving…and take care of Janet. Later."

Byron was solid. He would do as Jack asked. He would comfort Janet, probably better than he would. Bryon would make sure the projects got done, he would keep things moving, and he would keep Phillips, Nelson, and Adams out of trouble.

Jack headed back to the city to his condo near the German Village district south of downtown. He would pack and get going to Atlanta. He would talk to Meg first, but he would be on his way.

Millicent, his cat, needed attention. Jack had almost forgotten about her. At a time such as this is when a pet is a pain in the rump. He hated to call on Mrs. Brady again. He muddled with that issue as he packed. When he had everything set that he thought he needed, he went to the closet and pulled out his gun safe. Unlocked, he pulled out the Glock 21 nestled neatly in its holster. He ran his hand over the smooth polished leather and wrestled with the idea of taking it with him. At the bottom of the safe were two other pistols he could choose. He debated, but finally settled on the Glock. He dropped it into his suitcase and zippered it shut. But something bothered him. He had the carry permit, so that wasn't it. Would I need it? Who knows? A premonition, an instinct connected with him and he decided to take it.

The report said J.W. was a suicide. What if it were not? Then what? Was it murder? He felt better about having the Glock with him.

Millicent appeared as he moved to the kitchen and sounded a quiet voice as if to ask what he was doing, why the hustle-bustle. It would have been easier to take her with him than try to find someone to care for her on such short notice, except hotels don't like pets. Perhaps Mrs. Brady was the answer. After all, he didn't have many choices. He found Mrs. Brady's number on a note pad by the kitchen phone. She answered on the first ring.

"Hello."

"Mrs. Brady, this is Jack Phillips...your upstairs neighbor..."

"Oh, my...Mr. Phillips I'm so sorry...I was watching the news this morning and heard about your son. It is upsetting...you being so close..."

It was strange hearing her say the words. The reality pushed at him again as if it were a test to see how well he was holding up with the tension of grief lurking. Somewhere in the background grief was waiting to pounce on him. For now, he was keeping it at bay.

"Thank you...it is shocking, yes. I don't think it has sunk in yet. But I'm in motion, in action...to try to find out some things. I'm going to Atlanta and I...I need your help, if possible."

"Of course. Take care of Millie?"

"Yes, ma'am, it would help."

"That's an easy request to handle. Bring her down....and some food."

"I'm not sure how long I'll be gone...probably not more than a few days, but..."

"Bring her down," she repeated. "Go do what you have to do."

"Thank you...thanks a bunch."

Jack grabbed some cat food, threw one of his old golf sweaters over his shoulder, tucked Millie under his arm, and went down to Mrs. Brady's. Millie took it well, as she always did. Living with Jack had conditioned her to be ready for the unexpected. She was, for a cat, a one-man cat at that, quite flexible. She had learned she had to be. When Mrs. Brady opened the door Millie walked in as if she owned the place. Mrs. Brady put the sweater he was carrying in a spot near the kitchen table and Millie got contented digging her claws into the soft cotton. Mrs. Brady already had a dish of water on the floor by the refrigerator.

Jack had this feeling for Mrs. Brady. She was probably about eighty, widowed for years, living alone except for her own cat, Bradley. She and Jack had become friends over the years, the time he had lived in the building. He knew that she didn't approve of some of his lifestyle, but she never said anything directly. Once in awhile she gave him some kind of shot that stung his consciousness, poked at his sense of morality, and tended to bring him up short. She rebuked without rebuking, scolded without enumerating his offenses, and generally tried to keep him in line. Jack had to admit, he had led a life somewhat outside her rules of conduct. He considered himself a better person now, but in the past she had her points. He had listened, understood, and accepted. He had this feeling for Mrs. Brady. He cared about her a great deal. She sensed his vulnerabilities and cared back. Jack knew this was some kind of love affair, only she didn't know it.

"Sit down a minute before you run off. Have a hot tea."

Jack's shoulders slumped.

"Yes, I know, Jack, you're not that crazy about my tea and you want to get going. Sit down anyway."

Jack sat at the kitchen table and she poured the tea and placed the cup and saucer in front of him.

"Thanks."

"You're so polite. That's nice. These days manners seem to be a thing of the past. And you are a nice man. I'm sorry this has happened to you."

There was silence for a few moments.

"The emotion has to come sometime."

"I know, but not now. Got things to do, there's no time right now for emotion. I'll get to that later."

"What is your plan?"

"About what?"

"Rushing off to Atlanta. You should know what you're about before you get there. What can you accomplish?"

"I'm not sure, Mrs. Brady, all I know is that it's highly unlikely that my son killed himself. That's my opinion. Therefore, he was murdered. I can make sure the cops look for a killer and not just assume he committed suicide. I can do that much for him. Suicide carries a stigma that I figure he would not want attached to him. Just another assumption."

"That sounds like a plan. Good luck. And stay out of trouble. If someone did kill him they won't want you muddying the waters."

"I've got my Glock…it's a semi-automatic pistol."

"Oh, my, I don't like the sound of that."

"I'll be careful, believe me."

She pushed off from the stove where she was leaning and came to him and hugged his head, burying it in her substantial breasts.

"You worry me."

"I'll be okay.

"Don't get yourself shot."

"I'll be okay.

She kissed the top of his head.

2.

Jack needed to call Meg.

Janet Nelson was his close woman friend, but Meg was his special woman friend. Theirs was an even closer relationship, although maybe she was not a friend, come to think of it. He had yet to determine that, but in any case, she was the woman he was intimate with and the lover Janet was not. Meg was soft and sweet and determinedly coiled, ready for anything. They had met through mutual friends and that was a good thing, the getting together through dual recommendations. They had gone out on those restrained, sophisticated adult dates for six months before she asked him if he wanted to make love to her. When he leaned forward and stuck his tongue in her ear she laughed. They spent the better part of the next two days in her bedroom. Jack lost seven pounds and could barely do his workout routine at his health club.

Meg made few demands on him and he couldn't decide if that was a good thing or a bad sign. She ran her own real estate company and was very successful financially. Her dear departed husband, fifteen years her senior, Walter H. Ferrell, was also in real estate, also very successful. He dropped dead on the golf course and left Meg nicely well off. She thought it was wonderful he had died there, doing what he loved to do. She was clear with her feelings by declaring that after all, it was better he died there than in some whore house or in a damn car wreck.

"Meg Ferrell." She had answered on the second ring.

There always seemed to be a lilt to her voice, even if it were forced. Her voice was resonant, controlled, and very articulate. There was seldom a time when she could not be understood. No mumbling, no mushed phrases or thrown away sentences. Pure, understandable communication was her hallmark. He was surprised, however, that she answered. Usually, he got the voice mail recording, left a message, and she called him back.

"Surprised to get you…"

"Oh, I'm sitting here in my car, pissed, waiting for a client to show up who is twenty minutes late. This screws up the whole day and I don't have time for this kind of delay. Sorry. How are you doing?"

"I'm on my way to Atlanta. Wanted you to know where I was. J.W. is…"

"What's going on?"

"J.W. is dead…"

"What? What do you mean, dead? How…what happened?"

"Suicide they say. Happened in Atlanta. He was down there on business, I guess."

"Oh, Jack, I'm so sorry."

"I'm going to find out what happened. It's been on the TV news…wire services. They didn't contact me, of course, they contacted his wife. The Dispatch has the story, I'm sure, and they're probably after Angelina, but she's already on her way to Atlanta."

"It's awful. Jack, I'm really sorry. What can I do?"

"Not a thing. I'm already packed and ready to hit the road."

"Wow, such a shock. Are you okay?"

"I think so. I'll take some action and then I'll find out if I'm okay."

"Hey, I don't like the idea of you leaving town without my seeing you. You can't just waltz off like that. Meet me at Jerry's…twenty minutes."

He hesitated.

"Fifteen minutes," she revised.

He didn't say anything.

"You cannot leave without talking to me…in person…face-to-face."

"Yeah, okay, I get it."

He was reluctant because he did not want to get into all of the potential emotion that he knew could come with their seeing each other. The emotion could come later; he had to keep it at bay. He felt he was on a mission and did not want to be slowed down. But…she insisted, and he relented.

He snapped the phone shut, grabbed his bag off the bed, and headed for the car.

As Jack pulled away from the parking lot he spotted Millicent in Mrs. Brady's arms on her deck. It was as if he were leaving a child, a child who had to watch you go. Millie cried a deep, plaintive sound that emanated from some sort of primordial emotional abyss and he knew that he should also be crying. He was on the road again and Millie knew it. She had suffered through this with him many times before and she hated it, but each time she sensed after awhile she would survive. This time he wondered if he would survive.

Jerry's was a strip mall lounge and eatery on the west side that catered to the bored housewife crowd and young professional women on the move. It was a place Meg preferred to take her clients to schmooze. It did have a very sophisticated feeling about it and because it was primarily frequented by woman it was more sedate than any male-dominated bar. And no TV tuned to sports. There was one set behind the bar that was always checked in to Fox News or CNN.

He arrived in less than twenty minutes and got a booth towards the rear where it would be quieter. The lunch crowd buildup was still well off. He ordered a diet cola and waited another half hour for Meg. He knew what her fifteen minutes really meant and accepted that. His cell phone rang and he could see it was Kari. He shut off the phone. He wanted to be cut off from the office for awhile. He couldn't help them now, anyway. His mind was a long way from the advertising business.

Meg commanded attention when she came into the place. Attractive is the word. Tall, lithe, athletic, well-groomed, well-dressed. All the right hip criteria dialed in, expressed to the max. And brown. She was, in the politically correct term, African-American. She was African black diluted by Caucasian, coffee with some cream, a caramel delight, beautiful in any context. She had never been accepted by J.W. and summarily rejected by J.W.'s wife, as Jack eventually learned. J.W. had prided himself on being accepting, on being enlightened, racially blind, and so on, liberal in thought and action. But he had a hard time with a brown woman as his Father's special friend who just might become his step-mother. He wasn't liberal enough for that possibility.

Meg was part of the reason the estrangement between son and father continued. It was an easy excuse to keep Jack at arm's length. Jack remembered the phone conversation when he introduced the idea that he was seeing Meg.

Something like: *"If we get together I want you to know about the woman I'm currently dating. I'm pretty serious about her."*

"Who is she?"

"Name is Meg, Meg Ferrell. She's a big-time real estate broker."

"Yeah, so."

"And she happens to be Negro-Caucasian."

"Oh."

They never got together.

Meg put one finger on the table to balance herself, bent forward so her face was near his, and kissed him on the cheek. It was a kiss of endearment, of support, of sympathy, and without passion. She slid into the seat opposite him, ordering iced tea as she did so from the waitress who stood by as the kiss was delivered. Her moves were effortless, with style, and an élan that distinguished her.

"I'm sorry. You don't deserve this." Her voice was soft and comforting.

She reached for his hands and held them in her long entwining fingers. There was a look in her eyes that said something. In retrospect, her look was a foreshadowing of their relationship.

"His choice, I guess. If that is the truth," he said as he took a deep breath.

That was glib, Jack thought, but it jumped out. Probably a quick reaction for self-protection.

She looked at him quizzically, tilting her head slightly, the body language of accusation.

"What are you saying?"

"I don't know. I don't see him killing himself."

"Oh. Why not?"

"Doesn't fit somehow. It doesn't …"

He faltered in what he wanted to say because he did not know how to express the doubt he had about what happened to J.W. He could not figure his son to do that to himself. Kill someone else, maybe, but not himself.

"It's possible…you have to face that," Meg said softly.

She was being the realist, but what she said was not comforting and he figured she was not following his thought process.

"I know, I know…but…"

"But what?

"That's why I need to go to Atlanta and find out what happened.

"Are you flying?"

Again she had a curious look on her face.

"No. I can drive there in a few hours. I couldn't get on a plane until later today or tomorrow. I'll be there tonight and I'll have my car with me and…"

He didn't want to tell her about the Glock.

"…and it will really be easier."

"Have you talked to Angelina?"

"Yeah, I went out to the house…"

"You did? That's a first, isn't it?"

"Yeah. The kids weren't there. She was just about to leave for Atlanta. She didn't seem to have any remorse or sadness. Maybe upset at being inconvenienced. I would guess that was her emotional state. Aggravation. Put out at having to go deal with her husband's death. It fits, I think."

"Where's your sadness?"

He just looked at her. Her question was one of those body punches, a hard, stiff right to the ribs that took his breath away and made him wonder what kind of fight he was in and how to counter punch. Meg cheated, she caught him off guard. Internally he stumbled, but he caught himself and regained his stance.

"I have it under control…right now. I know what I have to do. I've called on the widow to offer my condolences, and now I have to go find out what happened to my son. My sadness can wait. I'll deal with that issue sometime in the future. Like when you and I are sitting in the quiet shadows of a summer evening, sipping a fine wine, and when I am better able to deal with what I can not now comprehend."

"Sadness can crush you, can take away your sense of reality, and it can distort your reasoning. Beware the devil of depression and mental distortion. You are vulnerable."

Those were wise words and her eyes bore in on him when she said them. These words, too, were not comforting, but they did give him a reality perspective. Funny, that reality stuff.

"I am indeed vulnerable."

Here was this wonderful woman, this voice of sanity, this vision of balance for his life. Yet, something was missing.

"I can go with you."

She said it, but it was tentative and it was not as affirming as she would have wanted. There was a slight catch in her throat. She wanted to help and support. She could not.

"I know. Thanks. Forcing me to see you and feel your support has been enough. Right now I need to get to Atlanta, get with the authorities, and find the truth about my son. The truth is somewhere there in Atlanta and I have to get there. No way around it for me."

"I understand."

She said the words he probably would have said, but he knew she didn't fully understand what was motivating him.

"I've got to go. I can't stay to eat, can't take the time. I've got to be on the road."

"Okay," she said quietly.

Her eyes looked away as if that would make it not true, as if now, she wanted to form a new reality. She didn't look back to him right away and he wondered what she was thinking.

"Thanks for understanding," he fudged.

He knew she didn't. Not really.

"Oh, my gosh, what about Millie? Do you want me to…?"

"No, that's okay, she's with my neighbor…Mrs. Brady. She'll cope just fine."

"You sure?"

"Yeah, trust me. I know the cat."

Meg walked with him to his car.

"I can pass lunch," she said. "I just wanted to see you."

"Thanks."

She stood close to him as he unlocked his car and then reached toward him. She took his face in her hands and leaned against him as she did so. He could feel her and could feel the tension of her emotion and it was exciting and scary at the same time. But it was different from any time before and he wondered why.

He could not let go of his emotions and release to her and he backed away slightly to ease the tension. It was tension that was fortifying and supportive and sexual all at the same time. He had trouble with it. He had to move on with his mission.

Meg caressed his face and softly whispered.

"I care about you. Does that help?"

3.

Leaving Meg was difficult, but a relief. Too much tension. Right then, at Jerry's, he would have wanted more conversation after she told him she cared about him. To get some meaning, some definition, some inkling of the parameters of that caring. She had never said anything like that to him before, so it was a surprise. A nice surprise. And the caress? The caress did not seem to fit the words; the caress seemed more like the mothering to a child rather that for an adult man with whom she had a sexual relationship. Her caress should have promised something more, something more intimate, more passionate. It didn't do that and he wondered why. What did it all mean…this business of saying: I care about you? The whole thing with Meg made him confused, uncertain about what their relationship meant. Maybe something less to her than to him. And maybe he didn't know where he was with it. He knew this was not the time to try to sort it all out.

He was way beyond Cincinnati, almost half way through Kentucky, on his way to Atlanta, a tad above the speed limit on cruise control, and Meg's words were still hanging with him. He said to himself again that this had been the first time she had said anything like that. Before today, their relationship had been sensibly superficial, physical, non-intellectual, mutually satisfying, and socially convenient although distracting to his friends who wondered what he was doing with this tan colored woman. He wasn't sure how to answer their unasked questions, so he didn't try. No one ever said anything directly to him, but word gets around. The chatter of speculation and prurient interest leaks away from the hushed conversations and gets fed back in subtle ways.

He ignored what got back to him and he and Meg and his friends just continued to have fun, all of them.

Meg's marriage to Walter was an added bonus to her own success in business. That success was sweetened by her sizeable inheritance when Walter dropped dead. The total result was that it contributed to a lifestyle of privilege, contacts with important people, and the press of demands on her time. But she found time for him. He liked that, he had gotten used to that situation.

Driving from Ohio to Atlanta on the I-75 Interstate is a monumental chore. Trucks constantly clamor for control of the lanes. They stack, they swerve in and out, they block, they aggressively threaten, and they refuse to recognize that cars also have a right to proceed to the their own destinations. Jack made the necessary stops, drank the required water, ate some silly snacks, and pushed ahead.

He wished he had been able to turn off his thinking brain as a human and flip over to some kind of robotic cruise control. Questions about what he was doing stabbed at him. What was he going to do once he got to Atlanta? Who would he see? Who would help him? Where would he begin? What would Angelina do when she got there? She had all the rights and responsibilities. What would happen with that? His mind tumbled all of these questions searching for answers as he made the drive. He found himself unable to answer any of them right then.

Jack's cell phone rang and he saw that it was Byron.

"By, everything okay?"

"That's my question to you."

"First rate. Cruising along, making time, wishing I was already there."

"Everything, and I mean everything is under control here. Do what you have to do and don't worry about us."

"Thanks.

"Stay in touch…

"I will…

"And be careful."

"I'll try."

He clicked off and the night that shrouded him made him feel comfortable and at ease. He liked driving at night.

Jack arrived at the Marriott Marquis in downtown Atlanta just after ten thirty that night. He had called the hotel on his cell phone for the reservation, and once there was relieved to be checked in and settled in his room.

Here he was in Atlanta. Now what? He looked out over the city lights, fully aware of the contrast from his view of Columbus, Ohio. This morning from his office he had looked out over an energized and diverse cityscape that melded with a ranging suburbia. Only hours later, he was taking in the city of Atlanta, another rambling panorama of sprawl. It was a significant time warp through space. He was exhausted by the time he got to his room and knew he had to sleep.

Sleep was the redeemer for his aching and tired soul and then the sound of buzzing brought him awake. He had set the alarm for seven, but it had not been enough time to recover from the drive. He felt whipped. There was that brief, scary sense of disorientation when he was trying to determine exactly where he was. In a darkened room someplace, but where?

He recovered his sense of place, chastised himself appropriately for not being quicker on the uptake, showered, dressed, and headed for breakfast with his briefcase in hand. He scanned the *Journal-Constitution* while he ate, looking for a follow-up story about his son. Sure enough, there it was on page seven, first section. **Foul play suspected in death of Ohio man.** The article went on with a rehash of the details, how J.W. had been found in Piedmont Park, an apparent suicide, gun by his side, blah, blah, blah; the Medical

Examiner's office tentatively revising the initial police report saying the death may be a homicide. Official cause of death was still to come. The impersonal tone of the story was to be expected, he figured, but it made him feel crummy. J.W. was just another victim to others reading the story. That is, if they even bothered to read it. It was Jack's personal anguish, his singular consideration. His son was just another statistic in a city full of statistics. Everyone else concerned with this death had other issues, even his son's wife, the newly created widow who scorned us all.

For the first time he felt that his coming to Atlanta was not so silly after all. Someone needed to do something about his son. What, an advocate? He was now…yes, an advocate for a dead man. The dead man was his son.

J.W. was the Ohio man in the article. An Ohio man; that was how they referred to him, just another victim, a body to warrant determination of death, an official case number, a new persona in creeping crime statistics, a factor of the statistics that are disliked by the authorities and generally disregarded by the public.

He had no desire to go to the sports section and dropped the paper on the table across from him. He reached down into his briefcase that he had dropped next to the table.

As he had driven, he had made random notes on a pad that he kept in the car just for this reason. Referring to those notes, he now developed a check list of what he wanted to do. The cops, the coroner, and the company. That's right, the company. J.W.'s company. He would not have been here other than on business. What did any of them know and who were the players here in town?

Jack knew he had no clout, no standing, and certainly no platform to deal with anyone on any basis. Angelina held that power. Perhaps sympathy and understanding could be his passport to revelation. It was revelation he wanted…needed. His wanted his son to be more than just a statistic.

The concierge gave him directions to police headquarters which was the beginning point on his list. He followed his GPS and drove. He had the nagging sensation that maybe this was a waste of time, but chucked that doubt and kept going. Zig-zagging through downtown streets, he reached Peachtree Street, SW and headed south. Police headquarters was housed in a five-story, brick building that was part of a complex near the Atlanta City Detention Center. Jack had the feeling the unexceptional building was probably designed by one of those functionary architectural firms with some kind of political connection to the established city bureaucracy.

The area surrounding the building was generally shoddy and worn down, with bail-bond offices and a few tattoo parlors predominate as he looked around.

Jack walked into the Atlanta Public Safety Headquarters, noted the name, and wondered if there wasn't some kind of irony in that title. He told his name to the uniformed officer handling reception and that he wanted to talk to the detectives handling the case about the Ohio man, the one found in the park. He might as well have been searching for his lost dog the way she looked at him.

"Phillips?" she asked. "You related?"

"The father."

"Uh huh."

She picked up her desk phone and punched in a number, the click of her inch-long finger nail sounding with every stab she made.

"Detective Moss? Yes, Monica…got a Mr. Phillips here, says he wants to speak with a detective working on the park suicide. Yes…uh huh…yes."

She hung up the phone, making sure not to let her nails rub against the cradle and gave him directions. After getting through the metal detector and the scan of his briefcase with no problem, he moved towards the elevator.

"Excuse me…I heard what you said to the officer. I'm Spence Colby…with the Journal-Constitution…I handle the police action for the paper. At least, I'm the primary writer…"

Jack turned as the man spoke to him and took his extended hand. He was a short, stocky young man, with long blonde hair that flailed at the world, and a flat, perpetual smile that sometimes broadened when he talked.

"Yes?" Jack was on guard.

"I'd like to interview you when you get done with the detectives…maybe we can have lunch…"

"You didn't use the word reporter…"

"Well, no…I…I think I'm more than that. I'd like to help if I can."

"I'll talk to you when I'm finished upstairs. Will you be here?

"No. Come to the deli a couple of blocks away. At Central and Trinity; you can't miss it. I'll be waiting. And thanks…for not blowing me off…"

Jack rode the elevator to the designated floor and found another uniformed officer. His badge indicated he was a police cadet. Cop in training, nice experience. Jack waited for more than ten minutes for Detective Moss. He gave the cadet an evil eye as if the young man had control of anything.

"Detective Moss will be along soon," he assured Jack in response to the taut grimace directed at him.

It wasn't long and the door to the floor offices popped open and a tall, blonde woman stood facing him.

"Mr. Phillips?"

She wore a gray pinstripe pantsuit with a white blouse and shuffled her feet in black pumps that were appropriate for her dress. She was lithe and sensual and commanding in her posture. He was impressed and was caught in a sense of attraction that betrayed the nature of why he was there. He mentally shook that off and tried to view her in a cop scenario. She was his starting point to find out about his son and that was the way it had to work.

"Yes, I'd like to talk to you about my son. The news said he committed suicide in one of your city parks. I came down from Columbus, Ohio, to see what happened. I...I know I have little standing in this, but I need to know something about it. I thought you might be able to help me. I don't believe he committed suicide. I don't know any of the facts, but suicide was...I don't think suicide was in the picture for him. My guess is that he was murdered; my guess is that it had something to do with someone or something here in your city. I just need to know why...I have to know. I was estranged from him and his wife and...and...she has the authority to deal with this, but I have to know what happened. I thought I might be able to work with you. I'm not sure his wife can...or will..."

"Come on in, Mr. Phillips, let's sit down and talk about this."

She led him to a small conference room that was dimly lighted and indistinctively furnished. He slumped into the chair she pointed to and dropped his briefcase beside it. She sat down across from him.

"Like some coffee?"

She was being polite.

"No...thanks."

"The widow identified the body yesterday."

"I assumed she would. I talked to her before she left Columbus...not a satisfactory conversation, I can tell you that. Could she help you in any way? About my son…what might have happened?"

"No, she was not helpful. I understand your situation…your lack of standing. I understand you want to find out what happened. The widow did not seem to care. She ID'd and left the ME building without saying anything. There was no…no grief; at least none that showed in her face or with her voice. She simply walked away. What do you make of that?"

"Not surprised. But I can't give you a reason without going into a lot of sordid detail about the relationship, their backgrounds, and so forth."

He said the words numbly. He was not surprised by Angelina's reaction. He felt her marriage to his son was always one of convenience, a way to escape the Green Card rules that would have sent her packing back to Italy. Marrying his son had been her salvation at the time, although her distaste for the U.S. was easily provoked and readily expressed by her.

"Why do you think your son did not kill himself?" she asked quietly.

"Not in his makeup…at least as I knew him. Perhaps he has changed, perhaps something is different from when I knew more about him. That is, when I thought I knew him better. Perhaps I didn't know him very well, but I still want to find out what happened."

She sat and listened and looked at him intently. She didn't say anything, but you could see her brain going clickity click and she was intrigued by the whole situation. He figured this was a case where she might want to get involved.

"Go on," she said, softly prompting him.

"I was worried that he might…might shoot someone…with provocation…out of necessity. But not shoot himself."

"Why did you think about that?"

"He had an extensive gun collection and I think…I think he was an angry person…felt frustrated about some things…and got caught up in the culture of…"

"Yes?"

"Oh…anarchy…of some supposed fear of the government. He was armed to protect himself against a repressive government…against the unknown, I suppose."

"Really?"

"Yeah. So I thought shooting someone might be in the cards for him, but shooting himself was not. I believe he was murdered. That's why I came to Atlanta. I wanted to make sure you folks got it right. I want to make sure you get the person who killed him."

She looked at Jack closely, with her lips puckered, brow furrowed, and a fist to her cheek. He knew he had touched a nerve.

"We're working on it. And I…"

"Look, I saw the paper this morning…the medical examiner doesn't believe in suicide either, so don't give me the usual bullshit. I know how it works in a big city police department. If I don't' press for an investigation it won't happen. Another dead body, another suspicious death, maybe murder. Maybe suicide…what the hell, there's a lot to do in this city. The bad guys keep moving on. I want my son to have your attention, because I'm going to be hanging around and nagging and poking. We're going to find out what happened. You and I are going to work on this. We are going to know."

She sat back against the table and chuckled. It was the sound of knowing where he was coming from, it was the sound of acceptance. But she still had to be the cop.

"I understand your concern and your emotion We're investigating and…"

"Come on…"

He yelled in frustration, a snap rebuttal; it was a visceral reaction, and he wanted her attention.

"I'll…" she paused, "I'll stay on it. The medical examiner says it was not suicide, so you're right about that. Like I said, I'll stay on it."

She had looked at him carefully and knew that he would not go away. She would do her job. With some more intensity than she might otherwise have given.

"Thanks," Jack said, "I'll get back with you tomorrow. I'm going to talk with his business associates. They may know something. You do your investigation…I'll do mine. I won't get in your way if I can help it, but let's compare notes tomorrow. I'm not going to let this thing with my son just drift away. There will be answers…I want answers."

Jack shook hands with the lovely and confident Detective Moss and walked out of police headquarters, determined to get with the working associates of his son and find out what they knew.

He had been correct with his speculation that J.W. had come to Atlanta on business. The Southeast Home Furnishings and Building Design Conference was in progress at the Convention Center. His company, Mondrian Industries, had a gigantic booth at the show.

It had been easy to check. He called the local Mondrian office and the ever-so-polite girl who answered the phone directed him to the trade show. No, she begged off, Mr. Phillips would not be at the conference…he has a problem and will not be available.

"He's dead," Jack said without compassion or sensitivity.

"Oh, my. Why…I'm sure…I don't know. Perhaps you need to speak to Karen Bowen, our PR director.

"No, that's all right…I'll check out the conference."

Jack went across the street from police headquarters to the pre-pay lot where he parked and using the GPS arrived at the deli Colby had indicated. With a bit of a struggle, he got into a parking spot on the street. He found Spence Colby drinking coffee as he was slouched over a table furiously making notes. Colby was startled when Jack touched his shoulder and spilled his coffee on some of the papers he had in front of him.

"Shit."

Colby mopped at the spill with a napkin.

"Sorry to startle you."

"That's okay, it's okay. I was just sort of deep in thought…"

"You asked me to meet you here. Can you help me?"

"I'd like to. Sit down."

Jack pulled out the chair across from Colby and dropped his briefcase close by.

"Sit, sit."

Jack eased onto the chair and kicked his briefcase under the table.

"How did it go with Elaine? Nice looking, isn't she?"

"Not very far," Jack answered, reluctantly, not willing to reveal much at this point and unwilling to comment on Ms. Moss' looks.

"Medical examiner says murder…she confirm that?"

"Yes, she did."

"That's good, playing it honest…"

"It was in this morning's paper…"

"Yeah, someone else wrote that piece. It's okay, though, we got the word from the ME's office late yesterday. Word's now on the street. Killer knows the investigation is after him…or her…it's under way even though they don't know who it is. The killer now knows they are looking; makes it interesting."

"What do you want from me?"

Jack was always suspicious of a guy like this, angling for something. Didn't matter what the issue was or what the circumstances were, reporters had killed him with ridiculous articles that needlessly hurt his clients. This bozo could screw up a murder investigation.

"I want to get a story. Maybe I can help sort this out…your son's murder. Find out who did it."

"Okay. I don't know what the next step is for the police…Detective Moss. But my next step is to get to my son's work associates. He was here in Atlanta on business, I'm sure. He came here frequently, I understand. The killer might be a business connection maybe or a link through one of his customers. Or maybe it was more personal than that…an unhappy lover, perhaps, an angry lover's spouse…"

"I'm with you…"

Colby spilled his coffee again as he spoke and grabbed at more napkins from the dispenser. He dabbed at the spill.

"There was probably something going on here…business related or involved, the business and something else like business plus a side deal, or…or maybe something deeper…more…more all inclusive."

"Business plus? Like stealing from the company, kickbacks…what? Now, I'm not with you."

Colby frowned and shrugged his shoulders.

"In situations like this drugs always come to mind. They're a powerful motivator…for money…for power…for control."

"Control…?"

Colby tapped his pen on the table and waved at the waitress for more coffee.

"Yes, life control."

Jack hadn't intended to wax philosophical with this guy, but the words rolled out reflexively. He had thought about such a proposition for years in connection with product positioning for successful ads. What was the maximum effect the ad could have for motivating the purchase decision? Our research showed that people wanted control over their lives. Anyway, he hadn't meant for that to creep out now, but he continued.

"I suspect the desire for life control may be the most powerful motivator of all for some people. The money, the status, those things become secondary. Control over others is a fiendish director of action. I thought about it a great deal on the drive down and my guess is that drugs could be at the heart of my son's murder. And, unfortunately, I make that particular comment with some misgiving. The truth is that drugs equate to big money, more money than you can make as a sales manager. It's just a guess, but I think that may be it. Right now, I'm suspicious of everything."

Colby sat staring at Jack as if he had said something profound, eyes intent, pen poised. He seemed to take what Jack said as gospel and nodded slightly as the waitress filled his cup.

"You want something?" she asked, looking at Jack.

"No, thanks."

Jack's reaction to himself was that his mind was now full bore in problem solving mode. He was the detective and had his detective brain in gear. The advertising world would now be way off somewhere.

"What's next for you, Mr. Phillips?"

"Like I said, talk to some of his business associates. His company has a booth at the trade show over at the convention center. I assume I can find them there. Why don't you find out the hotel where he was staying and check that? There has to be something to work on from there."

"I got that already. He stayed at the Ritz-Carlton. Big bucks, right?"

"That's what an expense account can do for you."

"I'm on it."

"Good, I'll get your check…"

"Hey, that's not necessary."

"My pleasure. Let's get back together at lunch time. Meet me at the Marriott…on Peachtree Center…downtown. Whatever any of the reasons are, something is not right about this. Let's try to find out what it is."

Jack gave him his card that had his cell phone number on it, paid the bill, and walked from the deli without looking back. He returned to his car and headed for the convention center, carefully following his GPS as he progressed.

Jack knew pretty much where he was going, so it gave him an opportunity to look around somewhat. He had not been in Atlanta for several years and the grunge of the neighborhoods surrounding the downtown area surprised him. What he was seeing did not jibe with his memory, but he guessed a fast-growing city doesn't age well. Atlanta was an older woman with wrinkles and stress lines and sun-beaten skin that sagged unmercifully. Her success was her bane and time was unflattering in its affect. He didn't think it was fair to be too critical of big cities with all the problems they suffer, but they can present a starkly grim scene.

He had some trouble at first with security at the Georgia World Congress Center where the trade show was being held, but he explained his situation and mission in talking with Mondrian people. They made a call to the Mondrian exhibit space to determine if he should be allowed to their booth, received an okay from someone, and was given a special pass.

Chick Wilson greeted Jack as he approached the Mondrian exhibit space. Chick, he would find out, was the salesman in charge of the Atlanta area for Mondrian.

"You must be Mr. Phillips," He extended his hand with the exuberance of making a sales call. He couldn't quite do it any other way.

"Yes, I am."

"I'm Chick Wilson. Really sorry about Jim, Mr. Phillips, it's a terrible thing; just awful…you have my sympathy."

He continued shaking Jack's hand and put his left hand on both his and Jack's for emphasis.

"I was so shocked that he had taken his own life since…since he had everything going for him…and he was a terrific boss to me."

Chick wasn't aware of the morning news, obviously, and Jack didn't correct him.

"Thank you for your concern, I appreciate it. I need to ask some questions about my son, is there anyone here from management who can talk to me?"

"There sure enough is…Bart Lofton, our VP of sales."

He quickly got Jack to Bart Lofton and Jack was certain Chick was glad to be rid of him. Bart was J.W.'s boss, the guy with the power. Jack wasn't impressed.

"You know my son is dead?" Jack asked after the intro and hand shake.

"Yes, of course…terrible. I'm very sorry. We've tried to help Mrs. Phillips as much as we can. Brought her down on the company plane yesterday. Put her up at the Ritz-Carlton in Buckhead. Didn't want her at the place where her husband stayed. She's going back to Columbus this afternoon. We're trying to accommodate her as well as we can."

"How about accommodating me?"

"Yes, if I can...what is it?"

"Tell me about his status with the company, what was going on, the works. Then tell me what his connections were here in Atlanta. Someone here in Atlanta killed him."

"I thought that..."

He stopped abruptly, looked around to see if anyone had overheard them, and spoke to Jack again quietly.

"Why don't we go over there to our private office?"

He turned quickly, assuming Jack would follow him, and headed to the center of the large display area that held Mondrian products. There were several other employees chatting, drinking coffee when they stepped inside the special room within the booth.

"Gentlemen, ladies, I wonder if you would give Mr. Phillips and me a few minutes of privacy?"

The others moved quickly out of the room with nods and stares, mainly directed at Jack. They all knew about J.W. and more than likely were talking about his death when Lofton and Jack entered.

"Thank you, thank you, thank you," Lofton said breathlessly as they left, almost as if he were going to hyperventilate.

As the door closed, he followed-up on what Jack had said.

"We had heard it was suicide...you said someone killed Jim."

"It's in today's paper...the medical examiner says no suicide. Someone here in Atlanta killed him...shot him, murdered him, and more than likely threw his body in Piedmont Park. A public park where he could be discovered, a place where the killer assumed he would be separated from the real killing site, and in a way that the killer hoped suicide would be accepted as the cause of death. No, Mr. Lofton, J.W. did not kill himself, he was murdered, and perhaps someone you know is the killer."

"Well, I...no, I don't think...well, how could I know..."

"Because it was someone linked to my son some way, some how. Someone you most likely are aware of."

"That's difficult to believe..."

"Please tell me about my son and Mondrian...the business...what was going on."

Lofton started to explain things. First, that Mondrian is a privately held corporation manufacturing high-end cabinets, hardware, and shelving for the new homebuilding and remodeling market. They mainly cater to those who want quality, but who don't want to get their hands dirty with the work it takes to install. Interior designers, design contractors, and builders were sales targets. J.W. knew the products and the market well and rose through the sales ranks to be a territory sales manager.

Then there was the story of his son's phenomenal success in sales, his ability to work with dealers getting their cooperation carrying products, and the tremendous volume of products he was able to get to market. J.W. Phillips was the southeastern sales manager for Mondrian. Damn good, Lofton asserted, damn good. Worked well with Chick Wilson here in Atlanta also Luther Collins in Charleston, Seth Greer in Orlando, plus the dealers and sales reps under his command in Raleigh, Miami, Montgomery, and Baton Rouge. J.W.'s sales network did very well for the company and he spent a lot of time in those cities, but mainly concentrated on the Atlanta area. The Atlanta territory was the company leader, even better than Miami thanks in large part to the efforts of Warren Crawford who owned Custom Design Interiors in Marietta.

"Your son spent a lot of time working with Warren and it paid off, no question about it. Warren has a sensational business getting his designs into new high-end houses and tantalizing the remodelers with ideas that work. He should be on one of those TV shows with the stuff he's come up with."

"Warren Crawford?" Here was a connection, a link to possible information. "How do I get hold of him?"

"Yes, well he's not going to be here at the show…some of his people are…but let me give you his address and phone number."

"Have the police talked to you…a Ms. Moss?"

"Just on the phone…no interview or anything. He said his name was White, Fred White, a detective. Why do you ask?"

"I wondered, that's all. Have there been any problems…complaints regarding my son? You've painted a very positive picture about him, but there must have been some negatives."

"Why no, off hand I can't think of anything."

"He was murdered, there was a reason for it. I think the reason is connected to his business. Any word that he was having an affair here in Atlanta?"

Lofton was startled by the question and tried not to reveal it. Jack had struck a nerve of some kind and Lofton took too long to answer, those seconds of hesitation a give-away.

"Well, that's something…"

"You took too long to answer," Jack snapped. "What's your instinct tell you, what indication did you have?"

"I…I…I began to see something about his T and E reports that bothered me."

"Atlanta was a big producer, wouldn't his expenses be higher here?"

"Yes, they would…but I didn't think they should be as high as they were. Expenses are budgeted for each of the business areas like Atlanta, Miami, and so forth. In the last couple of years Atlanta was always over…quite a bit over. We talked about it a couple of times, but his reason was as you said, getting the business here required more in expenses. It was something we had to deal with in the coming year. As a result of the excesses, I started to take a closer look at the receipts attached to his expense report. There seemed to be a pattern that was strange."

"How so?"

"There were more of the receipts…both restaurants and gas stations…primarily from two areas. He always stayed at the same place…the Ritz-Carlton downtown…at least the last three years or so, anyway. I thought that was excessive, but he was producing so I let it slide."

"What two areas?"

"Around Marietta…a suburb north of here…"

"I know where it is. And the other?"

"Columbus…"

"Columbus?"

"Columbus, Georgia. He had only one dealer there…one that doesn't do that much business with us, so that it seemed strange to me that Jim would be there so much."

Now he had something to work on Jack realized. This was a start. A pattern that was outside the norm.

"I figured the Marietta stuff had to do with Warren and Custom Design Interiors. Their main office is in Marietta. They also have offices in Athens, Chattanooga, and Savannah, but none of the three showed up in any special way on the expenses. I assumed Warren was the reason."

"What did the receipts tell you? What did he put down on his control sheet for who he was entertaining? My guess is that they were phony-baloncy entries. Did you check them?"

"Yes. I finally got into the detail last week…in depth. It was one of those items I wanted to go over with him while we were at the show this week. They didn't seem to make any sense. I wanted to check them out. I give Jim the benefit of the doubt, but they looked strange. Names I didn't recognize, companies I didn't know. I thought we had a problem."

"You had a problem all right. How else could he chisel the company out of money? Promotional money, allowances, that kind of stuff?"

"Yes, but those expenses are very tightly audited."

"By whom?"

"Ned Flournoy, in our accounting department. He watches all of the promotion money nationwide. That's his primary assignment."

"Supposing he's on the take. You better check on him when you get back to Ohio."

"On the take? By whom…for what?

"To finance something he did not know he was financing."

"Like what?"

"Like a drug operation, for instance."

"Noooo…no way."

"Yeah, it was something. Drugs would be a prime choice."

"Mr. Phillips, I think you have jumped to conclusions about this. I don't think anything Jim did would suggest a drug operation."

Jack had indeed jumped to conclusions, but he wanted to shake this guy up, get him thinking about what might not be right, and press for an internal look at what had been going on with J.W.'s operation here in the Atlanta area.

"People get killed over sex or money, usually," Jack said quietly. "With my son it probably wasn't sex, so it had to be money. The best way for big money these days is the drug market…delivering big time to big time buyers."

"But how…what…?

"I don't know yet, but I'm going to find out. Somebody wanted to throw off the police by making it look like a suicide. That somebody is out there, connected somehow to Mondrian, to Warren Crawford, to Columbus, Georgia, and to my son. Those expense reports are very revealing. Thank you."

Jack walked out of the hot, closed-in office in the Mondrian exhibit space and left the Congress building wanting desperately to breathe fresh air. Lofton helped more than he had expected. Now, he had something to work with beyond the simple check list he had initially created. He was energized and wanted to get with Spence Colby to learn what he had found out and get him after some of the leads he had developed from Lofton. He also wanted to get back to Detective Moss. She had to get on this, also. And he wanted to find out who this guy White was. Maybe her partner, but she hadn't said anything about him to Jack.

There was time to run by the Medical Examiner's office before he got back to Colby at the Marriott, so, programming his GPS, he made his way over to their building on Pryor Street. He hadn't quite made the parking lot when his cell phone rang. Where have you been all morning? He had left instructions at the office not to call him, eliminating the business connection. Caller ID showed it was Meg, the real estate mogul who rarely called anyone who was not her client. They called her. He was able to get to a parking spot before he answered.

"I'm okay," he said by way of answering. "Things are fine."

"I figured as much," she said tersely, "things are always fine with you."

"I appreciate the call. I know you are concerned about me. But really, things are as fine as they could be under the circumstances."

That defused the tension. Jack meant what he said, but for him there was comfort in knowing she was connecting, thinking about him, and caring. There are few people who care about you in your life and when it happens it should not, cannot be taken lightly or disregarded. He felt that she cared and had a pretty good feeling about that.

"Made any progress?"

Her voice sounded professional with a capital P, as if there were others nearby who could overhear her end of the conversation. Nothing warm or conversational, just business, just getting the facts.

"I've got some leads and the paper this morning reported that the Medical Examiner's office revealed they did not think it was suicide. I feel satisfied about the fact my instinct was right…but he's still dead. No solace in being right in this case. I'm at the Medical Examiner's office parking lot right now. Want to see what I can find out here. Probably won't be much help, but worth the try."

"How you holding up after the long drive?"

There was a smidge of warmth in the question, but the real estate mogul tone was still there.

"I'm energized…"

"I know you're busy…call me tonight."

"I will. Thanks for checking in…and Meg…I really appreciate the call."

"I know," she said softly and clicked off.

Jack could see her face, her smile, almost feel the touch of her hand as she brushed it across his cheek, and an edge of loneliness and longing crept up on him, pulling him to a place of unwanted sadness, causing him to blink several times to keep his composure. The real emotion would have to wait.

When Jack came into the reception area of the Medical Examiner's building, there was Elaine Moss with a lanky, jivey kind of black guy next to her. They appeared to be in conversation with a dopey looking man in a white lab coat. He was ME staff, no doubt.

Detective Moss saw Jack come in, but waited for him to get close to them before acknowledging his presence. She acted surprised to see him. His being there irritated her a bit, he thought.

"Mr. Phillips…what are you…"

"Checking to see if you were doing your job."

He was trying to be glib, but it was the wrong thing to say. She didn't like it and red crept into her face and neck, but to her credit, she stayed calm as she replied.

"I…we appreciate your concern, Mr. Phillips. Meet Detective Fred White…my partner. This is Truax Johnson, the deputy coroner. He's dealing with your son's case."

Jack shook hands with both men and waited. There was a nervous pause.

"Hello?"

The way Jack said it was sarcastic, but he didn't care. He knew they were in the business of not telling him anything, so he wanted to deal with that right away.

"I told you this morning that I was here to find out about my son's death…with or without you. I am not going away. And I have a lead."

"Tru," Detective Moss said at her officious best, "thanks, we'll be in touch later if we need anything else. Mr. Phillips, why don't we sit down over here?"

She pointed to some chairs to the left of the entryway and the three of them sat down.

"Now, what is it that you have?" she asked as she eased into one of the stiff looking chairs.

Jack stood; he was too hyped to sit.

"First of all, what did Tru have to say? You first, then I go."

She looked up at Jack with all of the disgust she could muster, but did not speak. It was obvious she was recalibrating, reforming her assessment of him, and reevaluating what she was going to do with him.

"You aren't going away, are you?"

"Naw. I'm as serious as a heart attack. Not easily put off. I've been in sales a lot of years and heard a lot of folks say no, met a lot of sales resistance, and still came out on top. You can't kiss me off lady. I'm here to get something done."

"We have learned that your son definitely was murdered, that he was not killed in the park, that his body was brought there to make it look like he killed himself there, and we are now in the process of finding out where he was killed. Your turn."

"I'm not surprised at all. Anyway, I was over at the Congress Center where my son's company has an exhibit at the trade show there and talked to his boss. He tells me that my son had screwy expense records for the last few years…inconsistent with previous reports to the extent it caught the attention of his company's management. There are patterns to the expenses. Those patterns, I think, will get us headed in the right direction to find his killer."

"Like what?"

"To Marietta. J.W. spent a lot of time and money there. His best customer has a design firm in Marietta. Name of Warren Crawford. Someone who should be checked out. And to Columbus; your Georgia Columbus. J.W. didn't have enough business from Columbus to be down there much, but he was. Disproportionately to any business need…any legitimate business, that is."

"Interesting," Detective Moss said. "Fred, why don't you check on this guy Crawford? Get some background, check our database, the usual stuff. Maybe there is a link."

Detective White nodded, headed for the door, and she turned back to Jack. As she eyed him, her look took on a different quality, as if for the first time it had sunk in that he was serious, that he wasn't just some Yankee jerk who had barged into her job to muck things up and get in the way.

"I'm probably jumping to conclusions, but I already have a theory about what might have been going on."

"Theories save a lot of work," she replied. "It's about lunch time, why don't we grab something to eat and we can discuss your theory...and you can tell me about your son."

"Well, I'm supposed to meet a newspaper reporter named Colby over at the Marriott."

"Let him wait. Come on, let's get some lunch."

She wanted Jack to drive, so they left her unmarked police car in the Medical Examiner's parking lot, and she directed him to a crowded joint half way to police headquarters. It was noisy, full of uniformed cops, detectives, and attorneys, which she explained as they headed for a booth near the rear. Two other plain clothes detectives were already in the booth and didn't seem to mind when she commandeered one of the seats. She motioned for Jack to sit and introduced him as he landed. They were unsettled at having a civilian in their personal and private midst, so they didn't say much at first. Detective Moss explained the situation. Both men expressed their sympathies and although their manner was gruff, Jack could tell it was sincere. Each of them had seen enough death to know the experience of loss.

"Mr. Phillips has already been at work." She wasn't sarcastic when she spoke. "He's turned up some information for us and has a theory. I wanted to get a better take on that...thought lunch would be a good time to hear him out. These guys work homicide like Fred and I do, so they could be a good audience for your ideas..."

The waitress rushed up to take their orders.

"What can I get you to drink? You boys all set?"

"Coffee, no cream," Detective Moss offered.

The other two detectives shook their heads no.

"Diet Coke. Throw a chunk of lime in it."

Jack knew he wasn't going to eat here, but he was thirsty.

"Menu's on the board," the girl pointed, "if you can't read it, ask me for something when I get back. Y'all can have just about anything y'all want."

There was no printed menu, Moss told Jack. The day's offerings were on a chalk board and in this girl's head. Just ask for something, hopefully they could match what you wanted. It didn't matter much because the waitress was gone for the drinks.

Then Moss looked at Jack for a response. The three of them waited for him to speak. He felt as if he were on the witness stand ready to testify, ready to be pounced on regardless of what he said, regardless of validity, regardless of value. He was the outsider butting into their deal and he had no credibility. Jack supposed this is why she brought him here, to get his comeuppance, to set him straight. He had been lulled into thinking that she had changed her attitude about him and here she was setting him up for the big put down, a way to get him in his place and send him home and out of their way. She wanted the upper hand and here in this stinking sandwich shop with slopped beer on the floor and loud voices of frustrated cops and inane country music twanging away, she could be in control. Flash item, Ms. Moss, he was not intimidated.

"I'm either going to puke or lose my mind," Jack said casually. "I'll see you around. This place is too noisy and it stinks. Check with me at the Marriott Marquis after you've eaten, if you still want to talk. I'll pay for my drink."

He threw two dollar bills on the table and got up to go. The two other detectives were laughing as he stood and they began sniping at Ms. Moss even before he got out of earshot.

Jack would have hated himself staying there and he figured she would catch up with him. He was glad he made the realization and decision as quickly as he did. It wasn't yet half past noon and Colby would still be waiting for him. As he made the drive to the Marriott, he reviewed the morning. One little aspect stuck out even though he wanted to discount it.

The business with the company plane bugged him. No, he would not have enjoyed a plane ride from Columbus to Atlanta with the widow Phillips, but it would have been nice to have been asked. However, that was an indication of the relationship they had over the years. Angelina – he called her Angie once and she blew a nut. 'My name is Angelina not Angie, Angie is American garbage talk for a wonderful Italian name, never call me Angie.' Angelina never tried to warm up to him. She didn't have to and she knew it. His son made no requirement on that score.

He let go of the memory and headed to the Marriott to get with Colby.

Colby was seated at a table in the hotel restaurant nursing what looked to be a martini. He was slouched over again, intently making notes, oblivious to the world around him. He sat up and his face brightened when he saw Jack approaching.

"Hey, Mr. Phillips, I almost gave up on you…"

"Call me Jack," he said casually as he sat down, "we've got work to do and you don't need to be so formal."

"How did it go at the trade show?"

His reporter's cloak came on and he was all business.

"I think pretty well. Tell you about it in a minute. I went from the World Congress center to the Medical Examiner's office and ran into Elaine Moss the detective I met with this morning at the cop house. I told her I may have a lead and she invited me to lunch and took me to this place…"

"Julie's…"

"That's the place…"

"Cops hang out there. Some of the defense attorneys, also…"

"She just wanted to yank me around…in front of an audience of two other detective guys so she could one-up me. Show me what's what for sticking my nose in where she doesn't think it belongs."

"Figures…"

"Why?"

"Well…she…"

"Tell me about her. What do you know?"

"She came sideways into the department. Well-schooled, never was a beat cop. Always was part of the detectives. Passed all the tests and everything, but not street cop experience. She had been in the military so she had some tough credentials in her background. Was some kind of investigator for the Army. Special intelligence, that kind of stuff, I think. Regardless, she had a lot of savvy and she has busted a number of big cases for APD. She's good…knows how to get on an investigation. There couldn't be anyone better working on this case with your son. She also knows how to plow through the BS. She maybe had some fun with you, but she'll come back and you'll need her."

"Thanks."

"She's tough…no doubt about it. But good."

"I'll keep that in mind. What's the word at the Ritz-Carlton?"

"Zero. Cops have it buttoned down as far as your son goes. I was able to get with a bell hop who knew your son was a regular. Once a month, maybe more. Your son flashed the cash, had everyone hopping when he stayed there. Something funny about this guy, though…name's Gary…Gary Manor…worked there a couple of years.

"Like what?"

"Like he was holding back…knew something, but was reluctant to say. You know what I mean?"

"I do. Like he was involved in some way?"

"Maybe. I mean…not in your son's death…something else…"

"Perhaps they had some kind of…of arrangement."

"You got it."

"That makes sense."

"What did you get from the company guys?" Colby asked the question, pen poised.

"I think you can help me with this. I was ready to tell Moss, but never got the chance, or at least I took the chance away. She'll get to me…I think. Anyway…my son's boss told me that he was in the process of checking out J.W.'s expenses. His expense reports had signaled something was not quite right. Seems there was a tight connection to Marietta…Warren Crawford and his interior design company…"

"A fag?"

"What?"

"A fag. Usually those cutesy designer guys are fags."

"Isn't that a pretty broad generalization? Stigmatizing without knowing."

He may have been right, but Jack thought it was a needless characterization. Surprising, too, from someone in his position in the newspaper business. Jack thought he would have been less biased.

"They're always into something in the shadow world. Was your son…ah…was your son…?"

"What are you trying to ask…was he gay?"

"Yeah, gay."

"I…no…I don't know."

Jack didn't know. But the thought had crept in several times in the past because of a variety of circumstances. He had discounted his thoughts. Here was a time of confronting the issue for him, perhaps, a gut-check on what might be the case. Let's wait to see what we find out before jumping to that assumption. Jack had already taken a leap way ahead on this other theory about the drug stuff.

"Possibility?"

"Wife…two kids. Anything is a possibility, I guess."

"Yeah. But it might be an aspect in this case…"

"Let's not assume something, Spence, we don't know about. Okay?"

"Sure, sure…sorry."

He scowled at Jack and Jack knew he wasn't convinced.

"You used the term shadow world…"

"You bet. There's a whole universe out there that lives in a shadow. Business and pleasure under the covers…in the darkness of anonymity, privacy, and secrecy. Stuff like illicit sex, cheating sex, kinky sex, drugs, drug dealing, fraud, white collar crime, the meth business, growing marijuana…all that stuff that's not out in the open. Takes place in a shadow world where the business dollars are not tracked in the GNP, the cops haven't caught up with it yet, and wives don't know what their husbands are doing, and husbands likewise don't know about their wives that are screwing around with all kinds of stuff. There used to be whore houses for cover of some of this business, now there's the shadow world that's always on the move, not in one place, highly mobile, very lucrative, bolstered by technology, and thriving. Man, is it ever really thriving, and leaving few tracks."

"Except credit card receipts, checking accounts, cell phone logs, and…juggled expense reports…to name a few. Tracks that is."

"And your point is?"

"My point is that I found out J.W. was being checked out about his expense reports. He appeared to be cheating. At least that's what I think his boss thinks. Regardless, the reports show that something was going on with one of his dealers and he was spending too much time in Columbus, Georgia. The expense reports are a reflection of the out-of-the-ordinary. We know that the out-of-the-ordinary is what we are looking for, not coincidental based on what happened to him, and a sure-fire start of an investigation. Tell me more about Ms. Moss."

He looked at Jack quizzically, trying to fathom why Jack would be asking about her again.

"You didn't finish about her…your assessment. Not just the "she's a good cop" routine. Spell it out."

"Well, like what…personal stuff?"

"Yes. Her make up."

"Like I said, tough, efficient, demanding…"

He saw the look on Jack's face.

"You mean…is she married, has kids, like that…screws around?"

Jack nodded assent. Colby was reluctant, but had the answers.

"Divorced. No kids. Ex-husband dumped her for a model who went to Vegas to make it big. He was an APD cop also…detective working vice. That's how he met the model.

She was involved with a play-for-pay deal for visiting businessmen. He got involved keeping her from getting busted, became her manager, and then left the police department. He and the model left town soon after that. The divorce was a proxy deal and Moss was not quite the same after that. During the week she lives in a little house off of Ponce de Leon about four blocks from where police headquarters used to be located. Has a place up on Lake Lanier…about an hour and a half drive from the city. Spends the weekends there when she's not involved with something or on duty. Likes the booze, likes…male companionship…"

"That means sex."

"Yeah, I understand that she's a hot number. She…she has a group of admirers…sometimes at one time."

"Yikes."

She didn't seem the type, Jack thought, but who the hell knows about these things.

"Have you considered that maybe your son was in the shadow world?"

"I would not have used that terminology until you suggested it, but all things considered it's probably a good bet that he was."

Colby sat back, admiring Jack's candor.

"Listen, Spence, I appreciate what you are doing…I need the help…but it means spending a lot of time on this. Why? Why would you want to do it?"

"I want the story…I need more background on you and your son. I want something big for Sunday."

"I understand, but I am whipped. I can give you more tomorrow. Not more than half the day is gone, but it has been big for me. I just need a little rest. Get with me tomorrow."

"I understand. Just give me the name again in Marietta. Craw…"

"Crawford…Warren Crawford."

"Yeah, that's it. Crawford…Crawford. Sounds familiar somehow. I'll check it out and I'll get with you tomorrow. Get some sleep, you look plumb tuckered out."

"Thanks, I think I will."

Colby gathered his stubby body into a walking bundle of briefcase, rumpled sport coat, disheveled pants, flying hair, and was gone.

Jack went to his room. He was exhausted. Yesterday's drive had finally caught up and the day caved in on him and he collapsed onto the bed. He was too tired to take off his clothes, too tired to even think about the rest of the afternoon, what he wanted to accomplish. He reached for his cell phone, clicked it off, and let his eyes close. He floated in space somewhere thinking of J.W., wondering if he would glide by, a heavenly body, an apparition he expected and wanted. They had not spoken much in five years. Jack's eyes flicked open and he stared at the ceiling, light forming a vague geometry of patterns, soft day-ending light that has little energy, but yet is wistful about day ending and coaxes the coming night.

4.

Time stood still as if there was no time at all; no past, no future, just an unrelenting now that dragged on into the night. Life circumstances seemed foreign; the uncertainty of events imposed on Jack's attempts for stability, his struggle with the burdens of adulthood, his understanding of duty, of caring, of nurturing created a fog of self-doubt. Somehow this sweet boy-baby was there in Jack's arms and he was the nurturer. J.W. was his responsibility, an integral part of his life. There was no turning back; no other choices perceived that could be made. There was only the moving forward in a new way. It was difficult at best. Jack was learning that nothing collides with immaturity like the responsibility of a baby.

Jim Phillips was that frightful baby with colic. What an ordeal. Surely this had to stop at some point; the crying, the unrelenting crying. The restless surge of awakeness when there should be sleep, the distended stomach, the fitful spasms of body arching outward to somehow ease the pain, the burbling gas that passed and that which did not, the overriding struggle to survive when survival was not the only potential outcome. Mother Nature works wondrous ways for providing protection, if we can but understand and match her challenge. Something was not right with this baby Jack held against his chest, but the answer was still in the future. The suffering was here with this baby and Jack, for awhile. The knowledge of a milk allergy would come later.

He had carried him from his crib to the living room and the antique rocking chair that could be their resting place. Holding, cuddling, gently rocking as the torment continued. They were alone in the night world; mother fast asleep recovering from the day, others in the household quiet, hopefully unaware of his struggle with this little being.

Jack held him to his chest as he carefully, slowly rocked the chair back and forth to form a rhythmic pattern of movement. This was the gentle sensation that has pacified babies for eons. His soft, wispy hair traced Jack's chin, a delicate feedback of sorts from him as he started to relax a bit.

The open drapes of the picture window allowed the light from the street lamp across the street to feed into the room as if he and Jack were being highlighted on stage, living performers in a tableau of desperation for relief.

Suddenly, there was a strange army marching after Jack, relentless in their pursuit. He ran, of course, holding this baby to him as he charged across a plowed field, stumbling, forcing himself to go on without falling, knowing somehow deep within that he could outrun them, that he could carry his child to safety. He reached the woods and the army came on in disregard, sure of their conquest, sure of their target. Suddenly, he realized that he had powers that he had never before possessed and he turned to face the army. He raised his hand forcefully at them in a salute of containment and they stopped, and then they vanished, quietly, swiftly, as if they were but a poof of smoke that had been sucked away and up the flue. The child had remained asleep throughout the episode and never awoke and he knew that he had escaped something predatory and he was relieved.

The walls seemed close to him as if he could reach out and touch them when he knew he could not. How could he survive this?

In the distance the signature, plaintive whistle of a train called out to the night world that it was in motion, ready to cross its own controlled space, ready to run over any late night idiot that transgressed its path. For Jack, that whistle was a sound which brought back childhood memories of lying in bed waiting to go to sleep, a lonely signal that meant sleeplessness, and a warning for the world that could hear its expressive call.

He longed desperately for compassionate sleep. He had an all consuming need for rest and relief from this child. Visions of the past and memories of what he wanted would not work for him; they would not console him nor divert his attention from this situation.

Where was that train going and where was that army headed? Both impacted him with powerful resonance beyond their vague existence only because it was night and he was tired and vulnerable and wanted some answer of relief.

In the middle of the night, sounds are magnified, thoughts are exaggerated. It is a distorted world. This must be one reason why so-called night people are out of sync with things.

Eventually there was no sound, no vision, no crying, and no motion. Father and baby had both succumbed to peaceful sleep, a blessing, a wonderful blessing that would let both of them last the night.

There was an end to the peace for Jack. There came a cascade of soundless, penetrating light as the sun surged forward and the new day became ready. He carried the bundle that was his son to his crib and laid him carefully in a place where he curled into comfort and continued contented sleep. Jack showered, shaved, dressed, ate one piece of toast, and headed for work. He understood he was part of a social system that for the present kept him contained in menial work and understood that there was more for him in this system at some point in the future. He knew that had to be true; it was what kept him motivated. If he could only survive this baby and other frustrations he would make it. He thought about surviving the day, tired as he was, and whether or not he could make it. Such a thought was silly in context with what his father had endured. How limited he was. How much he had to work to surpass the notion that he would somehow cave and retreat in submission. Success does not accept that and he wanted success. He would have success and his son would benefit somehow.

This was a time of turmoil for little Jimmy. Did his own turmoil match J.W.'s? Who knows? He was trying to finish college at night school, working full time days, dealing with a less than stable wife who was now a reluctant mother. J.W. was struggling, he was struggling. Neither of them really knew the severity of their struggle right then and what it might mean long term.

That's how Jack and J.W. passed many of those early nights when he was a precious baby.

5.

The phone rang in the distance, a vaguely familiar sound, muffled in the fog of sleep, and somehow Jack knew he should respond. He had intended his nap to be short, but a quick glance at the clock showed he had been asleep more than two hours.

"Hello," Jack said hoarsely.

"Were you asleep? Sorry. This is Detective Moss…Elaine Moss. Remember me?"

"Vaguely."

He didn't hold back on making it sound unwelcome.

"Sorry, again. I was feeling ornery, I guess, being pressed about your son…by you. You came on pretty strong. I know you're very concerned and I'd like to meet with you…let you know what we've found out while you were…."

She hesitated, searching for what she wanted to say. She sighed slightly before she continued.

"…while you were recovering from the drive down yesterday. And I would like to hear what you were going to tell me at lunch…your theory…and sort of compare notes. I'm in the lobby. All you have to do is come downstairs. Say five minutes?"

"The Marriott lobby?"

"Yes."

"I'll be right down."

He dropped the phone onto its cradle on the desk set and took a look in the mirror, realizing he needed to comb his hair. No sooner had he picked up his comb than the phone rang again.

"Yes." He wasn't hoarse, but he was curt. "Who is it?"

"Colby. Let's get together. I've found out a few things. Some interesting stuff."

"Okay, but I'm meeting with Detective Moss in a few minutes in the lobby…"

"Oh really? How nice. What does she want?"

"I don't know. She says compare notes…let me know what they have found out since this morning. I shouldn't be too long with her."

"Call me when you get free of her and we'll meet. I think we might want to take a ride up to Marietta."

"Good idea. Her partner Fred White said he was going to check on Crawford, but I want to do that, too."

"Yeah, the smell of this thing is coming from there. Warren Crawford lives there, has his business there. Your son spent a lot of time there."

"Yes. What did you find out?"

"Call me when you're through with Miss Moss, or when she's through with you."

Colby gave him his cell phone number and Jack carefully entered it in his planner.

Elaine Moss was standing by the concierge's desk when he got to the lobby. She saw him coming and smiled, belying her impatience and her eagerness to be someplace else. There was this feline quality about her, the trim athletic body, and the look of female satisfaction that he usually interpreted as the look of seduction. That probably was not the case with her, however, since he hardly thought of himself as a prospect. She shot out her hand as he approached.

"Sorry about lunch," she said quickly as she shook his hand, "but I'll make it up to you."

"I'll live."

The somber tone a hint of his feelings as he hurriedly tried to factor what was going on with this woman cop. She was in a rush as he suspected.

"This is a lousy place to talk. Why don't we get your car and I'll take you to a nice place for dinner. Not a cop place. We can talk better there…my treat. Okay?"

He didn't answer, but just looked at her. She held her broad smile, teeth showing slightly, a glint in her eyes, almost mischievous, certainly trying to be amiable.

"Come on, let's get your car."

"Where's your cop car?"

"I had one of the guys drop me off," she said in partial explanation.

"Pretty sure I would comply weren't you?"

"I hoped you would. Otherwise…"

"Otherwise what?"

"I would have had to…to figure something out."

Jack's guess was she never counted on his refusing. She knew his desire to learn more was too overwhelming.

Valet parking got his car and they were on their way. He followed the directions she gave and they headed north away from downtown. She was chatty, running on about the city its problems and potential, the challenges cops faced, drug issues, the weather, and the crummy way cops are thought of by the public. She steered clear of J.W.'s case.

Jack had enough of the inconsequential tour guide stuff and cut her off with a look.

"Let's get back on track. What have you learned?"

"Well…for one thing, we found out where your son was killed. We have some forensics and we're working on some other things. We're not standing still on this. We're active on your son's killing." She paused for a moment then said, "And I want to hear about your theory, maybe it will help."

She didn't say much more and it wasn't long that her directions got them to the Buckhead Diner. After a surprisingly short wait they were seated.

"Satisfied?" She asked.

"Yes, nice place."

Buckhead Diner was bright, glitzy chic, upscale like everything in the Buckhead area, filled with expensive people, and too loud for his taste. Not the sort of place cops frequented, but then he was beginning to think Ms. Moss was not your usual cop.

She tensed up and looked around as if she were expecting to see someone she knew, some suspect not found, a girl friend and her date, a good-looking prospect to hit on, some ex-boy friend, perhaps. For a few seconds she was totally disconnected from Jack as she gazed around, swiveling her head left and then right. She raised herself ever so slightly to peer over his shoulder. And then she was satisfied that whoever it was she might discover was not there. She relaxed.

"Everything all right? He, she not here?"

"Ah, yeah. I…I…"

"Forget it. Let's get to the reasons we want to talk. Fill me in…"

"Right."

Now she was concentrating on him, full in the face, serious, her face scrunched up a bit, a tad of biting the inside of her lip.

"I need to know" she went on with intensity, "that I can trust you not to repeat stuff to the press…Colby, any others. The electronic folks will be on you soon."

"That's a given; I understand."

"Good. I need to have your word on that because I'm not supposed to tell you anything. All info to the outside is supposed to come from our Public Affairs office. I'm in real trouble if it gets to the press. But I understand your situation…your anxiety about your son's murder. I know you want to know what's going on."

"You have my word on it. I know guys just like Colby, I know the media. It's my business."

"What is your business?"

"I'm a partner in an advertising agency in Columbus, Ohio. That's where my son lived and it's also the headquarters for his company."

"Oh…okay."

"You said you found out where J.W. was killed."

She didn't get to answer before a young waitress appeared to cheerily get their drink order.

"Martini," Ms. Moss said quickly, "very dry…up."

"Your house Chardonnay, please."

The waitress smiled and was gone.

"His hotel room?" Jack asked, impatient to get moving on the information.

"Yes, how did you know?"

"I didn't, but they wouldn't have killed him at any of their places or near them. Downtown, away from them, in his hotel room, that would work."

I had for some time recognized that J.W. struggled with a matter of personal identity and realized the irony of dying in the Ritz-Carlton would have been preferable for him than dying in a city park; loathe to have been found in such a place, suffering such an indignity.

"And the move to the park?" she asked.

"They wanted it to look like a suicide, confuse the issue, and make things more difficult. Crazy thinking, but what difference does that make?"

"You keep saying they. Are you speaking editorially?"

"No, I'm not. It gets to my idea…my theory of what was going on…what happened."

"Let's hear it," she said softly.

She gave him a look as she spoke, tilting her head slightly, raising her eyebrows somewhat, a look that seemed to say, "I dare you to come up with anything that makes sense." It may not have been what she was thinking, but it was his perception. His gut told him that Ms. Moss was caught in a bind about helping him, in the context that she was sympathetic to his position, but couldn't quite release herself from defending her turf.

The waitress was back with their drinks.

"Ready to order?" she said hurriedly, eager to take care of them.

He wasn't and nodded to Ms. Moss. Neither of them had checked the menus, but he let her respond.

"Give us a couple of minutes," she said without looking at the girl.

"Sure," the girl said and spun away.

Ms. Moss concentrated on Jack and the eyebrows went up again. She took half of the martini with the first swig.

"J.W. made good money with Mondrian Industries," He began to explain, "but there's a way to make even bigger money…in drugs."

"Are you saying your son…you think your son was a drug dealer?"

"Perhaps…I don't know…I think it's possible. That's the simple answer to his death. Undoubtedly it's more complicated than that, but yes, I think he was involved with drugs…with others…the *they* you asked about."

She was taken aback and furrowed her brow as she stared at him.

"Didn't you think of that?" Jack asked. "You should have because it answers a lot of questions and directs the investigation in the right way. What prompts murder? Passion and money. Sometimes both. Think about it. Think about drug operations where someone cheats and you have a scenario for murder. Think about all the time spent here in Atlanta and Columbus, Georgia. Something more than selling cabinets got J.W. down here and down to Columbus where he got little business for his company. It was something that meant money, big money. I came up with drugs. What would you come up with?"

Ms. Moss chuckled before she spoke. She finished the martini.

"You think something went wrong with a drug operation? You watch too much TV. Respected business people are not usually into drugs. Why should they be? They're making so much money legit. Cheating the IRS is a more likely crime for them."

"What makes you think Warren Crawford is a respected businessman? Or my son, for that matter. My guess is that both of them were cheating the IRS, but not in the way you mean. I think you need to get your drug task force guys involved. Atlanta Police has a drug task force, I assume."

"Yes. Yes, we do. But I need more than your guess to get them involved."

"Ready yet?" The high powered waitress had reappeared.

They quickly surveyed the menu while she waited, gave her their orders, and Ms. Moss ordered another martini. The aggressive waitress hustled away, happy to keep them moving along. Turning tables a high priority for this gal.

Ms. Moss must have been mulling over what he had said because as soon as the girl went away she took a note pad and pen from her purse and started writing. She held the pad in her hand in a way that kept him from seeing what it was that she scribbled. A practiced habit, he assumed, but he would have liked to have seen what she wrote.

"I'll get with Fred, find out what he's turned up on Crawford," she said flatly. "Now, tell me something about your son."

"Crawford's in Marietta. How can you…?"

"We work closely with the other law enforcement agencies around Atlanta. We have a contact in the Marietta police department. He'll let Fred know about Crawford."

"I see." He wondered how well that worked. No choice, however, but he figured he would touch base with them on his own, anyway. "Who's that?" He tried to be casual when he asked and she responded.

"Larry Davis. He's one of their detectives."

Jack nodded, took a sip of his wine, fumbled with his napkin, and looked away as he mentally logged the name.

"What can you tell me about your son that might help?" she insisted.

"His wife wasn't much help, I guess."

"She was no help, really. ID'ed her husband, answered the basic questions, and walked away. She said she would be available by phone in Columbus…Ohio…if we had further questions. She said she had to get back to her kids…."

"Her kids?"

"Yes, she said her kids, not their kids or our kids; it was *"her kids."*

"Yeah, that sounds about right for her."

Jack didn't pay much attention to what he ate, but he did have another glass of wine and talked about his son as much as he knew might help her.

He was limited because J.W. and he had not talked much over the last several years. There was this chasm between them, an odd circumstance considering the relationship they once had that was founded on mutual caring and respect. Or at least Jack had thought that was the case. However, in one of the last conversations they had, J.W. expressed something counter to that, something quite unlike Jack's perceptions, something so negative and critical it stunned him as if he had been bludgeoned. Critical of Jack's efforts as a father, J.W.'s remarks were of feelings that poured out like a dropped bag of sand that splits open on pavement. He had said that Jack was a lousy father and scolded Jack with his claim that he had never ever really been emotionally connected to Jack. The words stung like a whip lash, tearing apart their relationship, rendering Jack mute, without retort, and groping for an answer. Eventually, Jack would have little feeling for something he could not understand. Jack's emotions were like the spilled sand, scattered and useless, easily sent away by any stiff breeze that came along, ephemeral, and meaningless.

Jack was so shocked by J.W.'s assessment that he did not even ask why, ask for clarification, or at the least, counter his claims. The words had been spoken by J.W. and all Jack could do was numbly scribble them on a yellow pad.

What were the reasons? The lingering anger and pain that J.W. felt from divorcing his mother? Childhood slights or misunderstandings? Presumed slights and misunderstandings as an adult? What were his perceptions? Jack had always been solicitous and polite toward J.W.'s Italian wife. The reasons were within J.W. and he struck out at Jack because of them, whatever they were.

Over time, the sting went away. There was this lack of meaning from not being able to relate to or understand his comments. Essentially, Jack was busy building a business, life had to move on, and the issue was no longer important. The pain from J.W.'s castigation eased.

Jack's friends fretted for him, suffering in silence for awhile before carefully trying to gauge what anguish Jack might have. Eventually, he could level with them about what had happened. Most of them were supportive, but he was not sure they understood his resilience and his toughness in not responding to his son's accusations. He merely moved ahead with his life without J.W. As is often the case in matters such as this, some friends respected his position and others were quietly critical. Jack didn't blame those who were critical, but, of course, their support would have been a better reaction. Some of them were still a part of Jack's life; friendly, but not friends.

So what he knew to tell Ms. Moss about J.W. in the present were merely generalities from observations and perceptions based on past contact with him. They were highlighted by the contradictions in his personality, namely that he was capable, but unsure of himself; successful, but unhappy; intellectually curious, but unfulfilled; disdainful of those who have achieved and have things, but grasping tenaciously to the right house, the right community, the right neighborhood, the right car, and a long list of material imperatives. Jack had decided some years ago, even before their falling out, that J.W. was a person adrift in life who did not know who he was; without identity and essentially without character. It was a deadly assessment that Jack had not shared with J.W. On the other hand, perhaps J.W. had indeed identified himself and he didn't like what he saw.

Before their relationship degenerated Jack knew that J.W. was a rising star at Mondrian. Top management loved him while his peers hated him for his facile success, his glib demeanor that bordered on arrogance, and his suck-up behavior with the bosses. He was a sales leader and gloried in that accomplishment.

"How was his marriage?" Ms. Moss asked.

She had been listening carefully to what Jack had been saying, making a few notes, and letting him expound without interruption until this question.

"I guess it depends on whose standards you use."

He was dodging the issue. She knew it, probably saw it in his face, and heard it in his voice. But Jack wasn't sure how he wanted to answer that question. How would he, should he, be the judge of J.W.'s marriage? He had never liked J.W.'s wife, although he had never had any direct conflict with her. He had been a bystander, a witness on the sidelines like watching an auto accident that occurred in slow motion, agonizing and painful to observe, and then hoping against hope that you aren't called upon to be a witness by the police.

"Marriages come in all shapes and sizes."

He gave Ms. Moss that platitude that he assumed she wasn't buying. What was the straight answer? He probably didn't know. He only thought he knew. What should he say?

"Not good, I guess."

She didn't look at Jack, but rather doodled among her notes. He was watching her now and realized she was hip to his discomfort at making the assessment, or at least, in stating it out loud.

"Not the way I assume a marriage should be," Jack said flatly.

"Figures. She didn't seem to be the grieving widow when she was here to deal with the body. Pretty cold."

"You said."

"What else?"

He looked at her. They weren't on the same page. What was she digging for, what did she want?"

"About your son...what else can you tell me?"

"Like what? I think that I..."

"Something on the side? A girl friend? With a wife like that it wouldn't be surprising. Perhaps that was what got him down here to Atlanta so much and to Columbus. Maybe a couple of special friends? He used the extra expense money to take care of his girl friends, have a good time. A better time than he was having at home. Had you thought of that?"

Jack had thought of that, but not in the context she was surmising. A far different context, one suggested by Colby that he had privately not discounted and that he had kept to himself. He didn't know why, but he had suspected for some time that J.W. doubted his masculinity. There were a number of little things that in themselves weren't much, yet taken in total presented a different picture. And then there was the cousin once removed who was gay; his mother's cousin, a symbol of homosexuality who had comported himself with his lover throughout J.W.'s formative years, an exemplar who might well create anxiety about one's own sexuality.

J.W. never had many male friends. Jack didn't take notice of that at first, but it was later on, when he was in his twenties with no close male friends, that he began to wonder about the reason. Perhaps an overreaction on Jack's part? Fear of the truth springing forth? Fear of dealing with reality because of what J.W. might say? These had been his thoughts, his concern for J.W., a subject he felt he could not broach with J.W. even though he believed it would have cleared the air. Also, Jack's divorce and career used up the energy he would have needed to deal with what was essentially J.W.'s situation. It was a situation Jack saw as removed, remote, and not his highest priority. Anyway, J.W. seemed to be moving on with his life in those years, albeit sans partner, so it wasn't a preoccupation with Jack. The circumstances of retrospect are wonderful in their seeming clarity.

During that time of moving on with his life, he and Jack were in contact, talking by phone and periodically in person, writing letters, and generally building on a relationship Jack thought he had established when J.W. was younger, when he was still married to J.W.'s mother, and when they had continuous contact. There were few recriminations by him, few complaints, and almost no animosity that Jack discerned. They had some good times, enjoyed mutual interests in special books and movies and music. Jack really didn't worry much as J.W. got older and was unmarried and unlinked with anyone.

Along came Angelina like an unexpected natural disaster. It is a story in itself how that came about. A depressing story, Jack thought.

"Where are you?" Ms. Moss asked quietly, almost a whisper.

"Um...away, I guess. Someplace else. Sorry, I got wound up in my own thoughts."

"I could tell. We ought to get going. I know you're worn out from the stress. I'd appreciate it if you'd drop me off...at my house."

Jack didn't argue. He was ready to move on to get with Colby. He paid the bill over her protest and drove to her house several blocks from the old APD station. It was a threadbare neighborhood of small single-family homes packed tightly on each block. A numbing dreariness about the area matched the stolid brick building where she once reported for work. There were some better sections in the area that looked more upscale, but it didn't help alleviate the general feeling of depression these houses gave.

As they had driven and she gave directions, Jack determined that White had dropped her off at the Marriott. He would pick her up in the morning. When he pulled up in front of her place she looked at her watch.

"You plan to get back to the hotel and get a good night sleep?" She asked the question with an air of familiarity that Jack hadn't realized they had attained.

"Yes, I'm tired," he lied, "It's been a long day."

"Touch base with me tomorrow, maybe I'll know something. See what Fred's turned up. By the way do I have your cell number?"

"No, but here's my card. Cell number is on it."

"I'll talk to you tomorrow then…good night."

She got out of Jack's car and walked to the door without looking back and went inside. There was something about the walk; graceful, athletic, and sensuous in its fluidity. She knew Jack would be watching and was very deliberate in her carriage and step. She didn't do anything as blatantly obvious as wiggle her rump, but the effect she wanted was reached nonetheless. He had this idea that when a woman is interested in you some strange link takes place, some invisible wire is formed that runs directly from her calculating brain to the pit of your stomach with branches that run to your gonads. Jack could feel the signal as she walked away from him; in both places.

6.

Jack drove to Ponce de Leon Avenue, headed west to the upscale mall across from the former APD headquarters, and pulled to a stop by one of the shops. He had not wanted her to see him on his cell phone and this was a good chance to contact Colby. He was not sure why he was playing it so close to the vest, but for right now he didn't want her to know what they were doing. Let them dig stuff out on their own. Besides, he had his gun-in-holster nestled at his side; another reason to not let Ms. Moss know what was happening with him. He wanted to be prepared for…for whatever.

When Colby answered his cell phone Jack could tell he was eating. There was the slurred muffle that indicated he had some food in his mouth.

"How'd it go with Moss?" Colby asked, swallowing, and then clearing his throat as if Jack wouldn't notice.

"Okay. Where are you?"

"Marietta. At Shillings; having dinner. It's on the town square. I've learned some things, Mr. Phillips…most informative. Got some names; found out about the players. Why don't you meet me here. We need to move on to a place called the Sublime. We might be able to find out some stuff there. Where are you?"

Colby was excited when he spoke and it energized Jack even though he was as tired as Ms. Moss suggested. Colby had discovered some things. They would probably be doing what the police would not do which had been Jack's suspicion all along. Not that they wouldn't do their job, they would, its just that it might not be as thorough as it should or could be.

"I'm here by the old cop headquarters on Ponce de Leon. I took Ms. Moss home; she lives nearby. Give me some easy directions."

Colby did and Jack got up to Marietta in less than half an hour. He stumbled a bit trying to find the town square, but his GPS got him on track. Minutes later he was parked across the street from Shillings. Colby was at a table in the rear. He smiled when he saw Jack making his way to him and Jack could see he was pleased with himself. He had finished eating, although still working on a glass of white wine.

"Mr. Phillips," he began as Jack sat down, "you're going to like the progress I've made…" He paused. "Or maybe not."

"What have you learned?"

"Lots," Colby said, with real struggle against breathlessness, "and I haven't gotten to Crawford yet. He seems to be out of town…on business. In Columbus, the receptionist said. How about that? But one of my contacts told me about his friend Collier French. He's an architect here in Marietta and has his own firm, French-Siddons. Uses a bunch of Mondrian products in his projects and, as a result, has a heavy-duty connection with Crawford's design company."

"So what's this place you wanted me to go with you…the Sub…"

"Yeah, Sublime, the place where, I understand, French hangs out. Also, Crawford. Also, your son. You've eaten…have a wine, we've got time."

He had the waitress bring two more glasses of wine and in a self-satisfied way slumped back in his chair and looked at Jack with the appraisal of a butcher checking a slab of newly procured beef. How did Jack fit in his ambitions? He wanted this story – about J.W. - that was for sure, and he was driven for some reason to forge ahead without knowing the outcome. Although Jack suspected Colby had some sense of what he thought the outcome might be.

Colby was a man who would be obscure in a crowd; average, mild, medium, and nondescript by any accounts, a man blending with the world around him, a man lost in the condition of being unspecial. But on the other hand, he was diligent in his pursuit of the news, dug for information, and a reporter who had, for almost ten years, cultivated a myriad of sources around Atlanta that could get him to the heart of an issue very quickly. That included sources from the underbelly of the city in the unseemly goings on within its social structure to all aspects of the counter-culture and the denizens of borderline legal to full-blown illegal. His blandness was a distinct positive for the manner in which he ferreted out what was important on any story and for getting a handle on the salient elements that needed to be revealed and presented. He was a fooler who could come away with the answers, the confirmation of notions held, and the discoverer of what was bad and awful and ugly in a city where only the nice and good and pretty wanted to be accepted.

After a while, Jack realized that ordering the wine, taking their time, and commiserating about the essentials of this situation were merely stalling tactics. He finally called Colby on it.

"Why the hell are we still sitting here? Why don't we get to the Sublime?"

"Action doesn't get started over there too early," he answered carefully, directly, "nicer to stay here where no one will pay any attention to us before we take on the Sublime. It'll seem low-keyed, but it's not really. It's really pretty intense. Finish your wine and we'll go."

Walking into the Sublime knocked Jack out. The place was supremely gorgeous, the most exquisite combination of restaurant and night club he had ever seen. It presented a magnificent first impression as he entered. His followed-up detailed examination gave him appreciation for the subtle extravagant quality of design and workmanship that was exhibited throughout. Once he had absorbed the profound impact of the place, the overall impression was a realization of softness and sophistication which epitomized the décor. Muted earthen tones and cleverly arranged indirect lighting cast a warm glow that was almost a signal for something impending, perhaps some exciting occurrence of artistry, some revelation of creativity not before seen. The sense he got was that this was intended to be the center of the creative universe and that if some wonderful artistic thing were to happen it would emanate from this place. There was plush carpeting throughout, except for the dance floor, and few hard surfaces so that when he and Colby spoke to each other it was as if they were in a special chamber for sound testing or quite like a hushed, sound-deadened recording studio.

Yes, the Sublime was a club where intimates could meet and whisper to each other, where intimacy could take place with a sense of privacy.

The dance floor appeared to be teak with a floral design in its center created with variety of lighter woods using a marquetry technique. The curved lip of a raised stage was at the edge, large enough to hold a small musical ensemble. There was a featured female singer shown on posters in the lobby. The name said Mickie Gillonde, a stunning blonde dressed in a red strapless evening gown à la Monroe. However, in this case Mickie was a man. As it turned out, he was a very handsome man in person without the costume, attractive well beyond the stilted publicity photo on the posters.

The Sublime bar, an island located towards one side of the room, was enormous, yet not garish. Probably forty feet long and tended by four men and a young woman. Jack later learned she only had one leg and didn't cover as much of the bar as the four men, but she seemed to be very popular with those who ordered and attracted large numbers to her station. The five were neatly dressed wearing dark blue slacks, light blue button-down shirts with blue and cream striped ties, and light gray sleeveless sweaters. They were professional to the hilt. Shortly, Jack noticed that all of the wait staff were dressed accordingly. There were no females among the waiters, only young, very handsome men.

The Sublime was quite an experience and lived up to its name. If a night club can be such a thing this place was it. Jack figured it was like a well-groomed whore house, only classier, where style and good taste and a low-keyed atmosphere were its hallmarks.

Colby had the foresight to make a reservation and when he gave his name to the maitre d' they were escorted to a booth away from the dance floor. Colby craned his head looking around, eyes darting about checking for anyone recognizable.

"Not here yet," he mused.

"French?"

Jack assumed he meant the guy they were there to meet, but he clarified it anyway.

"Yeah, he'll be here," Colby confirmed.

As Jack followed Colby's eyes continuing to scan the room, he suddenly noticed the lack of women other than the young barmaid, and the realization hit him. This was a spot that must be for gay men. Colby seemed to notice his look and apparent lock-in on what Sublime is.

"Yep...it's a gay club, alright. I thought you would get it right away, especially based on our previous conversation...about your son. They all frequent this place like I said; Crawford, French, and your son. They're real tight; this is their spot."

"This guy French, what do you know about him?"

Just then their waiter approached, requesting an order. Colby asked for a club soda, Jack did also, and the young man was away.

"I know a lot more than I did two days ago. My source…sources, really, were able to give me some good juice about him. And Crawford…"

"And J.W.?"

"Yeah…yeah, also about your son."

Jack watched as Colby turned away slightly, stare at something across the room, and pucker his brow. He was reluctant to say much about J.W. quite yet, afraid to hurt Jack's feelings, more willing than not to let discovery be a revelation for what Jack needed and wanted to know about J.W. Jack could assume what the links and connections to the two other men might mean, that they would substantiate his conjecture about J.W., and bring to light what had been hidden away.

"Let's start with French and work backward."

"Right," Colby said. "French is an architect. Top notch. Partnered up with a straight fellow name of Doug Siddons who is an engineer by profession. French does the designing, Siddons figures out if and how it can be built. They've developed a very successful and well-respected business in the Atlanta area. They specialize in big homes for the ultra-wealthy and small commercial developments like small shopping malls, medical centers, that type of thing. Siddons is married, three teen-age kids, church going, respectable, and completely out of the social world that French travels in."

"Yin and yang." Jack was really thinking out loud when he said it, not intending for Colby to even respond.

"Sort of, but without the tight connection."

"How so?"

"I'm told they only meet occasionally when a project makes it necessary, otherwise they communicate by email or notes. French has his assistant take the plans to Siddons, Siddons does the engineering, and then sends the results back to

French via his assistant. They do, however, make joint presentations to prospective clients and established clients, that sort of thing, and it goes very well. They work in the same offices everyday, but you wouldn't say they work together. I should say Siddons is there every day, French is seldom there. He mainly works at home."

"How does he link to Crawford?"

Their drinks were delivered by their waiter without a word and he was gone.

"Easy. They met in college when they both were studying architecture. French went on to get his degree and got licensed, while Crawford never finished the program and took a jog off into interior design. I hear that Crawford is considered one of the top interior designers in the southeast. He has projects going on all over besides Atlanta. He has stuff going in Charleston, Jacksonville, Charlotte, you name it. Big time, big bucks."

"How did they both get to this area? I doubt if it were a coincidence."

"Nope, they were more than just college buddies. Roommates all the time they were in school until Crawford crashed and burned. Both southerners, Crawford from here in Marietta, moneyed family, father had been in some kind of importing business. French was from Macon, I think. They both came to Atlanta after college, got successful, and moved to Marietta to have their own businesses. They lived with Crawford's mother until she died. The old man died years ago; had a heart attack in Greece when he was there on business. I understand they lived together up until about five years ago…about the time your son came on the scene. French moved out of the old Crawford mansion and has a condo a mile or so from here. You can see how it worked for them…compatible businesses, I mean. French brought Crawford in as the interior designer for his projects. Crawford also had a number of product lines he represented and sold that would go into the jobs. It was a sweet setup for the two of them. Crawford started handling Mondrian stuff and that's how your son got involved with these two guys."

"Crawford took a liking to J.W., I assume."

"Yeah, seems so. I thought we might find out something from French. He agreed to meet me here tonight. I think he wants to separate himself from your son's death, maybe explain how he's not involved. At least that's the idea I got when I talked to him on the phone."

Jack's thoughts drifted away from Colby for a moment while he tried to sort out how he felt about the implications of what Colby had said. Jack got the meaning. His visions of memories of J.W. were blurred with the overlay of such meaning. He could see J.W. as a sturdy, capable athlete, solid public speaker, hard-working businessman – all in normal terms. Yet something was awry, not what it had seemed for his concept of this young man; his son. Not at all what Jack had believed, even though the suspicions of another kind had crept into his thoughts. There must have been attraction to this man Crawford, reciprocated or not perhaps, but a relationship ignited. What kind of relationship? One that strayed from amorous to illegal; that contained both? Why, and for what reason? The thrill of it; the money? Ah, yes, the money. Was the satisfaction money? Jack supposed it could be that for J.W. Being a top salesman, making gobs of money wasn't enough satisfaction. Jack could not relate to that answer. In his work it was the job, the challenge, the process, and the solution that gave him satisfaction; the big income was incidental and great results for the client was frosting on the cake. He didn't understand hungering for money, although he saw it often enough. He just never thought it would be part of J.W. Maybe there was another answer, more complex, something else he might not understand.

"He just came in," Colby whispered.

A dapper, well-dressed man in his mid-fifties stood in the lobby chatting amiably with the maitre d'. He soon turned and headed toward Jack and Colby. He was ruggedly handsome with looks and stature that might indicate a former football player or boxer, but his movements were fleetingly feminine, although that might have been Jack's own prejudice. In any case, his bearing wasn't manly enough to match his looks. Wearing an obviously expensive tailor-made gray suit with a hand-made white shirt and muted gray and black tie, he gave the impression of a successful businessman. Here was a businessman who wasn't very aggressive, but talented and perhaps on the receiving end of good fortune or a significant inheritance. God love a nice inheritance.

"Gentlemen, good evening," he said graciously as he got to their booth, "you must be Spencer Colby…and you must be…"

His voice still carried the overtones of what had once been a Georgian drawl, now smooth and precise in its practiced delivery. He had luxurious gray-streaked, curly black hair that, upon closer inspection, maintained it's magnificence with an intricately achieved comb-over. It surely must take him forever to get every strand in place; deft with a comb, to be sure.

"Jack Phillips," he helped.

"Yes, indeed…Jim's father. You have my condolences, sir, heartfelt condolences. I grieve for your loss…and mine."

Colby slid over, gesturing a seat for him as he did so, and Collier French sat down next to him.

"My name is Collier French. I was very fond of your son, Mr. Phillips, I hope you don't mind my saying so. Very fond, for sure. And I suppose that I might have contributed to your son's demise. I'm not positive of that, but that is certainly possible if not probable."

Colby casually slipped his note pad and pen from the inside pocket of his sport coat, and then slid it on the table slightly to his right, away from French. He was poised and ready. French was looking at Jack for some kind of reaction to his confession of affection and didn't notice Colby.

"You and J.W. were lovers?"

The bluntness of Jack's question shocked French terribly and an appalled look came over him as he struggled for an answer. He was trying to factor just who the hell Jack was; what kind of man he might be who would ask, and who might react violently with the answer. He had no idea how Jack would react, he had no idea how calm Jack was about the potential revelation.

French exhaled before he spoke.

"Yes," he said slowly, quietly.

Their waiter appeared next to French as if had simply materialized and leaned toward the man as if ready to share a matter of confidence.

"Your usual, Mr. French?" the waiter asked politely.

"Yes, yes, please, Connie…thank you."

Connie disappeared as quickly as he had appeared.

French was relieved by the interruption, able to gather himself, and able to right himself to continue.

"Mr. Phillips…"

"Jack…its okay, you can call me Jack."

"I…I really don't know quite what to say…really."

The old drawl crept in now more than before. He had lost his composure a bit and the drawl betrayed him.

Jack made it easier for him and picked up on what he had said a moment before.

"You said you may have contributed to J.W.'s death. How did you mean that?"

"Well, Jim had been involved with Warren Crawford and I got in the way of that relationship. Warren was furious. He threatened me, but I figured that was nothing to be concerned about. It can't be denied, however, that he has a vicious temper. After all, Warren and I had been very close and that, too, was a factor."

"You and Crawford had been lovers?"

He hesitated again before he spoke.

"Yes. Over years ago, however."

Well, there it is; another slap in the face. Jack's son was a man with two different male lovers. He was caught in a male love triangle. Somehow that isn't what Jack expected when he came to Atlanta. It was supposed to be suicide, then murder, which he expected, and now this. The alienation that he felt from J.W. was surely complete. J.W.'s life was a formulation of style and experience for which Jack had scant knowledge. His sexual proclivities were at the forefront of the entire episode and Jack could not, in all honesty, relate to them. Oh, sure, he could be magnanimously sympathetic, but he really couldn't relate. Walk in another man's shoes and all that. It would take some serious reflection on his part to sort out all of this. And it would take some time.

This was a situation Jack never would have imagined as part of his life. He was sitting across the table from one of his dead son's lovers. Now, if this were to have been a supple, young woman, appropriately attractive and bright, the consideration would have been significantly different. The assessment would be the kind he could and undoubtedly would make of the opposite sex with whom his son was involved; cheating on his wife to be sure, but certainly understandable in the context of the kind of cheating with which he was familiar. But this, this was something far different, far removed from the context of his experience.

Jack studied Collier French. He concentrated, focusing his considerable intellectual skill within narrow constraints outside the bounds of his prejudices and life knowledge which made up previous perceptions. He tried to make it a new look, a new assessment rather than revisiting old information. How should he feel, he wondered? How should he react? Life surely was replete with surprising twists and turns and here was one he could not have expected. The focus and processing were not enough, he could not come to grips with an answer to how he felt and what he thought. The prejudices and the old information were so overwhelming they stymied his mental gymnastics for new clarity.

For Jack, his answer needed to be netted out to the simplest form, which was the way he usually solved an advertising problem. The answer was that his son and this man had been lovers in whatever context and dimension that transpired. The sexuality of it was no more his business than if this person were the supple, young woman, appropriately attractive and bright who might be easier to accept. Collier French was handsome, articulate, bright, and highly successful. Jack let go of it and regained his contact with French.

Connie the waiter appeared with French's drink and placed it in front of him with an adroit affectation that bordered on silly. Jack had noticed his maneuver when he served Colby and him, but with French the manner was even more pronounced. He was performing, Jack figured.

"Yes, it got complicated...it is complicated," French continued.

"It's murder," Jack said softly, "and you know things that can help me get to the bottom of it."

Colby was now carefully making notes.

"Like what, Jack, how can I help?"

"Crawford and J.W. were involved in something," Jack said quickly, "beyond interior design stuff, something big…something probably illegal…like drugs."

"Yes." French paused and said nothing for a moment. "They had a…um…a drug…a drug deal going. I got in the way of that, too, in some respects, although I never asked Jim to get out of it with Warren. I really didn't put any pressure on him at all. No way; I didn't. It was something separate from us, his business deal with Warren. Oh my, it was more complicated than that. They were making huge amounts of money. I think that meant more to Warren than it did to Jim. Warren didn't want anything to change, that's for sure. I was the instigator of change. Jim cared more for me than he did for Warren; it was a terrible blow to Warren. He and I had words. 'How can you do this to me after all these years?' That's what Warren said to me. He was terribly accusative, very intimidating, and, frankly, very frightening. I did stand up to him, let me tell you. 'How dare you accuse me, you bastard, of doing anything wrong when you cast me aside without regard for all we had together?' He had his nerve, after all, playing the indignant one when I…I was the violated person…I was injured…I was the one who could make the legitimate claim of betrayal."

"What were they doing? How was the drug deal structured?"

This brought French to total silence. He sipped his drink, looked off to the bandstand, and glared into space. He knew and Jack knew that he knew, and Jack wanted him to ready himself to reveal. He could see Jack's resolve; he could feel the tension of Jack's question. No matter what, he would have to answer. He had to deal with Jack. There was no getting around it.

"He would want to kill me if he thought I told you this."

Jack waited.

"They…"

Jack remained quiet. Colby sat with poised pen. French sipped his drink.

"They...they had a sweet deal that they created. They found out that the Mondrian dealer in Columbus, Bill Shay, had a pipeline to drugs...illegal drugs that were easy to come by."

"Makes sense and explains what his T & E showed."

"Ryan Coleridge was the key man in this. I met him once. He's a nasty little man, dangerous, scary just to talk to. He was their big contact, he was the mastermind behind all of the drug stuff. He was the supplier and he made it all possible. He works for Bill Shay. Only as a consultant, mind you, a consultant who specialized in nothing. Unless you count illegal drugs."

The music came up and the entertainment was in place. Mickie Gillonde began to sing.

"Who killed J.W.," Jack asked calmly.

"I don't know."

"You don't know?"

"I don't know."

"You will tell me, Mr. French or I will make life very unpleasant for you. Not by bringing in the police, but by making you hurt physically. I can do that, believe me. Who killed J.W.?"

French sniffed and sucked in a deep breath and looked away to the band.

"I don't know."

Jack figured French didn't really know, but he wanted the man's speculation.

"Well, guess. Give me your best guess."

French finished his drink before he answered.

"I would guess Dixie Hamner," French said solemnly. "He would be the one to do it."

"Who the hell is Dixie Hamner?" Jack was furious.

"An awful man who works for Warren. He is so stupid. He would do anything for Warren."

Mickie Gillonde knew Collier French very well, had been in his home, had sex there, felt welded to his persona. He worked his way over to them as he sang "Ten Cents a Dance." How appropriate. He was being sexy as all get out and moved the heat of his performance to their table and sang passionately to French.

French was impressed with Mickie big time and forgot about Jack, his questions, and the link to Crawford.

Mickie rubbed against French, caressed his face, and ran his fingers through French's hair. He sang to the crowd as he pretended to seduce him. It all seemed strange to Jack, but it was effective.

Jack felt exhausted. Mickie was electric and even up close Jack could hardly tell the singer was a man. The makeup, the clothes, the body language, and delivery were that good. And Mickie had a terrific voice. Jack needed to get out of there. It was late, he was having a hard time organizing his thoughts, and besides, he had lost French. He could get to French again if he needed more, but he thought they had plenty to pursue. He had a suspect – Dixie Hamner. Jack bet the cops didn't know about him. He would talk to Elaine about him tomorrow. Right now he needed some sleep. Colby nodded to him and they said good-bye and thank you to French and to Mickie and headed to the lobby.

"Call me when you get up," Colby said as he pushed out the door and was gone.

Jack listened as Mickie worked his way back to the stage and began to sing "My Funny Valentine." It was still hard for him to believe Mickie was a man. But there was a lot about this shadow world that Jack didn't know. In the next few days he would come to learn more.

As he left the club he paused before walking to his car and felt at his left hip. This was a conscious comfort check to make sure his Glock was there. He did not know this neighborhood and did not want to be a victim if he could prevent it. He felt better knowing it was there, just in case.

The drive back to the Marriott downtown was a blur. His exhaustion forced him to concentrate on the driving. He had to find his way to I-75, get off on the correct downtown exit, and get parked without getting into trouble. Trouble would have been getting lost or having an accident. This was a situation where both were possibilities. But Jack made it without incident.

The exhaustion was more than just physical, he knew that. A great deal of it was emotional, that struggle within him to stay calm and composed, to be understanding and accepting, the struggle for patience and forbearance. It took a great deal of his energy and he was showing the signs of weariness from that effort. What had transpired at the Sublime helped him to understand what was going on and where to look for the killer, but it left him whipped. Jack couldn't remember taking off his clothes or brushing his teeth or getting into bed, but he must have done those things and rocketed into sleep.

7.

Sorrow was deferred, that pain subjugated, put away in some corner of Jack's mind so he could concentrate on what is rational. It will have to be dealt with at some point, but not now, not when he was most vulnerable, not when the hurt would be so intense. He would bear up better by overriding that impulse to collapse inward with sadness and grief, and perhaps some self pity. Stifle the memories, stifle the memories, cut short the thoughts of times ago, those scenes of tenderness, of joy, of love interacted, those exquisite memories. There will be time enough to cry.

Venturing out into the world can be tricky at any age, but for a five-year old it is monumental. No one totally loses that feeling even when they get bigger and older. It's a scary world and we know it, we've known it all our lives and it takes a great deal of learning and nurturing to supercede the feeling of helplessness that the unknown can cause within us. We spend our whole lives overcoming that issue and the successful among us know somehow intrinsically that it is a mirage of mysticism and nonsense that motivates such feelings. The cave man challenged the unknown by going out after the saber-tooth tiger and it was real and it was dangerous, but it was not mystical and it was not a situation outside one's control. Back then it took courage and planning and cooperation to get the cat. Today, it takes courage and resolve and perseverance to succeed in a dangerous world. Our younger generations were forced to understand that and to act accordingly. They survived the demands, but a lot of them didn't like how that played out or how it felt. And they were weaker in character as a result.

Little five-year old Jimmy Phillips could not yet tie his shoes on his first day of kindergarten. He and Jack had worked diligently on that task almost every day in the weeks leading up to school opening, carefully folding and looping the laces, pulling them taut, trying to create a bow, avoiding making a knot. Jimmy repeated and repeated and repeated with little success. He had cried in frustration with his inability to master the tangle of laces that were to him so complex, so mysterious, and so unassailable. Try as he might, at this point, he failed to conquer them.

And Jack was frustrated. He had been unable to teach Jimmy that seemingly simple task. Jimmy had appeared to be ambidextrous, but shoe lace tying and kindergarten exposed the left hand dominance. It was only later that Jack would become aware of the struggles of those who are left handed. Back then, he could not figure out what was the matter.

Here was the big day and Jimmy desperately wanted to tie his own shoes this first morning of school. He tried and tried, but it just would not happen. Jack was culpable in contributing to his desperation and frustration, he remembered, because in those weeks leading up to school while he was trying to learn, Jack had suggested that perhaps he might not be able to go to kindergarten if he did not learn to tie his shoe laces. Tears streamed down Jimmy's face as his mother did it for him and Jack stood by with camera in hand ready to record the momentous day.

Now, tears wiped away, ripe with the excitement of venturing off to school, he beamed from the thrill for whatever it was that waited for him. After the picture taking of laughing, posing, prideful determination, and seriousness, he went to that first day of school hand in hand with his mother. As they sallied off like two free spirits, Jimmy turned and waved and laughed and Jack shot one more picture. It was a picture that has stayed with Jack all this time and he can still see it as clearly as if it had just happened.

Left-handedness became an overriding issue as Jimmy tried to learn to write. Teachers made an effort to correct his defect by attempting to get him to write with his right hand.

It was wrong, it didn't work, and it was useless. Jimmy would write with his left hand. Awkwardly, sideways, half upside down, and with an exaggerated scrawl, Jimmy dutifully scribbled the required assignments. He seemed unflustered by the chore and progressed through school over the years quite successfully and it became for all intents and purposes a non-issue.

Although unspoken by him, it must have been more of a burden than he revealed. Coping with a right-handed world must have been a penetrating burden of his school life that he did not share except for bits and pieces. The litany of life-functioning difficulties for the left-hander are so numerous that it almost defies a list. On and on and on go the tick offs of items that are geared specifically for the right-handed person that impact the basic skills of those left-handed.

And there are all the historical connections of negativity, those connections of deficiency, of clumsiness, of evil, of saneness, and of depravity to name a few of the conditions of affliction by being left-handed.

How that has been manifested with J.W. over the years or influenced his personality Jack could not say. It was not something they had ever really discussed. He supposed because J.W. didn't complain.

Research shows that left-handers are twice as likely to have inflammatory bowel problems. Isn't that a nice piece of information? Thus, the colicky baby? Perhaps. Perhaps a coincidence. Jack would never know.

8.

Vivid, highly detailed dreaming can be a great catharsis or a miserable experience depending on the circumstances. Running for your life is not fun, while, on the other hand, prevailing over insurmountable odds is especially wonderful. The sound of the phone interrupted the exhilaration whatever it had been. It was six fifty in the AM. Jack hoped it was Meg.

"Too early?"

Meg's voice was soft and assured and comforting. It was a gift he clung to for the moment, lost in its sensuality and its connection with his real life.

"No, I was awake," he lied.

"I thought I might have heard from you by now…I couldn't wait any longer. You okay."

"Yeah. Making good progress…can't give you any details right now…"

"Can't or won't?"

"Same thing. Anyway, I'm sorry I didn't call…been on the go…lots to do. But I…I'm getting somewhere with this. I'll fill you in later. I've got an Atlanta police detective working on it and I'm working with a reporter from the newspaper. We're finding out some things. The reporter and I. The cops are useless so far."

"Was it…?"

"Suicide? No, it was murder. I think we have a lead on who did it…we'll find out more today. It's complicated…yet simple, I guess. Anyway, I'll explain when I know more and get some things sorted out. I'm okay…I have my Glock."

"Be careful and call me tonight. We need to talk."

"I will…I promise."

She was gone and he missed her and wished she were here and knew that was silly. He also missed her comment about needing to talk.

Now some nagging sensation came at him. He had to be concerned with his own survival. Those bastards will do anything to protect themselves. He wondered when the sadness would overcome him. When does he collapse with the realization that his son was murdered; that there are those who know who the killer is and who could care less about him, his feelings, or even if he would come after them? They are assured in their own righteousness.

The *they* are Warren Crawford and his crew. Today, Jack had to go after Crawford and Dixie Hamner. French knows Hamner did the actual killing. Knows not as a witness, but as one who knows how Crawford does things. He uses Hamner as his stick of vengeance.

Elaine needed to know about Crawford and Hamner. Jack punched her number into the phone, hoping she was already at work. He got her voice mail and left a message. She had handed him her card at one point and he retrieved it from the pile of receipts and keys and coins he had thrown on the dresser. She had written the number of her home phone on the back. He punched it in and waited. She answered and was quite chipper for the early hour.

"Mr. Phillips…Jack…it's early, you must have something. Do you?"

She didn't seem in the slightest way surprised by his call.

"Yeah, I do."

"Breakfast?"

"That makes sense. I'm meeting Colby downstairs at eight. Why don't you join us?"

"See you then, Jack."

He had become Jack to her. That was interesting; up until now he was Mr. Phillips. She knew he wouldn't sit still, would bore in, and would hustle to find out something. She knew he was out front of her and Fred. She was playing catch up.

It was too early to call the office and Jack debated with himself if he even wanted to make contact. Kari wouldn't be there until seven thirty so he had time to reconsider. He showered, dressed and caught some of the news on TV. The office could wait.

Colby was buried in the paper, cup in hand, when Jack got to the table. He acknowledged Jack's greeting with a grunt.

"I asked Detective Moss to meet us for breakfast."

Another grunt before he looked out from behind the paper.

"Braves won in the ninth," he said, pleased with the announcement. "They'll win the division again, no doubt…little good it will do them. They'll crap out to somebody in the playoffs."

Jack ordered coffee from the little woman who charged over to their table. He waited for Colby to react to what he said. Finally, Colby did.

"She's going to have to work with the boys in Marietta. That's where Crawford lives…and Hamner."

"How long do you think it will take for them to find out we know?"

"Some time today there will be a report back to Crawford that we were at the Sublime with French. Crawford will assume something is going on; he'll want to meet with you, try to find out what you know. It's up to you if you tell him…"

"I'd rather let the cops pick him up and question him. In the meantime, I'd like to find Hamner. He gets wind of something he might run."

"To what end?"

"What do you mean?"

"Why do you want to find Hamner? Let the police handle it."

"I'd like first crack at him."

"Wrong…let the cops do their job. Besides, you might not like dealing with a guy like Hamner."

"Really?"

"Yeah, and if he finds out you're looking for him he just might come after you. I don't think you'd want that to happen."

"You're wrong there, Colby, I would like that."

"Columbus needs to be checked out, Colby said.

"I suppose."

Elaine Moss moved in on them as if she were about to make a bust. Her smile belied her body language. She was very physical, cat-like, seemingly on the attack, but her voice was a purr of congeniality.

"Good morning, thanks for the invite. I usually don't eat breakfast, but this will work. What's going on? Where'd you go last night, Jack? Colby take you some place bad?"

"Colby took me to the Sublime in Marietta, it was an interesting experience."

"Lots of fags, Jack, didn't figure you for a queer bar."

"Sublime is not a queer bar," Colby burst out, "it's a dining…"

Jack held up his hand and Colby caught himself and stopped speaking and picked up his coffee.

"Who did you meet at the Sublime, Jack; someone I should know about?"

"Yes, that's why I called you this morning…someone you should know about…a couple of guys you should know about. One of whom is our killer."

"Really? That was fast work Jack, we should have you working with us at APD. Fred will love hearing this."

She snapped up her cell phone that she had casually dumped on the table as she sat down and tapped at one number.

"My incentive is very high," Jack explained. "Besides I have Spence on my side. He's the one for kudos, not I."

She ignored him as she spoke into the phone.

"Freddy, I'm having breakfast with Mr. Phillips. Yes, that's right. At the Marriott. Sure. Why don't you join us? Mr. Phillips says he knows who killed his son. Okay. Sure. Later."

She poked again at the phone to end the call.

"Too busy, or has he already eaten?" Jack tried to make it sound sarcastic and must have succeeded because Colby smiled slightly.

"Freddy wouldn't miss a breakfast would he?" Colby chimed in with his own sarcasm. "Probably still at his girlfriend's and can't get away."

"Come on, you guys," Ms. Moss grinned, "ease up. He's at Headquarters and just about to go into a meeting with our boss. I'll catch him later. Now, fill me in about last night."

Between the two of them, Colby and Jack gave her a detailed rundown of what Colby had found out and what they had learned in their conversation with Collier French. They told her what French had explained concerning Crawford and Hamner; about the drug dealing action. She appeared to take them seriously and dutifully took notes. But she asked few questions. It was as if she were not trying to absorb what they were saying, as if they were telling her about some minor crime. She remained calm, but Jack thought she looked bored with it all, while they were needlessly overly excited. Jack was surprised by her reaction. He thought she would have probed for more details.

"Well?" Jack pressed.

She stared at him for a second.

"Yeah," she murmured, "that's interesting."

"Is that all you have to say?" Colby snapped.

"Sorry, but I think I've got it. We'll work on this. I'm just trying to figure out how I deal with certain parties at Headquarters and with the guys in Marietta."

"Problem?" Jack asked cautiously, wondering what "work on this" meant.

"Not a problem, not at all. I meant to imply that it's a kind of…situation. One that requires some tact and…"

"What's to work? You ask the Marietta Police to pick up these two for questioning."

It seemed simple to Jack.

Colby rolled his eyes and fiddled with his spoon and coffee cup. Jack tried to be patient.

Ms. Moss sighed one of those 'this is too complicated to attempt and you wouldn't understand' sighs, but she made an effort nonetheless.

"The guys in Marietta are part of a narcotics task force with Cobb and Smyrna Counties and are working with the Feds – the DEA. Those guys are heavyweight territory protectors; they don't like anyone coming into their jurisdiction. I found out the hard way last year. They have clout and they use it. I got chewed out for going after one of their dealers…and I was on a murder investigation, just like this. I was told to lay off, they said they needed him to get to Mr. Big. I think that might happen here if what you say is true and they have a bead on Crawford, if they know he's into drugs. They'd like to get someone like him. They like the high profile busts."

Jack was stunned and felt as if the inside of his head was starting to crumble into tiny granules, as if he were hearing dialog from a bad TV cop show and the sounds of it were pulverizing his brain, grinding his thoughts into bits of nonsense. What was she saying? If Jack had any doubts about the help she and Fred were going to give him running down his son's killer, her explanation confirmed that. They were useless, as he suspected. He looked at Colby scribbling in his notebook; to what end Jack had no idea.

"Will you try?" Jack asked, his brain regaining equilibrium.

"I'll do my best."

She smiled at him and there was this look, the look you get from a woman when she wants something. It was a somewhat longing gaze meant to penetrate his thick male insensibilities in order to inoculate him against terminal lack of understanding.

Jack knew that look; he'd seen it a few times. She wasn't particularly interested in pursuing his son's killer or killers, she was interested in him. Why the hell did her focus change and how did she get it directed at him? Her look, that doe-eyed show of vulnerability and loneliness, was meant to get him off target and connect with her. Colby was still intent with his notes, but Jack noticed he had also checked out the look she was giving him.

"I hope you do," Jack said quickly. "It's what I expect."

Ms. Moss stood up, yanked her tote bag with her, and rested her hand on Jack's shoulder.

"I'll get right on it. Have to check out the gun and so forth, check out your son's movements, there's stuff to work on. Talk to you later."

She started to leave, but abruptly turned to face Jack. The look was still in place.

"Where will you be?"

"Trying to find out whatever I can."

"Please check in with me and let me know what is going on. Okay? Please."

"Right."

Jack didn't sound enthusiastic, but it was the best he could do right then.

"She's a lot of help," Colby snorted after she was far enough away that she could not hear him. "And it seems she's got eyes for you, Jack."

"Yeah. So now what? Go with me?"

"Nope, I've got some other things to do and I want to check on this guy Hamner. I'm heading over to the office. I'll meet you in Marietta if you let me know where you are. On the other hand, you might want to run down to Columbus and see what you can turn up."

"Yeah, I think so. You said that's where Crawford is."

"So the girl said. Maybe turn up something."

Jack had only been away from Meg two nights, but he was feeling a sense of aloneness. He felt isolated and lonely and longed for the comfort that she could usually provide. He managed to get her on her cell phone and had a less than satisfactory conversation. Something was missing, something had changed from earlier; there wasn't the contact he expected. She talked and Jack talked, yet somehow they didn't mesh with what each was saying. The syntax for each of them did not connect with the other. It was as if two autistic persons were trying to explain something to each other that each felt was important. There were two different sets of feelings, two different sets of circumstances that did not relate.

Meg must have sensed it, too, because she wanted to end the call because the connection she said was poor. It wasn't. The communicators weren't getting it. They agreed to talk again that evening. She said she was blowing him a kiss before she ended the call. It didn't help.

Jack wondered what the hell he was doing as he closed his phone and watched Colby walking away. What could he accomplish in Columbus. He thought he'd give it a try; no plan, just bravado.

9.

Determination can be frustrating or it can carry you through. Often determination helps a person succeed where others fail. Determination provides a framework for doing well when it otherwise might not be so. Making that extra effort, that push to do better, and the toughness to perfect a skill or master a technique is buttressed by determination. And out of that determination there can develop a kind of potential aggression that might not otherwise be a deep-seated personality trait.

Aggression is not in itself a bad trait, but misplaced and overdone it can become tedious and anti-social. J.W. had a certain ferocity about his determination; as if his life depended upon what he wanted to accomplish. That aggression showed itself most prominently in sports of any kind. When he was learning to bat a ball, he wanted Jack to pitch to him over and over again, and then more. The perfect swing, the perfect batted ball. Throw the football a hundred times and a hundred times more. The perfect catch, the perfect form. Through gritted teeth, through tears, with aching muscles, with strained patience on his part, and unrelenting repetitions he became aggressive and compulsive and arrogant about his athletic skills.

He was still not yet ten years old.

That aggressive arrogance did not pass muster with his peers. Other kids hated it and resented his obsession with mastery and his desire to point out that he was better at batting or catching or kicking or throwing or whatever it was. He cared about that and they didn't care as much. He made sure they understood his superiority.

"You can't blab about how good you are," Jack had said, "the other kids don't like it."

He nodded and said nothing. But he persisted.

There were the organized sports and the neighborhood pick-up games, each with the same intensity of his participation, his drive to excel. He did excel, but he lauded it over teammates and foes alike. Of course, they resented his attitude.

That attitude, that arrogant aggression, transcended sports. It made its way into all aspects of J.W.'s life. He could read faster, do math better, write superior compositions, and all of that in his mind, his self-evaluation. He wasn't really superior, but he told himself that he was. It was his determination.

Jack had asked himself, did I do that? Did he create some aura of competitiveness that fostered J.W.'s attitude about this? Was he the reason for such obsessive effort? Had J.W. learned that from him? Jack kicked that around for a long time, wondered what it might have been that he said or did or what was said about him that fostered J.W.'s behavior. Learned or in the genes? Such is an age-old argument.

Such determination can be a perceived as a negative, and still be a certain positive factor in his life. Why J.W. did well in school, in the military, and in his career. But also why his peers, his fellow workers, did not like him.

As a child, the striving for some kind of perfection, of domination, and of monumental effort created within J.W. a heightened level of frustration when what was desired was not achieved. The result was tears; tears that came too quickly, too readily in light of the circumstances.

Looking back, Jack's hindsight assessment would say J.W. was fraught with insecurity. Had Jack caused that? He had accused Jack of a number of things he did wrong, but not that. Maybe J.W. hadn't thought of it before he died. Jack wondered?

What is my place in all of this, Jack questioned? There certainly are more questions than answers. Jack had not held himself culpable in the creation of this specific demeanor of J.W.'s because he made an investment in time and effort of his own which was directed to J.W. and for J.W. And that time and effort was not some overlay of Jack's own frustration for being a failed athlete, which he wasn't, but is so often the case. J.W. was not living Jack's athletic dreams. So where did the determination come from with J.W.?

Jack felt he must have had some kind of influence, but what is his place in all of this? He'd thought about it a great deal and was hard-pressed to sort out a good answer. Reflection is certainly jaundiced, the accumulated prejudice of time, occurrences, and their conflicts since childhood. They did not get beyond the growing up phase and did not form a satisfactory and meaningful adult relationship. Somehow, it always seemed J.W. wanted to remain the child instead of being an adult son. Jack had hoped J.W. would be another person in his life who could accept him as a person with all his faults, as Jack accepted him. Now older, Jack thought J.W. should be a grownup, but as Jack knew all too well, being older does not mean one achieves maturity. Jack surmised that for J.W. his father's faults were too great to accept.

10.

So his son was a homosexual. That thought had not gone away. The truth was he had to, in some way, digest the idea his son was gay. He had no choice. When he processed this fact, all of the different reactions he had ever heard voiced from folks floated through his mind as he coped with trying to understand. "Well, that's his choice." "No one in our family has been afflicted that way." "He's still such a wonderful young man." "Can you believe it?" "He was such a sweet child." And so on and so on forever. People try to be kind and accepting, but the sliver of "God, I'm glad he's not in our family" creeps out and entangles itself in all of the emotion of this circumstance. It's your problem Mr. Phillips; we want no part of it.

Jack again felt quite lonely as he drove towards Columbus, Georgia, home of Ft. Benning, home to a drug dealer involved with his son. Sure, it was French who accused the drug business crimes, but Jack accepted what he said at face value.

Time of reckoning could well be at hand. Jack did not have, at that point, some all consuming emotion for revenge or to seek retribution. Instead, he tried to get hold of some perspective about his son and his own life. Where did J.W.'s life turn? Where did his life change from what Jack assumed was a "normal" path, the straight way? When did his son decide he was homosexual? It didn't matter, really, but his mind was trying to get it sorted out, ordered, organized, and contained in a way that he could comprehend. The distance he had felt with his son in the last few years now took on monumental proportions. There would have been no easy reconciliation he might have thought could take place, no simple meeting of the minds. It would have taken some effort to find common ground for discussion. That time was gone and lost, but if it had come and there had been a discussion about his being gay, Jack would have been woefully unprepared to understand the gulf that lay between them. And it would have been Jack and the circumstances and his own biases, his own lack of preparation that would have intensified that gulf.

For Jack, homosexuality in a general sense was a non-issue. It was what someone was, or is in his realm. All of his working life Jack had been associated with homosexuals. Gays who were by no means gay. Supposedly liberated, but constricted socially in the worst way. Many of them cried on his shoulder, complained about the injustice of it all, and wondered how it could change. They had been creative, sensitive, artistic, and highly motivated as they produced a solid marketing campaign. They knew what worked, knew why, and were fully capable of instituting the tools which made the campaign work. Yet, they were fraught with self-doubt in the conflict for being right and successful. They knew full well that somehow they were conning everyone and the con worked. And there was no con for them. They could not be explained away, consumerized, packaged, and sold. They were naked and vulnerable and unaccepted. And, sometimes frantic. They worked for Jack and together they made marketing programs successful, made lots of money, and they cried with Jack and alone. He knew they cried alone, but he did not know what to do about it except protect and nurture them, and not pass judgment. What Jack did and how he operated wasn't wrong, but it didn't help. Time moved on and Jack realized he never fully understood their angst.

Jack was half way to Columbus, before he thought about the fact that he had no clue what he might find out or how he would go about learning anything. Heck of a detective he was. He figured that he would go to Columbus Quality Cabinets and ask for Bill Shay and see what happened. Their nondescript building was in mid-town just off a main drag with a barbeque joint nearby and a used furniture store alongside. Nothing flashy here to draw attention. The minimal showroom was common and unattended.

There was a receptionist and she was cute. And wary. A tall, skinny blonde, she stiffened when Jack asked for Bill Shay.

"Can I help you?"

"Bill Shay."

"Did you have an appointment?"

Jack could tell she was on the defensive without anything else being said. She was the gatekeeper, the one who ordered the drawbridge pulled up from the moat. She was obviously accustomed to being the protector of the lord.

"No."

"And you are…?"

"A man who wants to see him and speak with him."

"Your name…?"

"Jack Frost, working for the Snow Alliance."

She stared at Jack, transfixed. She had no clue he was making a joke.

"A matter of importance," he said. "Money-wise."

She looked long and hard before she spoke.

"Wait here, Mister…?"

"Frost."

"Mr. Frost, I'll see if My Shay is in."

"Thank you."

She turned and walked down the hall towards the rear of the store. About half way, she opened a closed door without knocking. She went into the office and left the door open. Jack made his move and came into the room right behind her without her knowing he was there.

"There's a Mr. Frost here to see…"

She felt his presence and turned.

"You can't…"

"Beat it," Jack said, and walked toward Shay's desk.

She had not moved.

"Scram, this is a private meeting."

She backed out of the office. Jack closed the door.

Shay stood up. He was not a big man and did not pose a physical threat to Jack. But that is what Shay intended.

"Sit down."

Jack said it quietly and Shay knew Jack meant it and he sat down.

"Frost? I don't recognize the name."

"I'm here to find out about Warren Crawford."

Shay winced.

"I'm also here to find out about Ryan Coleridge and drugs."

"Really, how does that concern me?"

"My understanding is that you were supplying drugs to Warren Crawford and J.W. Phillips for their operation in the Atlanta area."

He shifted in his seat and stared at Jack.

"That's crazy."

"Maybe, but I doubt it. Too many good resources know the action."

"I have a terrific business here. I don't need drugs. Why would I get into some kind of illegal stuff?"

"You know J.W.?"

He hesitated.

"Of course you do, you were one of his customers. You know he's dead?"

"I heard."

"You're a suspect. Probably have a good motive."

He stood up, again.

Jack waited, not saying anything right away.

"It's over," Jack said, not knowing what he was talking about, but wanting to put the pressure on him. "You're going to jail and Coleridge is going to jail. The drugs will do it."

Shay moved for a desk drawer, but Jack was ready. Suddenly, his Glock was useful. Jack pointed it at him.

"Where is Coleridge?

Jack said the words slowly and as sullenly as he could. He was thinking about Bogart when he spoke, but when the sound came out of his mouth it didn't sound like Bogie. On the other hand, he did sound sullen and sort of nasty. It was one of his better nasty voices.

Shay didn't want to tell him anything, Jack knew that. Jack had no authority and he knew that also. Only righteous indignation was on Jack's side. Ordinarily, Jack's first reaction was not one of confrontation and force. After all, he had made his success in advertising on being politic, on convincing, on getting the other person to see his point, and to sell that point effectively.

Jack was tired, he was frustrated. He wanted to find his son's killer and this jerk stood in the way right now. He was no longer the smooth talker, the slick ad-man manipulator, the conciliator, the maker of all things possible. Right now, he wanted to cut through to the answer of his question: Where is Coleridge?

Jack walked behind the desk and hit Bill Shay in the small of his back as hard as he could and Shay fell onto the desk. He made a slight oofing sound as he gasped for breath, but did not yell out.

"Now, I'm going to keep hitting you in the kidneys until you tell me where Coleridge is. Do you understand?"

Shay didn't move. Jack waited a moment without saying anything else. Then Jack hit Shay again in the small of his back and there was more oofing. Shay slid back from the desk, against the chair, and onto the floor. Jack bent over as if he were going to hit him again.

"My house," he whispered.

He mouthed the address, barely audible. Jack wrote it down.

"Very good," Jack falsely praised. "Now tell me what was going on here. How did my son and Warren Crawford…"

Jack hesitated. What was the word he wanted? Interfaced? That was stupid. Sounded like grad school.

"How did it work?" he went on. "Your operation here and Crawford and my son…how you worked it out with them."

Shay stared at Jack.

"The mechanics…how did it function? Your drug relationship?"

Shay licked his lips slightly and his eyes rolled back and he balled up on the floor in a sort of fetal position. Jack hit him with the Glock on the upper back behind his shoulder and Shay oofed and started panting. Perhaps he was having a heart attack, maybe a panic anxiety attack, but in any case he was a mess and he was not going to tell Jack anything more.

Jack couldn't just leave him there on the floor, he would notify Coleridge as soon as Jack left. He looked around for something to tie up Shay. A flash of gray tape came to him and he only wished he had a roll. What could he use? Jack decided on a lamp cord. He pulled the cord from the wall socket, took a pair of scissors from Shay's desk and cut the cord loose from the desk lamp. He tied Shay's hands behind his back, and then secured his ankles. Jack dragged Shay into his private bathroom just off the office, flipped the lock, and closed the door from the outside. Shay was now tied up and locked in his own bathroom. This should give Jack time to get to Coleridge.

The skinny blonde glowered at Jack as he came out of Shay's office.

"Sorry, But there are things that just have to get done."

She shook her head the way a diffident horse does when it does not want to be ridden. She even snorted slightly.

"Bill says he doesn't want to be bothered for awhile, something about working on his memoirs. Says he needs quiet time."

She did not respond.

Jack plugged the address Shay had given him into his GPS and it wasn't long before he was nearing Shay's house. Shay lived in the Green Island section of north Columbus where houses stood majestically on large properties and at significant distances from one another. Two cars were parked in front. Jack noted the license plate numbers and drove by. Two hundred yards further on, he stopped, parked his car off the road by a clump of trees, and made his way back to Shay's.

Shay's acreage and his neighbor's property had loads of trees. The area was not exactly wooded, but with enough trees to cover Jack's approach. No dogs, but probably a security system. He cut through the neighbor's frontage and stopped in a cluster of pines to survey the situation. The front door opened and four men exited, laughing and joking with someone Jack could not see. Probably Coleridge. Each of the men was carrying some sort of bag, like an athletic bag.

Jack knew this was a situation where he should have backed off and called the police. It would have been the right thing to do. Jack did not do that. In a fleeting, fractious debate with himself, he considered the alternatives and still did not do that. Jack wanted to get hold of this guy. Here he was, the fool, driven by anger that had been building within him. Hitting Bill Shay had not alleviated it.

Jack circled round to the rear of Shay's house. Now what? There was a large patio with several tables and chairs, an umbrella protecting each table. As he approached, a stout Hispanic woman was clearing away dishes and glassware, loading them on a tray that she carried inside without seeing Jack. A man carrying a briefcase came outside through the sliding door that she had just used. He was in shorts and golf shirt, sockless in loafers, and smoking a cigar. He sat down at one of the tables, opened the briefcase, and started counting bills that he pulled from the case.

Jack could smell the cigar and thought about cigars and the enjoyment of cigars and wondered about smoking one. It had been a long time since he had fondled a luxury cigar. He did not stop moving towards the patio.

The man on the patio clenched the cigar in his teeth as he counted. He made a note of the total on a pad and grabbed another wad of bills. He was engrossed as Jack neared.

"You Coleridge?"

The man reacted to Jack's question as if he had been hit and fumbled with the money, his face filled with shock.

"Aaah," was all he could say.

Jack was almost to the patio.

"You Coleridge?" Jack repeated.

But the man regained his composure quite quickly. He stood up and Jack figured he was going to pull a gun.

"Yeah. Who are you?

Yes, Jack thought, I am the fool. Again. Like some movie quick-draw sequence in slow motion, here was this guy getting the drop on me, or so Jack thought. But the man could not get his pistol loose from his belt and Jack had his Glock ready first. Aha, you bastard, Jack wins.

But the man turned, was through the sliding door, and inside before Jack could even react. Coleridge must have been able to get his gun out by then because the next thing was a shot coming from inside, the bullet tearing through the umbrella above Jack's head and to his right. Three more shots sprayed around him hitting chairs and a pot of flowers on a nearby stand.

Jack dropped to the ground and fired a volley of four shots at the house. Two went through the open doorway and two went through the glass alongside and he could hear the shattering of glass and smashing of other material inside. Jack rolled to his right expecting return fire that did not come. What the hell was he doing in a gun battle? Jack's vague question to himself edged through the stress.

Jack heard a car rev up and then accelerate. He knew Coleridge was gone. He punched 9-1-1 into his cell phone and reported what had happened. When he went inside, the Hispanic woman was huddled on the kitchen floor, too afraid to move, too afraid to speak. Jack told her Coleridge was gone.

"Mr. Coleridge has left the building."

She nodded yes.

"The police are on their way, everything will be all right."

She slowly reached for the counter with her left hand and with some difficulty tried to pull herself upright. Jack moved to her, took her right arm, and struggled with her until she was on her feet. She was breathing heavily. He pulled a chair over to her so she could sit down.

"Relax," he tried to soothe and she raised her eyes to the ceiling.

"Dios mio," she sighed.

"Stay here until the cops arrive."

Jack went back into the family room and saw shattered glass everywhere. A lamp was smashed and one of the bullets had ruined a large vase. He noticed splintered wood where one of the bullets had hit a wooden chair back. Outside, some of the bills had blown from the table and were skittering across the patio. He retrieved the mixture of hundreds, fifties, and twenties. He put them back in the briefcase and closed it. It was difficult for Jack to estimate, but with the combination of denominations there was probably anywhere from fifty to a hundred thousand dollars in total.

"Hold it right there," a voice twanged. "Police, get your hands up where I can see them."

Jack did as he was told.

"I called in the police report," Jack yelled.

For the first time in this whole episode Jack was apprehensive; not frightened really, more worried about getting an explanation understood by the authorities.

"What report?" The voice flipped back.

Jack slowly turned so he could face whoever it was and he didn't say anything as he moved.

"About the shooting here a few minutes ago."

"You got a gun?

"Yes sir, and a permit to carry."

"Turn back around."

Jack did. The cop came behind him, did a quick frisk, and took the Glock from Jack's holster.

"Sit down," he drawled.

Jack did.

"Put your wallet on the table."

Jack did. The cop picked up the wallet, fingered through it, and put it in his jacket pocket.

"Two questions, Mr. Phillips: Are you nuts and what the hell are you doing here?"

"I can explain."

"Damn well better."

Jack started to speak when two other men came out from the house.

"Clean," the one said. "There's a Latina cook in the kitchen, pretty scared."

"Yeah, get a statement from her. And Tiny," he said to the other man, "have the lab guys hustle over here as soon as they can. Make sure the front door is secure until the uniforms get here and keep any press away that might show up."

He sat down across from Jack.

"Dave Wooley, Columbus Drug Task Force."

He showed his badge.

"Go on, this has got to be good." He almost smiled when he spoke.

Jack told him most of his story and Wooley just stared; Jack the fool.

"So you were playing detective?"

"My son was murdered…"

"I understand," Wooley said quickly, and he held his hands up, palms toward Jack as if to say, 'relax, take it easy.'

Jack was tense, tenser than he had even realized. Coleridge had shot at him and he had fired at Coleridge. A gun battle of sorts, with a great deal of broken glass. Jack was tense, damn right.

"He was counting the money when I came up to the patio."

"You said."

"It started to blow away when I went inside, so when I came back out I retrieved what was going across the patio and put it in the briefcase and closed it."

"Well, for your information," Wooley said slowly as he looked at the briefcase, "we had this place under surveillance. The men who left when you came around have already been picked up. Just a matter of time and we'll have Coleridge."

"You knew about Shay and Coleridge?"

"That's right; we've been watching them for some time."

"I need to tell you about Bill Shay. I skipped part of that."

"What about Shay?"

"I tied him up before I left his office. So he couldn't alert Coleridge."

"Detectives are already on their way to Shay's," he said.

"I locked him in his bathroom."

Wooley chuckled.

"Anything else?" he asked.

"I don't think so."

"We'll need you to come downtown and make a full statement. Keep in mind that this Shay fellow might press charges against you. Assault."

"He was going for a gun and I drew first, then he ran. That's it."

"So you say."

When they got to police headquarters, it was a madhouse. Jack did manage to survive the time-consuming, mind-numbing drudgery that took place. It was quite a sight to watch. The cast of characters already there when they arrived was sorry bunch, but then they brought in the guys Jack had watched leave Shay's house. The uproar was beyond belief. The press was everywhere. Lights, cameras, action. Yelling and screaming for attention to them and to create attention.

As it turned out, there had been a major bust for some street gang members right before Wooley and Jack arrived and their entourage of thugs, punks, and attendant female companions of every stripe milled about inside and out of the headquarters building.

Jack's sensibilities were ruptured. He watched this primordial zoo of reckless animals until Detective Wooley ushered him to an office where a young female stenographer could take an official statement from him. In the relative calm and quiet Jack repeated what he had told Wooley before. Wooley probed a bit, inserted more questions, got Jack's answers, and the woman dutifully captured it all.

Although Jack had broken into their drug stakeout, he had not spoiled their case. The four clowns from the Shay house had the drugs with them that they bought from Coleridge, drugs were found in the Shay house, and Wooley had the cash that was in the briefcase. Hip, hip hooray for the home team.

"Nice for you, but I still need to find my son's killer."

"Let the Atlanta police do their job," Wooley said patiently to him. "Give them a chance to get it done. These things aren't easy."

Jack considered what Wooley said; perhaps he was right. Maybe he needed to back off and let the cops do what they do. Kicking that around made him think about Elaine Moss. What the hell was she doing right now to find J.W.'s murderer? Was she really after the case, interviewing, running down leads, digging into Warren Crawford's connection, checking on Collier French, and finding out something? He wished that were so. He doubted that was happening. Where was Ms. Moss and what was she doing?

11.

Friends can help define a person by deepening and refining personality, and providing solace in desperate times. Friends can provoke a balance of thought and conduct. They can support hopes and dreams. The lack of friends is a blemish, a negative mark, a reminder of a life incomplete, a life wanting something more. In the complex puzzle of life, friends make up some of the important pieces.

Friends for J.W. were in the abstract. Jack realized this later on when he reviewed their relationship and thought about his son's growing up years. Jack's hindsight assessment is that he believed the persons J.W. spoke of as friends were real, which was how J.W. referred to and spoke about them.

This posture was part and parcel of the unreality of self-perception for J.W. It was his denial of the non-emotional non-acceptance of his feelings, where he was saying to himself that "I won't get close, I won't be hurt, I won't be disappointed, and therefore I won't be sad."

Oh, my no, he was determined not to be sad at all. On the contrary, he was one who professed something else, one who tried to create an image of being gregarious and ebullient. The image was manifested by being vocalized. Talk, talk, and more talk with glibness and machismo and bravado. There was more than that; there was a sense of carefree playfulness that fooled all those around him, family and friends.

Looking back, in spite of this façade, he was in truth a loner, resisting the real aspects of having a friend. He was, Jack thought, alienated and disconnected and yet, not one to openly brood or lament.

Yeah, yeah, here Jack was playing the psychologist about his own son. But he had put a great deal of thought into this. After all, when you are rejected by one of your children, you spend plenty of time trying to figure out what went wrong. You do if you care.

And what Jack was really thinking about was that later period in his childhood when J.W. was older and when the selection of friends could take place and be observed. When younger, playing with and relating to the somewhat mob of children at school and in the neighborhood, there was no specific identification of friend or friends. There was merely a group that played together, tolerated each other, and sought out fun and adventure without friend consideration or selection. There was a band of playmates and J.W. was one of those and seemed to fit in with them. It was only later that the characteristics Jack identified came into play.

On the other hand, J.W. was emotionally attached to several teachers who seemed to impact his life. Jack remembered one, a Mrs. Marshall, who taught English and who challenged and nurtured J.W. to read voraciously and to think about and analyze what he read. She was kind and demanding, clever and motivating, and knew how to get the most from her students. J.W. talked about her in glowing terms and Jack knew he had this emotional attachment.

Then there was this math instructor in high school who had a Ph.D. and who had worked for NASA, and who instilled in J.W. an incomparable sense of being a mathematician to the extent that J.W. started college in computer science. J.W. failed at computer science, but that was not the point. The point was that he was caught up in the wonderment of mathematics and he could do it pretty well and was encouraged to reach for something.

Those teacher attachments were certain kinds of friends at a distance for him. Here again, they were in the abstract, devoid of friendship reality.

Yes, Jack could not deny that during the high school years one or two young men came around the house on occasion. They were nice enough, yet they seemed to be their own masters, polite and convivial with J.W. and not connected to him in a way that would indicate abiding friendship.

During high school when a young man is still not yet an adult, it is time for him to begin breaking away from parental influence to find independence and his own life clarity. But for J. W. there was this abject clinging to Jack and the household and to his sister. How strange, how conflicted he must have been, and how perverse an outcome in life circumstances. Here he was clinging to Jack with the future outcome to be his rejection of Jack. Clinging to what? Wanting something Jack was not able to recognize or provide. Wanting something J.W. himself could not identify and so could not share with Jack. And they became strangers to one another.

There was scant dating of the young women. There were those times he escorted a delightful young girl to the year-end proms, a token deference to the opposite gender. Nothing on a regular basis and there were no phone calls from inquiring females. Sports were important, backpacking with Jack was a focus, but friends and females were distant.

The bottom line must have been his questioning of "How do I fit in" and "Where do I belong?" In all these years of Jack's quest for answers, subtle realizations, and musings about all of the aspects of their past, it didn't make sense until now. When had J.W. realized that he was homosexual? When did he know that he was "different?"

12.

Wooley said Jack would have to come back to Columbus at some point; he would let him know. In the meantime, as Jack headed north back to Atlanta, his thoughts about J.W. were now centered on his involvement with drug dealing. Jack wondered whether J.W. fully understood what he had gotten himself into. The whole process must have seemed like such easy money. J.W. was smart and Jack thought J.W. knew how to analyze situations. How had he worked this out in his mind to justify that kind of illegal activity? How did he evaluate jeopardizing his career with the chances of getting caught and probably spending time in prison? And who was the instigator? Crawford? French? Hamner? Jack supposed he was being the biased father who assumes his son would not have started such a scheme. Not his boy. It had to be one of the bad guys. In any case, the temptation to get involved must have seemed so strong to J.W. that not participating was out of the question.

Did J.W. die because of the drug business or was that issue incidental to his death? Would he have been killed anyway because of deceit and jealousy? There were lots of unanswered questions Jack was trying to get his brain around.

Getting sidetracked as J.W. had obviously been was foreign to Jack. He did not consider himself a puritan or a moralist or a saint, but it was not in his makeup to steal, cheat, and look for a fast buck. In his way of thinking, challenging the odds on criminal stuff was worse than being in Vegas. You lose. Jack's picture of J.W. was that he held the same outlook as Jack did in that regard or at least he thought J.W. once did. Guess he was wrong about him. Again.

Jack's cell phone made him realize where he was. It was Meg calling. Her voice was stiff and somewhat hoarse, the way it usually sounded when she was really pissed about something. There was an edge, a bite to her curt, "This is Meg." He sensed that Meg Russell, his friend and lover, was about to tell him something he wasn't going to like. She never said, "This is Meg." Hell, she knew his cell phone already told him who was calling. She usually started with, "How ya'll doin'?" or something like that. This was not going to be good. Here comes another solid slap in the chops.

"I've been thinking. A lot."

That was a crummy beginning. "I've been thinking," she says, in a way that makes him cringe. Like she hadn't been thinking for a long time and now she was. "A lot," she says, as if it were a new concept and different and a burden. And maybe it was a burden. So, what gives? In that brief moment of speculation he knew what was coming. Instinct, a sense of foreboding rushed into him.

"Really?"

Jack tried to make himself sound relaxed and confident even though his throat had started to tighten.

"Yeah, I've done a lot of thinking since you left…"

"Two days ago."

He tried not to sound sarcastic even though that was his reaction. A glib reaction was easy for Jack. Sarcastic could come later.

"Yes…yes it was. About us."

"You've been thinking for two days about us?"

"Yes, about us."

"Okay, and tomorrow, will you be thinking about us tomorrow?"

"Probably."

"Okay."

"Really, Jack, I've been thinking about us for awhile, but more so the last couple of days."

"And…?

Now he was ready to go beyond glib, and be sarcastic.

"Well, the result is that I, that is we…damn, this is hard."

"Hard as a rock."

Very sarcastic.

"There it is…right there. Hard as a rock."

"I was being funny."

"I know…and you are."

Jack waited and thought about ka-ching as the cell phone computer monster recorded air time. He thought waiting with a pregnant pause was his best plan right there. So far their conversation was as if each were talking in their own kind of code. It was beyond incoherent, although he thought he knew what she was trying to say. But, he wasn't going to make it easy. Shame on me, Jack thought, but let her spit it out; let her say what she wants to say. He waited.

"We're not making it," she finally said softly.

There was the slightest drawl in her voice and the tone was tender. Just a sweet colored girl from Greenville, South Carolina, dumping her white man friend, and sometime lover.

"What does that mean?"

He knew what it meant, but he wanted her to say it, say it out loud, and direct.

"Our relationship is not working."

"I thought it was. Last I knew before I left town was that you and I were a hot item. I was wrong. How come? How come I was wrong? How come I didn't know this before I left? I'm not stupid and I don't think I'm insensitive. Am I?"

Now she waited and he could hear her take a deep breath. Has she been playing a game with me, he wondered?

"No," she breathed.

"Well then?"

"I wasn't honest with myself, Jack, and I wasn't honest with you..."

"What is it?"

"I need to be with a black man. I've thought about our relationship and I came to the conclusion it was wrong. I finally had to admit to myself that it didn't feel right and I felt guilty, I felt false. I felt I needed to be with a man my own color."

"Racist."

That remark was downright nasty. Jack hated it when the term racist was thrown around, but he couldn't resist. It was too easy.

"Jack, please..."

"Your own color. Let's see how that works. Light brown, coffee with cream. Just enough cream for the right light brown. Light brown it is."

"A negro man."

"You're more white than negro..."

"Jack, please don't make this any more difficult than it already is..."

"For whom? I'm down here in Atlanta because of the death of my son and you call me about this. I haven't even been able to face up to my grief, that bitter sadness inside me, and you take this opportunity to phone me to dump me..."

"Jack, I'm sorry…I admit it, I did it this way because I could not have told you face to face. I've wanted to talk about it for the last few months, for crying out loud, but I didn't have the courage. I just couldn't do it. I'm sorry, very sorry. And I'm sorry about J.W. and sorry about your sadness, but the truth is I'm separated from those feelings. I have my feelings to deal with, I can't and don't want to take on yours."

"That honesty is a sure-fire finality. Saves a lot of time. No arguments, no bitter recriminations, no agonizing apologies, and no comeback except thanks for the memories. Bye, Baby, and good luck."

Jack flicked off the phone and waited. It didn't ring back. It was over between them. Just like that. No warning, no prelude, no phony fight of some kind that wasn't the real issue. He had no clue this was coming and struggled to sort out his feelings at being blindsided. Damn.

There he was, buzzing along at seventy miles an hour, wondering what the hell was going on in his life. You talk about distraction, here was the height of it, but fortunately he was in the middle of nowhere between Columbus and Atlanta, the traffic was almost non-existent, and there were no complex considerations for his driving. His car was on cruise control and he tried to put his brain there, also. No thoughts, no deep analyzing, no memories, no flirting with possibilities, just blankness in his brain. Erase the blackboard, no pun intended, simply forget the time he had spent with this woman, forget the involvement, the fun, the closeness, the connection that they had, and the seemingly overwhelming emotional bond that welded their lives. Meg erased all of that in a phone call. Limited dialogue, minimal explanation. He was not a Negro man. That is the net result of their conversation. Nice, but a denigration of all that they had previously discussed and discussed intensively in detail and at length. Of course he was not a Negro man. She knew that and now it was an issue. She wanted a Negro man. He was not a Negro man. It was over between them. Over. What bullshit.

Jack could not conceive of a separateness and an aloneness for himself right then and wondered whether he should collect his senses, pack his bags, and head back to Ohio. There was still more to do here, but screw it. His life was in turmoil from several aspects. First of all, he wanted to find J.W.'s killer. That was a significant motivation for him. *And* he just got cut off from a person he thought was his love, that anger and frustration now resonating inside him so that he was almost immobile except he was moving in his car. *And* he had a thriving advertising agency that needed him right now. These were three directions of emotional pressure collapsing on him and it was as if his mind were in a vise being squeezed to a compressed funk. He could hardly swallow and struggled to breathe normally.

His cell phone rang. He believed that it was Meg calling to… To what? Change her mind? Give him solace? Hardly. It was Elaine, the cop he thought did not care, the cop he thought felt ambivalent to his cause about J.W.

"Jack…" She sounded tired.

"Yes…"

"I didn't know you had a gun…"

"Ah, yeah. I have a carry permit. I know how to use it. In fact, I'm quite good with it."

"Wooley called me."

"Yes, we had a little difficulty down in Columbus today."

"I heard. You okay?"

"I'm fine under the circumstances, just fine."

"Where are you?"

"The last mile marker I saw said I was twenty miles from Atlanta."

"Not far away, but you've got some traffic to maneuver through."

"I'm heading back to the Marriott, I'm sort of…sort of had it for today."

"I understand. You've been through a great deal. How about coming to my house…have dinner?"

"I don't know. I'm strung out a bit. Lost in my own…dark cloud."

"I'll cook, you'll eat and relax, I'll fix you a drink; it will be low-keyed."

I hate to say no, but…"

"Don't say no. I'll make it worth your while."

"I…"

"Say yes. You won't regret it."

The offer was surreal. He had just been axed by Meg and now he was being hustled by Elaine. Out with the old, in with the new. The shuffle was almost too much for him, even though with the kind of business he was in he was used to quick changes. However, he wasn't used to being hustled. After all, he was the hustler.

In the span of a few days his son dies, he's in a gun fight, and Meg ends their relationship. It's been a hell of a week so far.

Elaine had given Jack her address and his GPS got him there unerringly, through the heavy traffic congestion, steady and sure. He recognized the area where he had taken her home, not far from the strange building that used to house police headquarters. He drove by the small, unpretentious single family homes, the facades hiding the many secrets of the private lives they contained. He found a spot to park and walked to Elaine's house and rang the bell. There was no answer. He waited a minute and rang the bell again. Nothing. He stepped off the porch and stood there wondering what tack he should take. Check out the rear? He trudged around to the back and stood looking up at a rear porch and the seeming deadness of the house. He pulled out his cell phone, punched up her previous call, and punched send.

"Where are you?"

"I'm by your back porch. There was no answer when I rang the doorbell."

She laughed and the phone went dead. An instant later she pulled open the rear door and came out on the back porch.

"Come on in. I forgot to tell you the bell doesn't work."

13.

When Jack got up on the porch their eyes met. He realized it was kind of intoxicating being looked at the way she appraised him, one of those movie moments when there is a crescendo of music that lets you know for sure that something special is happening. But a wave of apprehension rushed over him and he tried to stay cool, to not react to her look of approval and desire; that look of lust. Before he could respond in any way, she stepped close and put her left arm around his waist. The move was made with ease and smoothness; nothing awkward or strained. Her body was pressed against him with a familiarity that surprised him.

"Come on inside. You've had a rough few days."

She guided Jack into the kitchen, her arm still around him, and patted his chest with her right hand. Her hand lingered on his chest and she smiled at him.

"I have martinis made."

She stepped back, the appraisal still under way, and continued smiling. The smile turned to a grin. She went to the freezer compartment of her refrigerator and pulled out a stainless steel martini shaker and two very chilled long-stemmed martini glasses. She warmed the shaker with her hands, shook it a bit, and then poured quite deliberately. She handed Jack a glass. She was smiling again.

"To us and a nice weekend."

They clinked glasses.

"Let's sit down. Relax."

As she said this, she put her hand on his waist again, again to direct him.

They went into the living room of the small house. It was sparsely furnished as if she had just moved in or was getting ready to move out. A sofa, two unmatched overstuffed chairs, a plain non-descript wooden coffee table, and no carpet. There was no other furniture. The bare wooden floor appeared to have recently been refinished. An inexpensive abstract print about two feet by three feet hung above the sofa. That was it. The sounds of their footsteps on the wooden floor bounced around the room. Their voices seemed to echo slightly as they talked, quite like being in an empty warehouse. Certainly a strange aspect to the whole setting.

She flopped onto the sofa and rubbed her hand on the seat next to her as she directed him to sit down. Jack wasn't sure about it, but he did sit next to her. She kicked off her shoes and swung her legs across his lap. This was another move of familiarity that caught him by surprise. He rested his martini glass on her leg. Right now, there was no point in resisting. She was in charge.

"Well, cowboy, besides the chance of getting shot, you could have gotten yourself in a lot of trouble. Fortunately for you, Wooley talked to me." She had reverted to police detective status.

Jack furrowed his brow, but did not respond.

"You went to Columbus, why?"

"My son had a drug connection there. I went to find out about it."

"Find out anything?"

"Just that it was real and the cops there had a line on it."

"They were on top of it?"

"I guess so."

"Well here in Atlanta we're on top of stuff also. Your case in particular. I am, anyway. Stick with me from now on. Forget about the newspaper guy and work with me."

"I figured you weren't much interested. At least that's the way it seemed."

"Yeah, well, you figured wrong. Stick with me. Monday we'll get after it."

"How about tomorrow and Sunday?"

"You need a break, I need a break. The bad guys aren't going anywhere."

Jack stared at her. His inclination was to argue, to get up and leave, and move ahead by himself. But he didn't. She was right; he was sort of used up. Pulling back for awhile could help reenergize him, refresh his focus for getting this thing resolved. And there was this way about her. The inflection that packaged her words, the innuendo of intimacy that came from smoothness of familiarity she granted him. Her touch, the implications of her words.

"You know I've been a cop fifteen years and never been in a gun fight."

"Really?"

"That's right and glad of it."

They were silent for a minute as they sipped their drinks.

"What do you have planned for this weekend?" Jack asked.

Boy, was he being coy.

"I usually spend my weekends off getting drunk and staying drunk until I go back to headquarters. Helps me forget the stink and filth I'm involved in most of the time. The rotten mess that cops have to deal with. I thought maybe this weekend I could spend with you having sex. Maybe I wouldn't drink so much. Maybe I wouldn't feel so lousy about my life."

She wasn't flip or glib in the way she said it, just matter-of-fact. Very casual, very real. She wasn't looking for a reaction from Jack and he didn't give her one. He sipped his martini and looked at her.

"I thought we'd spend the night here. Tomorrow we can go by the Marriott so you can get some clothes, and we'll go up to my place on Lake Lanier. Come back Sunday night. Be refreshed and ready for Monday morning."

"You've got it all figured out," he said. "We get refreshed by drinking and screwing all weekend?"

"And relaxing, having some good food. I'm a great cook. I'm pretty good at a number of things."

There it was, all of the looks, the smiles, the innuendos, the implications, all laid out for him. There was the hustle; naked, unabashed, and certain. Take it or leave it, he felt. He had never had a woman so blatant about her desire, so secure in the idea her proposal would be accepted. He could feel her legs on top of his thighs, the intimate warmth part of her message. The message was I want you, you will be mine for this weekend, and you have no choice in the matter.

"You connected to anyone?" she asked.

That's an interesting way of putting it. Probing to determine what complications there might be. Jack was sure she didn't care if there were complications, she just wanted to know if they involved another woman. He was quite sure she would not have cared if there were another woman, she would readily deal with that issue. For her, probably a non-issue.

"Not now…"

"How so? What do you mean not now?"

"Well, as the fates would have it, driving back to Atlanta from Columbus I got a call. A dear Jack notice…you know what I mean?"

"I do."

"…from a lady in Ohio…Columbus, Ohio…"

"Splitsville?"

"Yeah, splitsville."

"She dumped you without facing you…"

"I know…"

"Man, this is a lousy week for you…"

"I know, I know. It feels…"

"Wow, Elaine *does* have the right solution for you this weekend."

"I…"

She reached for Jack, got him by the neck and pulled him toward her. She kissed his cheek as their martini glasses clicked together and gin spilled on both of them. She let go of him, slid her legs off, and stood up. She took his glass and headed for the kitchen.

"Let me fix these."

Jack sat there staring at the blank white wall across from him. Right then, the lack of art or pictures or anything else on the wall didn't register with him. Numb. All this stuff was jumping around in his head about Meg. He was confounded for the moment. How could he begin to explain what his feelings were about her, about her dismissal of him and the feelings of rejection that he harbored. And explain to whom? Himself? Why did he even need to explain what had gone wrong. Explaining, that construction of rationalization, was a grab-bar for the psyche, Jack guessed. We do it with some intellectual persistence with the idea that it will resolve the matter. It does not. Emotional hurts are not resolved by intellectual gymnastics. Emotional hurts are taken care of by time and soothing, the soothing that comes from being comforted and cared about. Elaine was willing to be the salve for Jack who was just flash fried by Meg. Screw trying to figure it out, he was willing to be comforted.

Elaine came back to Jack with a fresh martini and he slugged half of it with the first take. She sat in one of the overstuffed chairs across the coffee table from him. She was serious, the smile was gone, she wanted to connect.

"Feelings hurt?"

"Hell, yes."

"It happens that way sometimes. She probably didn't plan it, to wait until you were out of town. She probably had been considering the split for awhile and this looked like a good chance to get it over with. She give any reason?"

"I'm not Negro."

"Aha, she's a black chick?"

"Yes, but more light chocolate."

"With a touch of cinnamon."

"You make her sound edible…"

"Was she?"

"Almost, I guess."

"Look, when you're having sex with me you'll forget all about her. You'll feel better."

Jack smiled. Stupidly smiled, he supposed.

Damn, was he in a Russ Meyer movie? Elaine was so certain, so sure, it was unsettling. But it was titillating and it was invigorating. Perhaps she was right. He tried to stay on an even keel mentally. He wanted to sort out his thoughts about his relationship with Meg. He wanted to get his feelings about her straight. However, he now was confronted with the flagrant pull of sensuality from Elaine that cluttered his thinking. The physical over the intellectual, lust over reason, sex over sensibility. What a goddamn male he was and he was succumbing to the temptation. Has it always worked this way? The cave man was tough, but more than likely when the cave woman beckoned, he felt it in his loins and he fell prey.

"I have chicken in the oven. It'll be ready soon. Bring your drink and talk to me while I make salad and a vegetable for us."

She swept away to the kitchen and Jack dutifully followed. He could smell the tempting odors of chicken baking, a smell that made him realize all of a sudden that he was hungry. It had been morning since he had eaten. She caught him sniffing.

"Hungry?"

"Yeah, I just realized I am."

"While I cut up a salad why don't you set the table? There, in the dining room. And light the candles. Give us some romantic atmosphere. Plates and salad bowls are in that cupboard, silverware in that drawer."

She pointed out both locations and turned to the cutting board. Jack did as he was told.

This is interesting. Romantic interlude of intimate dining? Let's see, how does this work? Unabashedly she says they're going to drink and screw a lot this weekend. Does that remove the aura of romanticism from this encounter? He guessed that in her mind it was not so.

"You've led me to believe that we're going to drink and have sex all weekend. Doesn't that sort of temper the romantic mood? I mean if you take away the…"

"Not if you don't want it to. And I want our dinner to be romantic. Talking about sex doesn't necessarily diminish its pleasure or excitement or its romantic content. It's just another kind of foreplay. Don't you think?"

Don't you think? What the hell does he know right now?

"Why don't you open the wine?" Elaine said. "Corkscrew is in that drawer next to the silverware. Bottle is in the fridge."

Again, he did as he was asked and popped the plastic cork on the white wine she had chilled. She handed him two wine glasses and he put the glasses and bottle on the table.

"Now what?" Jack asked, as he went back into the kitchen where she was just taking the chicken from the oven.

"Why don't you pour us some wine and sit down. I'll serve."

Again he was dutiful and she served. She brought out some cloth napkins, yellow linen, handed him one, and sat down. She flipped the yellow cloth onto her lap and smiled at him. She was poised and sure of herself, she was sexy and knew it, knew she appealed to men who were comfortable with her air of confidence, her aggressiveness, and her command of her surroundings. She had assessed him early on, he supposed, probably when they first met. He was tabbed for acquisition, an invisible target inscribed on his back not unlike men do when they see a woman they want. Elaine had wanted Jack and now he was in her web of convenience. He was caught within the scope of her desire. He could walk away after dinner, excuse himself for being tired or having a headache or some such thing; he could make that decision if he wanted to do so. If he wanted. But her intrigue had taken him. He decided to see what would happen.

"Tell me about her."

"This is delicious," Jack said as he finished the first bite of chicken.

"Thank you, enjoy."

She paused.

"What is she like?"

Elaine circled her fork in the air as she said this.

"Who?"

"The unkind lady who dumped you today, that's who."

"Meg."

Of course Jack felt stupid. Why the hell did he say "who"?

"Wonderful Meg. What is Meg like?"

"I thought she was a terrific person. Lots of fun, smart, warm, and…loving. I thought she was loving. She was loving until today. And I thought we had a lot in common…"

"Except you're not the right color."

"I guess."

"How did you meet her?"

"Through my partner, Byron Adams. She's a real estate agent; she was his agent. He bought a new house, an estate actually, and Meg had the listing and handled the deal. He was so excited and pleased with the place that he had a humongous party to celebrate. She was there, I was there; we met. We hit it off. We sort of went on from there."

"Long time?"

"About three years ago. A little longer, I guess."

"Any complications? Like children?"

"She has two grown kids, a son and a daughter living in California. Never were an issue. Met them once. Neither married, no grandkids. The only complication was scheduling time. Time to be together, time to do things. She was very busy, very successful. I was and am very busy. Running an ad agency has its demands"

"Was she good in bed?"

That rocked him. How the hell do you answer that and not sound like a dope? Any answer you come back with is wrong. Let's see, you're a tattletale or a complainer demanding there should have been something there wasn't. Here was a woman on the verge of jumping on top of him wanting to know the quality of his sex life with the ex-person female in his life. None of your damn business. But that begged the question. Meg was a delight for sure. In bed, out of bed, a delight.

"When did you stop beating your wife?"

"What do you mean by that?"

"It's that kind of question, so that's my best answer. I hesitate to be impolite and tell you it's none of your business and I don't want to implicate me or Meg with any other response."

"So, it's none of my business and you're right, it isn't. Just curious, though."

"It shouldn't matter to you, since you have the weekend planned."

"It doesn't matter."

Elaine stopped in mid-bite, put her fork down, and poured herself another glass of wine. The bottle was empty and he still hadn't finished his first glass. She did not seem to notice she had killed the bottle, but then caught him watching her and realized what had occurred.

"Oh, sorry. Here, take this."

She slid her full wine glass over to him and got up. She went to the kitchen and he could hear her clattering ice and pouring a drink. She came back to the dining room with a fresh martini.

"I like these better, anyway."

Jack wondered how many of those she could tolerate before she went face down into the plasma of stupor. If she were as practiced as she says she is, it could take awhile.

"Where were we? Oh, yeah, you were about to tell me about your lousy sex life with marvelous Meg. Right?"

"Not really. I was about to ask you what if anything you have found out about my son's murder since last we were together."

"Oh, come on, let's leave that stuff until Monday. I'd rather hear about your sex life."

"That's not going to happen, that part of my life is…"

"Off limits…?"

"You bet."

"Well then, tell me this. Do you like it? Fucking."

"Somehow there is a distinction that I have, that I maintain, where I prefer the terminology of making love."

"A difference between fucking and making love?"

"Yes, of course."

"My, my, that's very cerebral of you. And you make that distinction because…? No, wait, let me guess. You prefer to think of it as love making because you believe that raises you above the level of a mere fornicating animal and, most importantly, you respect the woman you're lying on top of. Or has you in her mouth. Am I right, oh righteous one?"

He didn't answer. He looked at her and sipped his wine. She gulped down her martini and went to make another.

There was no getting around the fact that Elaine had that "sexy look." To him, there is in certain women an indefinable quality of facial context that no matter what expression these particular women have there exudes an image of sensuality, and, an almost wantonness. Funny as it seems, men seem to agree on this look even though they have no idea how to describe its effect or categorize its elements in any specific way. This was a Mona Lisa-like enigma; recognized, but elusive in quality. Elaine had this "look" no matter what her demeanor was whether it was serious or silly, she was still very sexy. He felt it was a look of availability that transcended her seeming toughness and her polished aggression. Available for sex, that was the connotation. The overriding sexual aura, no matter what she said or did. It was compelling. And no matter how crass she might act, the sexiness didn't go away.

Jack had finished eating when she came back into the dining room with her fresh martini. She didn't sit, but came behind his chair and leaned down against him and put her arm around him and rubbed his chest. She kissed his neck and nuzzled. He wished he could see the sexy face. He could see it in his mind, but he wanted the real image.

"Do you like to dance?" She whispered the question in his ear and kissed his check. "I love to dance. Slow and easy, smooth and sure. I like that."

"Yeah, I do…"

"Good."

She let go of him and went into the living room to a sound system she had. She punched several buttons and a few seconds later the quiet sound of sentimental danceable music filled the room. Quiet, modulated, and for their age group almost inappropriate. It was throwback music that their parents danced to and really appreciated. It was big band sound, slow, melancholy, and it was sensual. Almost as sensual as Elaine's look and just as indefinably so. She came back to him and held out her hand.

It was so easy to stand, take her in his arms, and begin the slow foreplay of 50's style dancing that created an erection and turned a man senseless and wondering if he were going to get laid. That was not an issue in this situation, but the mind-numbing senselessness still was overriding. Elaine's body was against him in a way that was not clinging, but damned familiar, as if they had danced like this many times before and she was used to feeling their bodies together; wanted their bodies together. And it intensified the sexiness of what they were doing, it made it electric, it was charged with anticipation. Hers and Jack's.

The piece ended, she slipped away from him, and retrieved her drink. She took a sip, gave him that sexy grin, and downed the rest. She stepped back against him as the music picked up and again they were undulating around her living room in tight circles of slow motion. Like two dancing puppets with some unknown, unseen hands directing the moves, they had no control of their actions and floated on the strings of raw emotion that propelled them. It seemed unreal.

She let go of him when the music paused for the next cut and went to the kitchen. She quickly returned with her martini glass filled. He watched her stick her tongue in the clear liquid. She kissed him and pushed her tongue in his mouth and he could taste the gin. Before he could reciprocate, she leaned back slightly.

"Have a taste…"

"I just did. I wanted more but…"

"No, I mean here, take a sip."

He did and put the glass down. She picked it up, slurped some of the Martini, and put it down. The music was well into the next selection and he pulled her to him to dance and she didn't move her feet. They kissed and this time their tongues met. How do you do, Miss Moss?

"Maybe that's enough dancing for tonight," Elaine said quietly. "Maybe we need to move on to other things."

"I can guess what you have in mind."

After he said it he knew it sounded insipid, but he couldn't erase it. Unfortunately, there is no erase button to reality. If there were, he figured, all of us would have a better chance at not saying stupid stuff. He wanted to be clever, but there just wasn't the well-scripted Cary Grant in his repartee. He could excuse himself, though, because he was exhausted and half whacked out on Martinis and wine. On the other hand, he didn't think she cared what he said. She was intent on her next move.

The transition to Elaine's bedroom and bed was dream-like in its sequence of events. Kissing, fondling, laughing, touching, excruciating touching, crawling some, and then stumbling the rest of the way as the orchestra played in the background.

They were finally there by her bed and were suddenly naked and kissing and caressing with an ease and sense of intimacy that overwhelmed him. In retrospect, that whole event breakdown astounded him. He was the hungry male animal. He assumed this would be fucking not love making.

The next morning, Saturday, Jack awoke to a dreary, gray pall that hung low over Atlanta as the prolog to the storm that would sweep over the city and steadily rain the entire day. Elaine was still unconscious, caught firmly in a cocoon woven from her passion for sex and Martinis. She would remain that way for awhile.

He turned on his side and looked at this unusual woman lying there next to him; she, his current dance partner and partner in wildly erotic pleasure. Elongated, prone Elaine, nude Elaine, breathing heavily, was eminently sexy in repose.

He realized that no matter what Elaine wanted to do in terms of going to her place on Lake Lanier, he was going to move ahead with his investigation. He had caved to her desire and her aggressive management of his time the last twelve hours, but he was yanking the reins back. He would be in charge of himself. And himself did not want to go to Lake Lanier today. Get back on the trail. He knew that was what he needed to do.

He went downstairs and poked around in the kitchen to find coffee and filters to use in the automatic maker on the counter. Cups were on a wooden rack next to the maker. Once he had the coffeemaker gurgling, he went to the front door to check for a newspaper. He could see it there on the front porch, so he fetched it inside with a quick swipe. He had been walking around the house with a bath towel wrapped around his waist, checking out the place, finding neither the front nor back door had been locked. It probably didn't matter since the neighborhood bad guys already knew there was a cop living here. Coming in unannounced they stood a good chance of getting shot.

Jack got a cup of coffee and settled in on the living room sofa. There it was on page five: **Distraught Father Of Murdered Ohio Businessman In Shootout With Columbus Drug Dealer.** The detailed story covered most of the page. Some of the facts were screwed up, but mostly it was correct. Was he distraught? He didn't think he was. Should he be distraught? Perhaps. Right this moment he felt quite calm. Some booze and heavy duty sex can do that for you. Or is that too cynical? He assumed it was.

He skipped from the article about him to the Sports section and spent some time there. Next, he flipped through the other pages to the Op Ed page which was dizzyingly stupid in terms of the subjects it wanted to op ed about and amazingly silly in its use of language and syntax. Our copywriters could do better than this mess, he mused.

He could hear stirring upstairs. Elaine was awake. A toilet flushed. Elaine was up. He could hear other sounds, the rustle of some kind of clothing. Seconds later, she fairly bounded down the stairs. She wore a frilly, flowered chemise that he saw was sheer enough for him to see through if he were paying close attention.

"I could smell the coffee." Her voice was full of energy. "Guess you found everything okay. God, let me have a cup."

She headed for the kitchen then turned.

"Hey, good morning."

"Good morning."

She got her cup of coffee, came and sat next to him.

"Well now, how was that last night? Don't answer. I know I shouldn't ask such a question, but it's hard to resist. I should…"

"It was rapture," Jack said flatly and didn't smile or offer any expression of emotion.

She looked at him and laughed.

"Thank you, I thought it was wonderful."

"I'm surprised you can even remember."

"Why do you say that? You mean because I had a few Martinis?"

"Yeah, more than a few."

"I have you to thank for how little I drank. If I had been alone I would have…I would have had more."

"Glad to see you're so spunky."

"This is a stinky day, though." She changed the subject almost as if she didn't hear him.

"Weather will not be a factor for what I'm going to do today."

Jack tossed the paper onto the coffee table.

"Oh, what is that?"

"I'm going to continue my investigation. I can't wait until Monday."

"I thought we'd go up to my place on Lake Lanier…"

"You thought. That I understand. However, I've got to keep working to find my son's killer."

"Okay. If you're so determined and are already tired of our sex life I'll help. I'm flexible, I can make the change."

Jack pulled on the clothes he wore the day before and Elaine got in a lightweight dark blue pants suit with a white blouse. She said that when she was working she liked a suit so the jacket would hide her semi-automatic. She still looked sexy. They took his car and she talked him into stopping for brunch at the nearby cafe in the strip mall. They ordered, sipped at their coffee, and she reached across the table and took his hand. She was serious for the first time since he came to her house yesterday.

"Not today, probably, but in the next few days we will arrest your son's murderers. Try to relax. A great deal more has gone on than you realize, more work than you think."

"I'm worried about standing still when whoever did it is not standing still."

"Yes, they are. They are because they think we can't catch them. We can, we will. You didn't think I was involved, that we weren't involved. I know more than you think."

"That makes me feel a bit better. I felt I was doing this alone."

With Elaine's seriousness came a look of vulnerability that hadn't been there before. At least he hadn't spotted it. The uncanny sexiness never left her face, the layer of vulnerability merely slipped over it and refreshed her image.

They finished eating and drove to the Marriott. There was gentle probing about last night. He guessed she still wanted a critique. That sort of 'was it as great for you as it was for me' routine, although those weren't the words she used. Did he like the music? Yes. Did he like the dancing? Yes. Did he like her dinner? Yes. He volunteered that he liked her bedroom and her bed. She laughed and that was the end of it.

Jack left the car with the valet, told him not to bury it because they would be heading out soon, and they went in the lobby.

"Wait for me here?" he asked.

"No, I'm coming up with you."

Once they were in his room, Elaine started taking off her clothes.

"And?" he said, surprised.

"I thought you would take a shower and I'd join you. I should have before we left, but you were in such a hurry."

She finished undressing, got to the shower, and had it steaming before he could get his clothes off. There was that continuity of familiarity she had and their naked bodies rubbing together in the shower seemed natural, without awkwardness or constraint. It was luxurious, it was a surprise, and it was comfortable.

"Do you think we've hit it off?" she asked as she washed his back.

"I don't think it matters," Jack said and she laughed.

14.

As Jack started the drive to Marietta he called Mrs. Brady on his cell phone. He thought it was about time to check on Millie. Mrs. Brady was her cheerful self and took several minutes to update him on how well Millie was doing. He listened in silence, periodically offering a "sure" or "I know" or "yes" or "isn't that nice" to let her realize he was still on the line. Millie didn't miss him, she had Mrs. Brady.

Mrs. Brady got Millie to meow and held her phone so Jack could hear.

"She says she misses you, Mr. Phillips. Isn't that nice?"

Jack said that it was and thanked her and told her they'd talk again soon. She did not inquire about what he was doing or ask how he was; she handled his call in return as simply as he had presented it to her. He did not want to bother her with what he was doing nor take the time for narration. It was enough just listening to Millie cry at him and certainly a more satisfactory call than the one with Meg. That bothered him, but he didn't want to take the time right then to figure out all the reasons why.

Jack's drive north to Marietta on I-75 took him against the grain of heavy going-into-the-city traffic so he got to his exit fairly quickly and started the process of wending his way to Crawford's business. It wasn't hard to find. Design Interiors was the largest store in a small up-scale line of shops that included a tea room and a cigar emporium. It was a neighborhood Jack appreciated, a neighborhood of refurbished older houses that gave the proper hint of affluence with their newly painted exteriors and clever landscaping, all neat and tidy, with a view of the appropriate Volvo or BMW or Mercedes in the driveway.

Jack parked in front of the store and squinted to read the hours of operation stenciled on the front door. It was dark inside and he suspected he was too early for Mr. Crawford or his staff. He grabbed his briefcase and got out to get a closer look. Ten; he was too early. He hadn't thought of that really; his agency started its business at eight. He had a hard time with retail hours. Oh, its not that they're not open enough, they are, but just not early enough for him. Of course, it was Saturday, but for the moment that fact escaped him.

He walked to the tea room a few doors down, which was open, and sat at a table toward the back where he could read their menu posted on a chalk board near the counter. He only wanted coffee, but he was curious about their breakfast fare. A spinach and mushroom omelet. Even if he hadn't had breakfast with Elaine he would have passed on that.

"You can place your order up here, sir," the young woman called to Jack.

"You have coffee?" He asked hesitantly.

"We sure do. Regular or decaf?"

"Regular, thanks."

He walked up to the counter.

"Is that all?" she asked politely.

"I think so…for right now, thanks."

"That will be one seventy-five."

He gave her two dollars and she gave him a quarter and smiled. She turned, filled a Styrofoam cup from a stainless container, and handed it to him.

"Cream and sugar's right there," she pointed.

He nodded to her, ignored the cream and sugar, and sat back at the table where his briefcase was resting. It was twenty minutes before ten.

A genteel-looking man was sitting across the room from Jack, intent with the morning paper. Whatever he was reading had his full attention. That could be Warren Crawford, he speculated, letting his mind hop about as he watched the man's concentration. He's checking the paper to find out where the investigation is going, wondering if he is yet a suspect. Little does he know that he is and that Jack was there to reveal who he was. What bunk, Jack thought, and looked away and drank his tea room coffee that was quite good. The man and he were the only customers right then.

The man broke away from his intensity with the paper and looked toward the counter to get the young woman's attention. She was too busy to notice.

"Teri, could I have some more hot chocolate, please?"

His voice had an interesting lilt to it, almost as if he were singing the words to her rather than saying them. He dragged out the please with full Shakespearean affect as if he were on stage and needed to emphasize: pleeeese. Please, please he says, with the words affecting like a cat rubbing against your leg. The way it sounded was not commanding, but rather cloying as if he were not sure she would honor his request unless he begged.

"Yes, Mr. Crawford, right away."

Damn, there he was in the flesh. And, for the time being, Jack had him all to himself. His silly speculation about Crawford had been correct and he wondered what the man was reading so intently. He would find out.

Jack got up from his table, grabbing his briefcase as he rose and eased over to Crawford's table. He pulled out a chair and sat down, not waiting to ask permission. He plunked his briefcase in the vacant chair near him. No question about it, he was being aggressive with the man; belligerent perhaps. He didn't care.

"Wondering how close the cops are?"

Jack looked directly at Crawford when he spoke and he said the words in a manner that mimicked jabbing his finger into Crawford's chest. The effect was the same.

"Who the hell are you?"

"J.W. Phillips' father."

Crawford was stunned, mouth agape, momentarily lost for words, and stared at Jack. He quickly gained his composure.

"Mr. Phillips, so sorry, really, so very sorry about Jim."

Jack nodded, ready to attack the man.

"Terribly emotional thing for me. I was…I was very fond of your son."

"Yeah, so I hear. So fond that in your jealousy over him with French, you killed him. That's some kind of fondness. Loving someone to death, it seems."

"No, it's not like that at all."

"No, that's right, you didn't actually kill J.W. yourself, you had your goon Dixie Hamner do the job."

"I don't know what you're talking about…"

"You're a lying son-of-a-bitch. Hamner works for you; that I have established. Don't play innocent with me, I've already talked to French."

"Hey, hey, Hamner used to work for me awhile back, but he doesn't now and has no connection with my business."

"What did he do for you?"

"You know, odd jobs, special assignments…"

"Like what? Protecting your drug business? Word I got is that he is working for you right now."

"Not true."

Sparring with Crawford about Hamner was a waste of time. Jack wanted other information.

"How the hell did you get started with the drugs? Weren't you making enough money with the legit business you had? I bet my son was."

"You know, I don't have to talk to you…"

"That's right…you don't. But if you don't, I'm going to kick your ass all the way down the street to your business. Then I'm going to make sure everyone knows that you killed my son. Hamner will love that, so tell me what happened. Tell me how the drug bullshit got started."

"Okay, okay, I don't want any rough stuff."

"Good, you know I mean it…"

"Yeah, yeah."

"Speak…"

"Okay. All of us were doing fine. Then Bill Shay got to Jim and convinced him there was a way to make even more money. It was easy money that he could squirrel away from the IRS, and his wife; especially from his wife. Shay had this guy Ryan Coleridge who had it all scoped out. He had connections to a guy who had a direct pipeline to Mexico. They flew the drugs right into the airport there in Columbus. The plane came in from Texas once a week. Somebody who had a business jet that went back and forth. All would seem like it was on the level; simply doing business."

"Doing business, all right."

"I cared for Jim very much, Mr. Phillips, and we…"

He paused, tears welling, and he caught his breath.

Jack eased back in his chair and waited for Crawford to compose himself.

"You were lovers?" Jack asked.

His voice was soft when he posed the question, not entirely insensitive to the man's feelings. Damn, Jack thought, how can I even relate to any of this? Murder, gays, and drugs were not part of Jack's everyday world. But he asked for this by coming to Atlanta to be the big deal detective. He realized maybe right now he had learned more than he wanted to know.

"He was going to divorce his wife," Crawford said as he dabbed at his eyes with a paper napkin.

"That's what they all say," Jack blurted.

Crawford laughed a bit at the remark, the irony not getting by him, and the laugh caught in his throat and he coughed and choked and sipped some of his hot chocolate.

"You know, they'll get to you, the cops, the drug guys. They got Shay and Coleridge…"

"I heard."

"Only a matter of time. So where is Hamner?"

Crawford's head snapped up from its self-pitying slump and the eyes glared.

"You could testify against Hamner and get easier prison time. Oh, yeah, you're going to do time, no doubt about that."

All of a sudden Jack saw that Crawford's attention was on something or someone outside the tea room. Almost immediately a huge figure loomed at the plate glass store front and glared at Crawford. The big man motioned to Crawford with his index finger. Crawford was paralyzed, mouth agape.

"Thought Hamner didn't work for you. Maybe you work for him."

"I…"

"He wants you to come outside it would seem."

"I don't have any idea what he wants…"

"He wants you. You better get to the cops before your boy kills you. You can see it in his eyes. He wants to kill you.

The whole thing has gone bad just because you wanted him to kill J.W."

"No, I..."

"Look, he's walking away. You're safe for awhile until he gets back to you. He will get back to you. You're cooked if you don't go to the police."

Crawford rose slowly and watched as the big man walked across the street and got into his car. The car did not move.

"Do you think you can get to your store before he gets to you? Maybe you better go out the back way, get in your car, and drive to Police Headquarters. You might stay alive."

Crawford turned away from Jack without responding and walked to the back of the tea room. He went down a narrow hallway and disappeared.

Jack rose, pulled at his sport coat to make sure the Glock was covered, and headed for the door.

"Was everything all right? I mean, Mr. Crawford left sort of in a hurry."

"Oh yeah, just great, sweetheart, we're doing fine."

Jack went out the door and the girl behind the counter smiled, glad to have satisfied customers. He walked toward the car the big man had gotten into and realized the motor was running. The car gunned away from its parking spot before Jack could get half way across the street. He could not get the plate number.

Jack wondered if Crawford had gone to the police as he had suggested or was holed up in his store. He walked down to Design Interiors and went inside.

"May I help you?" the officious salesman asked as Jack walked across the showroom.

"Mr. Crawford in?"

The man hesitated, his head turning slightly from the pressure of the lie.

"No, he's not in yet. How can I help?"

"Tell him Mr. Phillips from the tea room is here. Tell him the big guy is gone."

"I..."

"Tell him...now."

Mr. Officious turned on his heels and left the showroom through a door to someplace at the rear of the store. It took less than a minute for Crawford to show himself.

"Come on in to my office."

He turned, went back through the door, and Jack followed.

"Have a seat," Crawford offered, once they were in his office.

Jack dropped onto a leather sofa and put his right leg on a cluttered coffee table.

"I saw the gun when we were at Carol's, so I know you mean business. Let me tell you some stuff."

"Some stuff?"

"How it played out. And I know you are right. I need to get to the police. This has gotten out of hand; it's ridiculous."

"Okay, let's have it."

"Would you like a cigar?"

"And a snifter of brandy?"

"Yes."

"Thank you, I will. Haven't had a good cigar in a long time. I assume you have only the best."

"I do."

Crawford pulled two huge, somewhat ugly looking olive-brown cylinders from his desktop humidor and handed Jack one. He reached in the credenza behind him and brought out a superb cognac and two glasses. He poured each glass nearly to the brim. He clipped his cigar, lighted it, and handed the clipper and lighter to Jack. Jack fixed his cigar and lighted it. He drew on it and puffed and the revelation from Crawford began.

"I met Jim early on when he took over this sales territory. He called on me, we hit it off, and I recommended and specified a ton of his company's products for projects I worked on. So did Collier. We did a great deal of socializing. Collier, Jim, and I. By the way, I noticed you call him J.W. instead of Jim or James or…"

"Jimmy? Yeah, it goes way back to when he was a kid. His mother started calling him that; J.W. It stuck. Not sure I like it, but it's an old habit. Go on."

"Well, Jim and I became more than just client and salesman. We became very good friends, very good. One thing led to another and we were involved emotionally…intimately. For a number of years things were great. He spent a bunch of time here in the Atlanta area, here with me in Marietta, and we were making good money. Then Shay brought Jim the drug deal, an opportunity to make really big money. And like fools, we moved on it and the money we made was incredible. Jim stashed his, I don't know where. He said it was his hedge fund, hedging his life for the future when he split with Angelina. Said he was just biding his time until the right time when the stash was big enough."

"How much?" Jack asked.

"About five million dollars…"

"Are you telling me that somewhere J.W. has five million bucks hidden away?"

"Yes, I am."

"Where?"

"I said, I don't know where."

Jack blew a smoke ring and stared at Crawford.

"Look, I know what you're thinking…"

"No, you don't…"

"I don't know where the money is…"

"This really gets it complicated. Not only does my son get killed because of some bullshit fag reason, but there's a pot of money involved…"

"The reason…I didn't finish what I was explaining to you. The reason things became tense is that Jim decided he wanted Collier and not me."

"Jesus Christ."

"It's true. But Jim didn't deal with things honestly. He was playing both of us, using us, and then he wanted to take me out of the drug action."

"And you found out and, of course, were angry."

"I was. I admit that, but I didn't tell or order Dixie Hamner to kill Jim. Dixie knew how angry I was and he thought Jim would screw up the drug deal, so he took it upon himself to take care of Jim."

"Makes a nice story. You're innocent, absolved of the murder…"

"I cared about Jim. It could have been worked out."

"It was worked out."

Crawford winced.

"Hamner acted on his own?" Jack asked.

"Yes, I never would have…wanted Jim dead."

"End of story?"

"Yes."

"You loved J.W.?"

Crawford hung his head, his arm outstretched on his desk with the cigar over the ashtray ready to flick the ash away as he wanted to rid himself of the pain.

"Yes. I hated it that Jim was now with Collier. But I didn't want him dead."

Jack puffed on his cigar and listened and wondered what to believe. He decided it did not matter.

"You better get to the cops fast."

Jack stood and adjusted the holster where he carried his Glock. He stepped towards Crawford's desk and leaned forward, his hands on the front edge.

"It would be so easy to shoot you right now and then find Hamner and shoot him. But I am going to let the system deal with the both of you. I think I can take satisfaction from how that works out."

Crawford stared back at Jack as if the message did not compute; a blank look, no comprehension. He grunted in response, a primordial reaction to what Jack said, but without understanding the true implication of the words.

Jack walked to the door. He turned and looked at Crawford.

"There isn't a lot of time."

Crawford watched him leave and a wave of foreboding swept over him. Jack walked away and outside to his car, the cigar held tightly between two fingers; he flicked the cigar to the gutter and got into his car.

The short drive to the Marietta police headquarters took several minutes. Jack went through security without much of a problem, but they took his Glock. He was shown to the office of Larry Davis, the detective who was in and would talk to him. Jack realized this was the man Elaine mentioned.

"Morning, I'm Larry Davis, how can we help you, Mr. Phillips?"

Detective Davis was a small man, compact, bullish, rough around the edges, unschooled, but not insensitive to someone like Jack. He extended his hand.

"You have a guy, living here in Marietta," Jack started, "who is involved in drugs and who, with his hired hand Dixie Hamner, killed my son in Atlanta. They have a big-time drug operation going on, illegal drugs, happening beneath your noses, and they are getting away with it."

"Sit down. Please."

Jack slid into the chair in front of the desk.

"Relax, stay calm, and understand that the situation is within our control. We have them all under surveillance. Let me assure you again, sir, that we have this situation under control."

"My son is dead because of all of this."

"I know."

Jack sat forward.

"They will not get away with it. Believe me."

"Tough talk. Don't do that."

Jack slumped into himself as he pulled back onto the chair. He then got up and paced and this unnerved Davis.

"Why don't you sit down and let's see where this is going?"

Jack sat back down and tried to relax.

"Ms. Moss called me."

Jack knew better than to say anything. Let him talk, let it play out. Perhaps he had underestimated Ms. Moss. Davis looked at him. Jack waited. He won the silence standoff.

"Ms. Moss told me what was going on, told me who you are, told me about your son. I'm sorry for your loss, Mr. Phillips, it's a terrible thing to happen. Brings a lot of pain into your life, I know. Maybe you better give me an update. What's happened since you last saw Ms. Moss?"

Jack wondered how this should go and decided to play it straight with Davis.

"I spent some time with Warren Crawford, one of your esteemed citizens. He was involved with my son. He had reason to kill my son or have my son killed. Either way, he says he's not part of my son's death other than knowing my son and being upset with what my son did to him. Or what he thought my son did to him. He says he is innocent and I told him to get to the police before Dixie Hamner kills him."

"Hamner?"

"Yes. I believe Hamner is the one who actually killed my son.

"You said "involved with my son." What did you mean by that?"

Jack bristled.

"What do you think I meant by that?"

"Sounds like maybe your son was gay. This department certainly knows that Crawford is an openly gay businessman. Was your son gay?"

There it was: the brutal question.

"I guess so. Yeah, he was as far as I can determine."

This admission was difficult for Jack, but he knew he could not dodge the answer. He had been dancing around the edges of the issue and now it confronted him directly and he could not back away from the truth. His feelings fell apart within him and he wondered at that point if he would ever gain some kind of understanding for what his son might have experienced and how he, himself, could truly reconcile with an understanding of the complexity of meaning this might have. A social outlier was what he fabricated for J.W. in the past, the description he drew from marketing research lingo. Jack believed J.W. was a man who never learned where he truly belonged. J.W. was caught in the conventional world with traditional ideas of working, making money, and succeeding in his job, and yet drawn to some sense of reality about his own sexual preferences which conflicted with the conventional. What a terrible existence. Plus, J.W. had the added burden of having a shrew of a wife to make the complex seemingly incomprehensible.

"So, now what," Davis asked.

"So, Crawford gets to you and tells his story or Hamner kills him."

"Well, I don't think so; I don't think those are the options. The Drug Task Force is on this one and we're watching Hamner very closely. We have all of these people under surveillance."

"Really? Then tell me how they managed to kill my son with almost no evidence left to enable you or the Atlanta police to get after them?"

Davis stared at Jack.

"Let me tell you something, bud. Hamner will kill Crawford before you can do anything about it."

"I know you're upset, Mr. Phillips, but we're working hard on this and we'll get Hamner locked down and we'll close down their drug operation."

"I don't have a lot of confidence in what you can do."

"Let us handle it. We know what we're doing"

"I'm supposed to butt out."

"You're supposed to let us do our job."

"It's amazing the way you guys react. As if the only original thoughts about a case only come from you. Well, your original thoughts aren't original and you should accept what comes in from outside your box. You are going to have more dead guys on your hands thanks to Dixie Hamner. Get ready. Have a nice day."

Jack walked out of Davis' office, retrieved his Glock at security, and got to his car, still fuming at what he felt was the man's reluctance to understand what Jack was trying to tell him. He flicked open his cell phone, waffling on a decision which number he wanted to punch in first.

The sound of Phillips-Nelson-Adams which was voiced by Kari was quite a shock to him. Almost as if it came from another dimension, some other world, remote, strange, and alien. And he was stunned at his reaction to what he heard. What the hell is this?

The "this" was his office with the normal greeting, the regular introduction to the business. He realized his disassociation from them; his short time here in Atlanta that had transported him to another universe that he had been functioning in since he had arrived. This call intersected his new realm with his regular reality. It was a jolt, but he adjusted quickly.

"Kari, Jack."

"Yes, Mr. Phillips."

"I'm okay, I'm working on the case of my son's death, and I'll be at it until there are answers."

"Sure, Mr. Phillips, I understand."

"What are you doing there on Saturday?"

"Deadline, sir, lots of us are working today."

"Right, well anyway, I'm not going to call in again until I'm finished. This call was a mistake."

"Yes sir."

"Tell the guys."

"Yes sir."

"Ciao."

"Yes sir."

He clicked his phone dead.

Jack punched in Colby's number, but got the answering recording. He tried Elaine.

"Moss…"

"Elaine…?"

"Yes. Are you all right?"

"I am. Why do you ask?

"I hadn't heard from you."

"Been busy."

"I understand, I talked to Davis."

"He called you already?"

"Yes, not happy you showed up at his office."

"He wasn't very helpful; handed me the "let us handle it" line."

"That's good advice. I wish you would listen to it."

"And Davis gave me the impression they didn't care about Crawford one way or another…"

"The Task Force probably doesn't need him to sing for them in order to pull the string on the drug operation, although his story would be a big plus."

"Maybe you're right."

"I think so. Look, Hamner has dropped out of sight and you're probably a target. Come on back to my house. We'll go up to my lake place for the rest of the weekend and then we'll get on this Monday.

"Weekends off for murder?"

"No, Sunday lay low while the cops do their job and you stay off Hamner's radar. Monday we make some moves. Besides, I miss you. Miss your delicate touch."

"The Task Force calling the shots?"

"You've got it. Come on to my house. I'll protect you."

"Is that what you call it?"

She laughed.

"See you later…at my house. Bring an overnight bag. We're going to the lake."

15.

Dixie Hamner stood in the center of his living room trying to remember if he had forgotten anything. Four day-laborers had carried his furniture, numerous boxes of miscellaneous belongings, and three large wardrobe cartons to a borrowed truck parked in the rear of the building. The laborers he found in a Home Depot parking lot. The truck came from a near-downtown carpet company thanks to Denny somebody-or-other who owed Hamner money. Denny diverted the truck after he made a delivery, but it was worth getting yelled at by his boss in order to have his debt cancelled.

Denny drove the loaded truck little more than three miles to a house in a quiet mid-town residential neighborhood just off Peachtree. The truck was emptied into a carriage house behind the residence. Hamner had led the truck to the house and watched over the transfer with little comment and paid the four men when they were finished. They were happy with the fifty dollar bill he gave each of them. He had directed Denny where to pick up the men and now he would return them. Hamner didn't say anything to Denny; it was understood they were even. The truck pulled away and he walked towards the house.

Hamner had a career of being ex-everything. Most of it conducted in a sleazy manner in some way. Ex-Marine dishonorably discharged, ex-con – assault with a deadly weapon, ex-used car salesman, ex-carpet salesman, ex-con – some kind of drug rap, ex-real estate agent – without a license, and, of course, ex-something-or-other right hand man for Warren Crawford. He was a lean, tough big man slightly more than six feet four inches tall, with a well-proportioned two hundred sixty pounds distributed on his frame. He was mean, he was intimidating, and he relished conflict. Never married, as far as police records show, he had lived alone in the luxury condo he had just abandoned in Atlanta's Buckhead area. He had no visible means of support, but financed the condo easily and drove a new top-of-the-line Mercedes.

As Hamner approached the house, the rear door opened, and a man masked by a nasty scowl stood in the doorway. He wore boxer shorts and tee shirt, and his feet were slipped into suede bedroom slippers. A stained coffee mug was in his left hand. Daryl Binser held the door open as Hamner plunged up the stairs and lumbered inside. He was wheezing and began to cough as he threw himself into a kitchen chair.

"You're out of breath old-timer and you probably ain't done a thing except climb them stairs."

Hamner smiled at Daryl, the indulgent smile one gives a favorite child.

"How about a drink?"

"Whiskey, beer, orange juice...?"

"Water would be good. A little ice."

Daryl got a glass from the cupboard.

"So you're out of that place?"

"Yeah, it's empty. No going back. I appreciate your letting me store my stuff here for awhile. Temporary, until I can get myself situated."

Daryl grabbed some ice from the freezer compartment and dropped the chunks in a glass and filled it with tap water.

"Leave it here as long as you like. Me and Lilly don't care. Plenty of room for your stuff. Could use some money, though."

In the last decade, Dixie Hamner had developed a fairly sophisticated network of operatives promoting wide-ranging hits of low-grade theft while staying out of the way of the mafia. Daryl was a member of Hamner's network and also worked part-time for Warren Crawford.

One of Crawford's customers stiffed him on the additional costs for a project and Daryl subsequently overheard Crawford, in the shop area of the store, screaming into his cell phone at the customer. All the shop workers heard Crawford demand his money and make threats. It was Daryl who approached Crawford with a solution.

"I know someone who can get that money for you, Mr. Crawford."

"How? A lawyer?"

"Naw, better than a lawyer; a guy who knows how to collect debts. He's real good at it. I've seen him in action and I know he can get your money."

"I said, 'how.' What's his secret?"

"His secret is that he is very persuasive."

Crawford and Hamner met at a crummy neighborhood bar just off downtown Atlanta. After some discussion, they agreed: Hamner would collect Crawford's debt for a percentage.

Hamner was effective in his collection methods and got Crawford his money and then some for himself. That started a working relationship which covered a wide range of intimidation and coercion projects. Those efforts benefitted Crawford handsomely and added significantly to Hamner's income. This on top of the two-bit theft ring Hamner continued to operate throughout the greater Atlanta area.

"Are you on the run?" Daryl asked.

Hamner sipped his ice water before he answered.

"Unfortunately yes, Daryl, I am."

"What happened? What's going on?

"Jim Phillips is what happened. He and French got sloppy, tried to squeeze Crawford and me out of the deal. You knew that. That's why he had to be exed. Now, Shay and Coleridge are history; picked up in a drug sweep in Columbus. Phillips' old man was involved nosing around. He's done a lot of nosing around. It didn't quite work out the way I wanted with Jimmy. His suicide was pegged for a murder right away, especially with Mr. Phillips pushing the cops. And there's this reporter guy Colby from the *Constitution* sniffing around everywhere and getting information."

"What do you want to do?"

"First, I want to side track this guy Colby. Then we shut up French and Crawford…"

"And then what?"

"We disappear, Daryl, we disappear."

"What about our guys. They're waiting for word on what's the next hit."

"Get out now. Leave town. Pass the word. Leave town. It's over for the time being. We'll get together in six months…in Waco. The newspaper ad; they know the code."

Hamner's south-Georgia twang was fully apparent with that directive and Daryl could hear the implied danger and immediacy for action.

"Okay. And what about the newspaper guy…"

"Colby…"

"Yeah."

"I'll get in touch with him. Set up a meeting. Tell him I have inside information he might want to hear. A meeting out in the open so he'll think it's safe. You lift a big pickup or van or something heavyweight like that. Mr. Colby will then be involved in an automobile accident that puts him out of the way for awhile."

"I think we can do that."

"Good, let me call him right now. Got a phonebook?"

Hamner checked the number for the *Journal-Constitution* and punched the number into his cell phone. He knew the call could eventually be traced, but he didn't care. By the time that was accomplished he would be long gone.

Colby did not answer his extension and his answering machine asked for a message. Hamner did not leave one, but hung up and re-sent the call. The operator gave him Colby's cellphone number. Colby answered.

"Yeah, Colby."

"Colby, this is Dixie Hamner, I heard around that you wanted to talk to me."

"Yes, I do. Where are you? Where can we get together and chat about a few things?"

"How about this afternoon?"

"That's great. But where?"

"There's a Publix supermarket on Ponce de Leon. In the parking lot. At the back; farthest away from the store. Big black Mercedes."

"What time?"

Hamner looked at Daryl and mouthed the word 'time.'

Daryl held up three fingers.

"Three. Be on time."

"I'll see you there," Colby said.

"And come alone. I don't want any bullshit from this guy Phillips."

"Will do, don't worry."

"What kind of car you got…and color?"

"A white Honda Accord."

"Okay. See you there."

Hamner hung up the phone.

"Okay, now we need a crash vehicle."

Daryl called his buddy Rodney.

"Rod, this Daryl. Need a favor."

"What?"

There was little enthusiasm in the man's reply.

"Lift a truck or a van for me. Then help me with a small assignment."

"What's it worth?"

Daryl held his hand over the receiver and turned to Hamner.

"Rodney wants to know what it's worth."

"Ask Rodney if he'd like me to find him and kick his ass into his empty head."

Daryl took his hand off the receiver.

"Rod, I'm doing this as a favor to Mr. Hamner, so maybe you could just help me out on this one. Won't take much of your time. I'll make it up to you later."

"Yeah, shit, okay."

"Good. It's much appreciated."

Rodney stole a van from the Lennox Square Mall and met Daryl several blocks from Daryl's house. Daryl got into the van.

"What the hell is this for?" Rodney asked.

Daryl ignored the question.

"I guess your car is, what, where you heisted this thing?"

"Yeah, Lennox Mall."

"I'll take you back there when this is over."

"When what is over?"

"I'm going to drive this van and you're going to follow me in my car. We're going to the Publix parking lot on Ponce de Leon. Then I'm going to ram a car with this van and take you back to your car."

"How's that gonna work."

"Not sure, but I'm going to make it work once I get there. Now let's get going, we don't have a lot of time."

When Daryl and Rodney got to the Publix parking lot Colby was already there. He had parked near the middle of the last row of lined spaces with no other car nearby. It was twenty minutes to three. His car was headed into the parking slot. Rodney, close behind Daryl, stopped his car in a parking space almost as soon as they had driven onto the lot.

With the lone white Honda sitting there, Daryl saw his chance. He circled around so he could drive full bore at the driver's side of Colby's car. He gunned the van's engine and hit the Honda at the center of the left door. He was doing a little more than 40 MPH at impact.

The noise was horrendous. Plastic and metal chunks flew in all directions showering the area with bits and pieces that skittered away on the asphalt parking lot. Radiator fluid and windshield solvent dripped into a widening pool that glistened beneath the van.

Daryl had not reckoned on the van's air bag deploying and was knocked unconscious when it did. He sat, slumped forward, a limp rag doll in the clutches of the seat belt harness.

Rodney got to him before anyone else in the parking had realized what happened. Daryl was still unconscious as Rodney pulled open the door. He reached across Daryl, unlatched the seat belt, and pulled it free so it could recoil.

"Shit, man; are you okay?"

He shook Daryl's shoulder.

"Come on, we gotta get out of here."

Daryl was gasping for breath and could not answer.

Rodney shook Daryl again and he began to regain consciousness. Eyes glazed and unfocused, Daryl moved his lips, but no sound emerged.

"Don't try to talk, just get your legs around, and let's get you out of there."

"Whaa…" Daryl muttered.

"Come on, move your legs."

Finally, Rodney got the woozy Daryl out of the van and with considerable difficulty helped him stumble away to Daryl's car. He was just barely able to walk as Rodney tried to keep him steady. Then came the hurdle of getting Daryl into the car.

"Hurts…hurts like hell. My chest…my neck, face. I…it hurts."

Rodney opened the car door and eased Daryl onto the seat and pushed his legs around and inside. As he walked around the car to the driver's side, he saw that the first person had reached Colby's car. Others were following and soon there would be a crowd of gawkers. He got in and started the engine.

"How you doing, buddy?"

"Hurt bad…think I need a doctor. Take me…emergency room."

"Damn, sorry Daryl, but I don't think I better do that."

Rodney saw Hamner's Mercedes pull into the lot, but he didn't wait and drove out of the lot without being noticed. He headed for Daryl's house.

When Hamner came onto the parking lot he drove right to the spot where the large crowd had gathered. He buzzed down his window and called to one of the onlookers.

"What's going on?"

"I don't know exactly," the woman answered, "it looks like that van ran into a parked car."

"Anyone hurt?"

"I heard someone say there was a man in the car and he might be dead. No one really seems to have seen what happened."

"Gee, that's too bad."

"I know, it's terrible."

Hamner buzzed up the window and drove out of the lot. He wondered if Colby really were dead. It wasn't his intent, but what the hell, that wouldn't be a bad thing; no more snooping for him. Nonetheless, he knew he didn't have much time to do what he wanted to do.

Next up for Rodney was to get Daryl out of the car and into Daryl's house. There would be an issue, he supposed, with the girlfriend, but he would have to deal with her. He had witnessed Lilly's hot temper, but wasn't sure how she would react to this situation.

Daryl had bobbed in and out of consciousness all the way to the house, babbling mostly incoherent phrases. As Rodney eased Daryl out of the car and to his feet, he wondered if any of the neighbors were watching. The trip from car to the porch was a chore; now he struggled to get Daryl to take the first step up.

"Come on, man, we got to get you up these stairs. There's five of them. That's it, get your foot there, that's right. Hang on to me. Right, step up. Good."

They made it up the stairs and into the house. Rodney let Daryl collapse in a chair in the living room.

"What the hell is going on?" Lilly yelled as she peered around the corner from the hallway.

Before Rodney could answer, Hamner walked into the room.

"Come in here, sit down, and shut up"

"Don't you fucking talk to me like that."

In three strides Hamner was to the doorway, grabbed Lilly's arm, danced her like a small child into the room, and threw her on a chair. Her head snapped back and she stayed in that pose, eyes wide, mouth agape.

"Now, you sit there while we figure this out. Daryl, where's it hurt?"

Daryl's eyes fluttered open.

"Chest…neck. I think I…can't see very well."

"He needs a doctor. Anyone can see that," Lilly hissed.

"I told you to shut up. If you open that yap again I'm going to smack you quiet. Get it? Stay buttoned up until I ask you something."

"Give me a beer," Daryl slurred. "Thirsty...real thirsty."

Lilly started to get up and Hamner pointed at her and she slumped back into the chair. He motioned to Rodney.

"Get some water."

Rodney dutifully went to the kitchen.

"Who was that doctor took care of him when he got shot two years ago?"

Lilly just stared at him.

"Look, you talk or I'll kick you around this house like a bad dog. Who's the doc?"

"Colburn…Ned Colburn."

"Call him. Tell him to get over here right away."

"Phone book's in the den," she whispered.

"Get it, call him, get him over here."

Lilly rose carefully and left the room as Rodney brought a glass of water to Daryl.

"Drink this, see if it helps. Better for you than a beer."

Rodney handed the glass to Daryl. Daryl took a sip and coughed.

"Jesus, that hurts. Aaaah, god damn, it hurts bad. Give me a beer."

"Drink the water and then I'll give you a scotch," Hamner said as he bent over Daryl.

"Yeah, okay."

Lilly came back from the den.

"Doc Colburn says give him Motrin or something for his pain. Four or five pills. He can't get here for another hour…"

"What?"

"He will come, he just can't get here for awhile. But he will come."

"You got Motrin?"

"Yeah, I'll get it."

She went to the kitchen.

"Hell of a thing," Rodney said, "who knew?"

"Yeah, hell of a thing, all right. Look, Rod, I can't stick around. I'm counting on you to keep her here and keep her quiet and wait for the doc. I'll check in later."

Lilly came back from the kitchen with the Motrin bottle, shaking out tablets as she approached. She had four pills in her palm and fed them to Daryl one by one.

"You behave until I get back," Hamner instructed.

She plopped back into the chair and gave him the finger. He ignored her and walked away and out the back door.

"Fucking asshole," she yelled after him.

He made note of her cry as he went down the back steps.

Hamner had already factored the consequences of what had happened and the result was that he had a limited amount of time to get to French and to Crawford. He drove to French's house in Marietta.

When he arrived at French's neighborhood, he parked a block away and walked up the street. He got to the front gate, pushed through, and strode to the porch. He started to push the doorbell, but caught himself. He decided that was the wrong approach and walked around the house to the back door. He tried the door handle and it opened. He closed the door behind him and began the stealthy move into the interior of the house. He could hear voices and he moved to them. He recognized French, but could not tell what they were saying.

"Mr. Hamner."

Hamner was startled more than he wanted to reveal and lurched sideways into a hall table.

"Yeah, right…"

"May I help you?"

It was Gerald, French's butler and man-in-waiting.

"Yeah…Hi, Gerald, didn't know you were there."

"Yes?"

"Sounds like your boss is in the living room…"

"Should I announce you, Mister Hamner?"

"No no, I'll just slip in. Thanks."

Out of the corner of his eye he saw Gerald begin to pull a pistol from his waistband. Hamner was on guard after the initial shock of Gerald sneaking up on him and had his automatic out before Gerald could bring the revolver ready. Hamner shot Gerald once at close range in the chest. Gerald fell backwards through a doorway into the den and was dead when he met the floor.

French rushed onto the hall with a cellphone to his face.

"What's going on?" French yelled.

"End the call," Hamner ordered.

"I'll call you back, we have a problem here."

He shut the phone and stood squarely facing Hamner. Two shots hit French in the chest and knocked him backwards onto the hall floor, the cellphone flying out of his hand against the wall to the floor and then sliding away to the front door.

There was no one else there. French had merely been talking on his phone.

Hamner was satisfied with this part of his check list and walked out of the house back to his car. He called Rodney's cellphone.

"Yeah. He's going to be okay. Doc's here now working on him. That Lilly broad is a piece of work. She's going to get us killed."

"I'll be there as soon as I can. In the meantime, keep her quiet. Tell her I'll be there with money. She'll like the sound of that."

"I'll try."

"What's Doc say about Daryl?"

"Doc says he'll be fine, but he's got lots of pain. Broken rib. Face raw, neck kinda screwed up."

"I'm on my way. Tell Colburn to wait until I get there."

Hamner parked out by the carriage house, came in the back door, and stood in the kitchen, listening. He could hear the voices of Lilly and Daryl. The other voice must be Doc. He waited as they talked and then Rodney came into the kitchen.

"God, I'm glad you got back, she's driving me nuts."

"Stay calm, it will all work out. Let's see how the patient is doing."

They went to the living room where Daryl was lying on the sofa.

"Doc Colburn?"

"Yes. Who are you?"

"Hamner, we've met before. When there was a little trouble."

"Ah, yes, Mr. Hamner."

Hamner handed Doctor Colburn some bills.

"Here's a grand. Make sure he gets well. I mean…make sure."

"I've done my best, Mr. Hamner, but he's quite beat up."

"I'm sure you have, Doc."

"He'll need some time to heal. Going to be okay, though, with rest. I've taped his ribs and dressed his face. Neck's sore, but all right. Given him a couple of pills. About all I can do right now. I'll check back here with him tomorrow. Here's my card in case you need anything sooner."

Hamner put the card in his shirt pocket.

"Thanks, we appreciate your help…and we'd appreciate it if you kept this matter our private situation. Wouldn't want anyone else to worry."

Colburn nodded, picked up his bag, turned without saying another word, and walked down the hall.

"Lilly, how about you and Rodney getting us all some beers?"

Rodney started for the kitchen, but she glared at Hamner and didn't move.

Hamner pulled a roll of bills from his pocket and peeled off a sheaf. He thumbed through those, counting silently.

"Here's two grand for you, sweetheart. I want you to take good care of Daryl. They'll be more for you when he is healed up and can get around."

She followed Rodney to the kitchen without saying a word. Daryl was watching Hamner with a sly smile.

"You're going to be okay."

"Thanks. That's what the Doc says."

"When you get to feeling like you can travel and can get out of here, ditch her and get yourself to Waco. The ranch. We'll be safe there. There's ten grand for you in the small desk I brought over and put in the carriage house. I've got plenty of money in the Mercedes. Pay off Rod and get rid of her. I'll be there, you'll be okay there. Without her."

"Thanks, I'll make it."

"See you there."

Hamner walked out of the room and was gone. He figured his act was good enough to fool Daryl. When the cops got to him, Daryl would convince them he was headed for Texas. He had no intention of heading for Texas. Hamner had to take care of Crawford first and then he would disappear. First, he had to switch to a car that wasn't going to be hot.

16.

Making the drive to Elaine's house on Lake Lanier was surreal for Jack. While their conversation was pleasant, questions continued to flick in and out of his consciousness: What am I doing driving this woman detective to her lake house? Why have I allowed this? What have I gotten myself into? This is escapism for sure, but do I need that? Where am I going in a relationship with this woman? What is it, just the seduction and sex? What? What parallel universe have I encountered and now become enmeshed? Truth was, Elaine was easy to talk to, easy to be with, comfortable in a way that belied the fact he had known her but a few days. Quit trying to figure it out, Jack told himself, this is real, it's happening.

"So tell me about your meeting with Crawford."

Elaine had her shoes and socks off and sat with both feet hoisted onto the dash. She was staring off somewhere, seemingly disconnected from Jack and the moment, save for the question. They had been engaged in banter since they left Atlanta, fun banter that he enjoyed. Elaine had been clever with her quips, but she had handled her part almost anonymously. Her manner had kept him at a distance and he was yanked a bit by her question.

He looked at her before he answered and she didn't notice.

"I met him at the tea room near his office; kind of by accident. He was in there getting his breakfast, but I didn't know it."

"How did you know?"

She didn't look at him.

"The girl, the waitress, called him by name."

She said nothing and Jack decided just to tell what happened.

"We talked. I let him know who I was. He denied killing J.W. or even ordering it. Said Hamner did the killing on his own."

Elaine turned to him, said nothing, and waited.

"Crawford told me how the drug stuff developed. Shay brought the deal to them. Hammer didn't want it to end, J.W. changed sides and that changed everything…"

"Crawford was okay with that?"

"Probably not, but he let Hamner be the heavy. Now he pleads innocent. Who knows?"

"He was upset, too, with the change. Lost his lover besides. Sorry."

Jack didn't react to her comment. Elaine picked at her nails.

"Hamner showed up while we were talking. He let Crawford know he was there, but he went back to his car and then drove off. Crawford says Hamner did it on his own."

"What do you think?"

"It all stinks. Hamner killed J.W., but Crawford pressed him on it. They both had the same motive."

"Yeah, I figure."

She ran her fingers through her hair and tossed it and pulled it flat above her ears. She was very attractive, he thought, attractive in a way that registered with him. Earthy, sexual, available, and complex. No simple physical release with her; that would not be her sexual directive, her internal manager of emotions, the mental chart with tick-offs and accomplishments and self-delivered rewards. No, not Elaine. Elaine was deliberate in what she desired and she desired him. Jack realized it and was taken by that realization.

"I stopped into Marietta Police Headquarters. Spoke with Larry Davis. A detective."

"I know…"

"You said you talked with him."

"Yes, I did. And he isn't just a detective, he is the chief of police detectives in Marietta. The head man."

"What is it, these guys all report to you? Columbus police, now this guy Davis…"

"I wish. What did Davis tell you, leave the police work to us?"

"He said Hamner is still around, be careful. And yes, he did tell me to leave detective work to the police. Or something like that."

"Good advice all around, I think. I was afraid you were going to tell me you pulled your gun and went after Hamner when you saw him outside the tea room. Turn right at the next corner. Slow down, it's not easy to see right away."

"Never entered my mind."

"Good. Just because you have it doesn't mean you pull it out any time you want…

"I know that."

Elaine was content being the passenger and had been directing Jack as they drove from Atlanta. They were getting close to her place, now, and the directions closer together.

"Here it is."

Jack made the turn effortlessly.

"Okay, we go on this a ways until there is a jog in the road and then a fork. Take the left fork. Then another right turn and we're there."

"You need to be fairly sober if you want to drive this at night."

"I make it a point not to drive around here at night."

Jack made the jog, the left fork, the right turn, and at the end of that narrow lane Elaine pointed him into the carport behind her house. He glimpsed a view of the lake just before he eased into the carport.

"Well, that wasn't such a bad drive was it? We're here; my little home away from home. Actually much nicer than that place in Atlanta. I've got to get out of there, find a nice apartment. It was a good idea once. Come on, I'll show you around. We can bring our stuff in later."

Elaine jumped out of the car, went to the backdoor of the house, flipped the lock with her key, went in, strode quickly through, and onto the front deck that spread away from the living area. The view was a panorama postcard. The late day sunlight flitted through the trees, bounced from the water, and sparkled with glittering intensity. A person would squint, but would want to look.

When the Chattahoochee River was dammed at Buford, Georgia, years ago, the backfill of water created a reservoir with a long and jagged shoreline of sharp inlets and juts of tree-covered land that sliced back into the water. Elaine's house was built on one of those jutting promontories which gave a commanding position to the scene.

"What do you think?"

She put her arm around his waist as he leaned against the deck railing and then rubbed his chest. Jack accepted her closeness and stared out at the surroundings. There was little sound other than a boat motor in the distance and the persistent chirping of birds.

"The quiet is intense," Jack finally offered.

Elaine patted his arm.

"We're on sort of a peninsula. Let's take a walk around, I'll show you the lay of the land."

Jack didn't move at first and she didn't press it.

"An escape, wouldn't you say?"

Jack was quiet and looked.

"We have this part all to ourselves. No one is close by. Lots of privacy. We can nude sunbath here on the deck...when the sun is up above...around noon, one o'clock. Then its behind the trees."

"Very nice," Jack said. "Let's check it out."

Elaine took his hand and led him to the steps leading down to the front of the deck. She headed toward the point of land the house faced and followed a well-maintained path to get to the water. She still had his hand. She didn't drag him, but her aggressiveness made sure he was by her side. Ferns brushed his leg as they followed the path and the birds jumped aside to check out the aliens. Elaine knelt by the water and slid her hand back and forth on the surface as if she were making sure it was there, testing its temperature, evaluating its texture, and, as if she were testing its value, flicked it away with her fingers.

"I can see why you want to come here."

Elaine paraded Jack around the property, showing him her favorite places, pointing out the special vistas, naming the kinds of trees and some of the plants, and teasing his sense of vulnerability. Elaine was physical; she walked the ground as if she were stalking, hunting her prey. She touched him provocatively, brushed his lips with hers, and made him understand her lust.

They were working their way back to the house when she tripped and started to fall toward the water. Jack grabbed her arm to catch her and she got her balance. He slid his arm around her waist and rubbed his finger across her chin.

"How did you lock in on me?" he asked.

She moved away from him as she examined his face and Jack did not try to hold her. She turned away from him and walked on a few steps. She stared out at the golden water tinged with blue ripples. He could tell her brain was whirling, going clickity-click again, trying to form the right answer. He stood still, waiting.

"That question is probably a good example why."

She smiled at him as she stepped back to him and put her hands on his shoulders.

"I don't think I've ever known any other man who would have asked me something like that. What a great question."

"Thanks, I worked on it all day; actually for a couple of days. Why me? I kept asking myself."

"Did you answer yourself?"

She was grinning and even her grin was seductive.

"Yeah, oh yeah."

"What did you figure out?"

"No, I want to get your answer first."

"You're passionate, with tons of energy, and rippling underneath is a current of sexuality that's exciting. I sensed that; could feel it right here."

She pointed to her stomach.

"It was immediate lust, but I realized right away that you were smart, clever, and had strength of character. All the best qualities I want in a man. Hadn't met a guy like that in a long time."

"I'm flattered."

"Caught you at the right time; vulnerable and ready for some female…"

She stopped.

"Female what," Jack asked.

"Contact…naked contact."

She moved her hands to grasp his head and she drew him to her and kissed him. Jack embraced her and pulled her tight against him.

"You might be right."

"I am right, come on."

She pulled away from him, but grabbed his hand and led him back to the house.

"What do you think?"

They were back in the great room with Jack looking at the lake view. It was if he were mesmerized and she broke the spell.

"Nice. It's all quite nice."

"Hungry? I've made dinner reservations in Gainesville. The Barony Shores. It's very expensive, but I'm buying. You're my guest."

"What…where is Gainesville?"

"It's the big, hot Lake Lanier town. Not that far from here really."

Elaine sipped at what the menu called the Lost Souls Martini as Jack checked out the surroundings of the Barony Shores. The huge restaurant was packed with weekend tourists and homeowners from the surrounding area. The crowd din bounced around and off the walls and other hard surfaces, overpowering the silly music that floated from somewhere toward the bar section.

"Good Manhattan?" Elaine asked.

Jack read her lips for understanding as much as hearing what she said.

"Yeah, good, very nice."

"It's a little noisy, but we aren't going to stay here very long. We've got to get back to my place for sex."

Jack laughed.

"Maybe we shouldn't waste time eating," Jack suggested.

"No, no; I have to have a little something to keep my strength up. Maybe just a salad. Do you know what you want?"

She motioned to their waitress who quickly came to their table.

"Ready to order?"

"We are. I'll have the Caesar salad. Hold the anchovies. Darling…"

Elaine tipped her menu toward Jack.

"Steak, rare, and a side salad. And another Manhattan. And Martini."

The girl collected their menus and was gone.

"Thanks for thinking of me."

"I figured you wanted another one."

"Jack, tell me some more about your son. You've been chasing around trying to find his killer, but you really hadn't said much about him."

"At what age?"

"That's a strange response."

"Well, no, you see, I had this perspective and I come down here and it changes. I get a new glimpse of my son. Not what I might have expected."

She waited and studied his expression.

"I learned he was homosexual. Quite the revelation, don't you think?"

Elaine stayed quiet, letting Jack speak as he thought, letting the words tumble out, and giving him time to formulate what he wanted to say.

"Yeah, this little tow-headed guy of mine turned out to be a fag. When he was young he was cute, precocious, quick and bright and fun, and clever. We were good buddies and did all kinds of things together. As he got older, though, he became a tad tentative, not sure, wanted to be encouraged, needed to be supported, and more than willing to be helped. And passive. We still did things together like hiking and watching sports, but it wasn't the same as before."

He was silent.

"And then what? What happened?"

"I don't know. I lost regular contact quite a while ago; while he was in college. Then there was the divorce and…boom, the big divide. We never really ever fully connected again. Touch and go, fleeting, casual, a superficial relationship that was parallel, but not in tandem, never real. Maybe it had never been real, hard to say. I've been thinking a lot about that."

The waitress put down their new drinks and did a half-skip away to another table.

"It can't be reconciled," Elaine said as she sloshed the last of her first Martini into her mouth. She let the excess ice slide back into her glass and pushed it aside. "You can beat your brains out about it, but it won't matter. Life has those irreconcilable issues that crop up and we tend to try to set things straight, to make it different. It's like rewriting history trying to make a new reality and with the same result. You're just kidding yourself. You can pretend it's different, but it isn't. And that's not good enough for some folks and they end up beating their brains out trying to make it the way they want."

"Easily said."

"Right. It's like Cher said to Nicholas Cage in the movie "Moonstruck," *get over it*, and she whacks him one."

"Are you going to whack me?"

"Yeah, but not like that."

Jack drove them back to her house as the last edge of daylight shot through the trees and the horizon's orange glow cast an unsettling coloration on the surroundings. Elaine directed and he dutifully made the turns.

Elaine began to remove her clothes as soon as they entered the house, flipping a blouse, kicking a shoe, unzipping, and unbuttoning. More than a striptease, this action for her, it seemed, was more a release, a quest for some kind of freedom for her body rather than a move of temptation or flaunting her sexuality. Jack admired her motions and movement and ability to undress as she walked through the great room. He did not follow or follow suit and had some sense that she was invoking her right to such freedom even if it were an act of self-indulgence. She was naked by the time she reached the window wall and sat down and stared at the last bits of daylight that were creeping away.

"Will you fix me a Martini?"

She didn't turn around.

"Sure," Jack answered.

He went to the side bar and poured her Martini over ice he retrieved from the kitchen refrigerator.

"Fixed and ready to drink."

He stood by the side bar.

"Very funny, Jack. Would you bring it to me? Please."

He carried the glass to her and handed it over her shoulder. She still did not turn around.

"Thanks. Fix yourself a Manhattan. And don't get too close to me, I'm very hot. You might get burned."

He went for more ice and back to the side bar and poured his drink. He plunked down in a nearby chair.

"Don't worry, I can feel the fire from here."

Elaine laughed and stretched out like the Naked Maja, but with her back to him.

"Would you open the sliding doors. The evening breeze would be so nice."

Jack went to the sliding doors and pulled them open. When he did, Elaine disappeared, only to reappear from the master bedroom a moment later draped in a floor length diaphanous chemise. She again took the same prone position. Jack had already returned to the chair.

"The breeze might get cool."

The breeze wafting through the opened doors was evident as the folds of the transparent material fluffed and fluttered.

"Are you thinking about taking your clothes off?"

"Yeah, sure, I am. But I'm not certain it's safe."

"Oh, come on, we've done this before."

"Not this…

"We've had carnal knowledge of each other…"

"Now, you're mocking me…"

"I wouldn't do that. I just want to see you naked."

With that, she rolled over to face him.

"I want to see you take your clothes off."

"Well, I could never do it as elegantly as you did with your exhibition."

"Give it a try. I promise I will only be encouraging."

Self-consciously, Jack began to undress.

"I'm a damned stripper."

"Only because you want to be. Relax, you love it because you know the result. You want the result."

Jack was naked and moved to her side, on his knees, and touched her shoulder. He lay beside her and they kissed and there was the result. It was sexual encounter as ballet; exotic, ecstatic, exhilarating, and exhausting, a physical exercise of erotica. When the encounter was climaxed, Jack fell on his back, limp and near lifeless.

"You're nuts," Jack breathed, trying to keep from passing out.

It was dark outside and no lights had been turned on and Jack could hardly see anything in the room. He went to the kitchen without turning on the lights, feeling his way, groping for the doorway, and then was guided by the microwave clock. More than an hour had gone by since their ballet had ended.

Jack found his clothes and pulled on his pants and shirt. The night air falling into the room made him shiver. Elaine was knocked out and he pulled the chemise over her. There was a light blanket on the sofa and he put that over her also. She didn't move.

He walked back to the kitchen and proceeded to make a pot of decaf coffee. He figured that eventually the kitchen light and his bustling about would wake Elaine. But she was strictly zero in response to the light or the noise. A little music, he thought, and turned on the sound system and punched the jazz selection. Music filled the room and he toned it down and waited.

Jack sipped his coffee and wondered what the hell he had gotten himself into. He was in that drowsy half sleep when Elaine stirred and wondered what time it was. His watch, the one he had pulled off earlier, was across the room. He was too whacked to move to get it. There wasn't another clock in the room.

"God, what time is it?"

Elaine was now fully awake. He didn't answer right away, but struggled to his feet and found his watch on the coffee table.

"Twelve thirty seven."

"Damn, how was that? Don't answer; just tell me how you like my Lake Lanier house."

"Very nice.

Elaine sat up and was very serious; as serious as a woman can be sitting on the floor essentially naked but for a transparent fabric floating about her.

"No one has claimed the body."

She sighed.

"Your son."

Jack didn't respond at first, still caught in his own recovery from their encounter and he shook his head slightly.

"What do you mean?"

"No one has claimed your son's body. You'll probably want to do something about that tomorrow."

"Why the hell are you telling me that now…in the middle of the night…after we have screwed ourselves crazy?"

"I thought of it and figured you would want to know."

"Shit."

"Sorry…"

She came to him and enveloped him and caressed him and kissed him sweetly.

"I'm sorry. Sorry I told you now and sorry that it's the situation. We'll take care of it tomorrow. Make a decision tomorrow. Let's go to bed. You can think better in the morning."

She pulled him by the hand and led him to the bedroom and the ballet and the night were over.

Jack woke up and realized Elaine was not next to him. It was daylight. When he got to the kitchen Elaine was seated at the table with a group of 3 x 5 cards laid out in front of her.

"Coffee's made."

She moved one of the cards slightly.

"I work with 3 x 5 cards. Helps organize my thoughts."

Jack poured his coffee.

"There's cream in the fridge."

"Black is fine."

He leaned on the counter and watched as she fiddled with the cards.

"And what do the tarot cards tell you?"

"Go ahead, make fun of me, but this is one of the ways I keep things straight. Yours is not the only case I'm working on."

"Just teasing…"

"I know. How you doing this morning?"

"Okay, I guess…"

"Just okay?"

"Yeah, I'm all right, but I keep wondering what the hell I'm doing here with you."

"Getting laid and having a relaxing overnight get away. At least you should be relaxing."

"Well, I'm not relaxed."

"Bad sex?"

"No, not at all. Bad something, though."

"Bad karma."

"Yeah, right."

"Maybe there is bad karma. Beverly called me."

Elaine waited for his reaction.

"Beverly?"

"Yes, your daughter."

"How did that happen? I mean…"

"Well, she really called the Department and was transferred to me. She said she called the *Constitution* trying to get to Colby and couldn't reach him. Someone at the paper told her to call me. She learned of the news of her brother and came to Atlanta to find out what the story was or is. She's looking for you."

"What did you tell her?"

"I told her I didn't know where you were; which was the truth, because at the time I did not know where you were."

Jack shook his head.

"It is amazing…"

"How long since you've seen her?"

"I don't know, ten or fifteen years. Last I knew she was working in the music biz in Nashville. Some sort of singer."

"She gave me her cell number."

Elaine picked up one of the 3 x 5 cards and handed it to him.

"It must be upsetting…"

"No, not really. When there is a divide like this, time becomes the salve that soothes the wound."

"That's terribly poetic…about something so emotional."

"No, look, that's the thing; time has a way of taking the emotion out of the equation. Even with a child…with your own child, if there is a situation where your child disregards you, lacks respect, and gives you the finger at every turn, then over time you lose that emotional connection. They become just another person who has shit on you and wants you to accept it and feels they have done nothing wrong. There's an aspect of personality defect in all of that behavior…"

"You're a psychologist?"

"No, I'm the person who was crapped on and over time has been able to disassociate myself from the emotion of caring one way or another."

"Really? Not caring?"

"Really, yes, and not caring. By not caring I am able to move ahead with my life and not get dragged down by the past."

"Without culpability?"

"Have you ever had any kids?"

"No…"

"There's one shot at every situation, every decision; there are no instant replays. You make a judgment and it's your one chance at it, good or bad. That's parenting and you make some mistakes, but you do the best job you can. You never did it before and you do the best job you can. Sometimes, it doesn't work out; the relationship with the child. Sometimes, it's a bust."

"Is that all a rationalization?"

"I don't think so. And keep in mind that I wasn't the only parent. When the person you're married to, who should be your partner in this kid-raising business, works at cross purposes to you, then it compromises whatever you do, whatever decisions you make about child-rearing. That's an ugly little reality people don't want to consider. It takes two parents in tandem to make the child-rearing work well. Otherwise, it's a roll of the dice. I lost, that's the way it fell out and I accepted that and I moved on. I can't change the past."

"Will you call her?"

He did not answer right away and more than a few beats went by before he responded.

"Yeah, I think so. Why not? She cared about her brother, I think, I assume. She may be struggling for an answer like I was."

Elaine's cell phone rang. She pulled it from her bathrobe pocket, looked to see who was calling, and flipped it open.

"Good morning.

She held her fingers over the speaker and mouthed, "It's Fred."

"What's going on? Yes, up at the lake. Yes, he is."

She listened as he relayed some kind of report.

"We'll be back later today. Thanks. See you tomorrow morning."

Jack stared at her as she didn't immediately say anything after she closed the phone.

"Is someone else dead?"

"Colby. Yesterday."

"How, what?"

"His car was rammed in a parking lot and he died on the spot. He was parked. A van just ran into the side of his car. The driver got away. The van was stolen."

"Hamner. It had to be Hamner."

"I would guess."

"Hamner is not going to run away, he's going to stick around until he has killed everyone involved with this thing.

"There's more…"

"What?"

"Someone shot French, and his assistant, butler, or whatever you want to call him. Both dead. Marietta guys working on that one."

"And you take the weekend off? Let's get back to Atlanta."

They quickly packed the few things they had brought with them and Jack put the bags in the car. Elaine made sure everything was turned off and locked up the house. As Jack drove, she directed him to the freeway, and they wooshed along without speaking for several minutes. Finally Elaine spoke.

"It's all unraveling for these guys and we'll have the thing wrapped up in a couple of days."

"Good for you, but there are some loose ends I have to deal with."

"Like what…?"

"Like taking care of my son's body, like finding out what happened to all the money he was supposed to have made, like Hamner still running around killing people, like dealing with my daughter who I haven't heard from in years, and…"

There was a nagging, unrelenting pause as Jack gripped the steering wheel as if he meant to strangle it.

"…like what the hell I'm going to do about you."

"I think I'm the easy part."

"Yeah, well, nuts."

"I can't prioritize your stuff for you, but I would think you take care of your daughter first. I'll go with you to the coroner's office. Get those two items out of the way and then we can think about Hamner. Keep in mind that a ton of police agencies are looking for him. They'll get him."

"Bunk."

"He'll be caught, believe me."

"He will kill Crawford before we can do anything about it."

She didn't answer and they didn't say anything for a long time.

"Stay with me tonight and I'll help you tomorrow."

"You didn't respond when I said I didn't know what I was going to do about you."

"I know."

"Help me out on this. "I know" doesn't get it done for me."

"We can talk about it later. Not now. Riding in a car makes me want to sleep. Can't think clearly. Didn't get a lot of sleep last night, anyway.

Elaine's eyes flickered and shut and the subject was closed. Nothing more was said and she slept all the way to her house.

Jack wondered if she really was asleep all that time or playing possum. He gave her the benefit of the doubt and accepted the consulting GPS female voice as his driving companion. The voice made it easy for Jack to navigate the return.

17.

There is this animal need for intoxication; a core element connected to behavior and yet a flaw, leading to character destruction. With the pursuit of and devotion to intoxication, there is misuse, overuse, and extended use which forms a constant that diminishes function, distorts reality, and ultimately deprives one of life success. Circumstance matters not; intoxication is sought.

Jack was not sure exactly when J.W. began his love affair with drugs, but he figured it came about sometime during his senior year of high school. The discovery was made incidentally, quite by accident, in a way that only fate could arrange and then orchestrate. Jack had been out of town for several days ministering to clients at a trade show in Vegas and returned home a day earlier than planned. For whatever reason, part of fate's hand in things, he chose not to open the garage, but instead parked in the drive. He caught the telltale marijuana odor as soon as he entered the foyer and stood still, listening for the voices of the culprits. He waited; nothing. After a few moments, there was laughter and conversation from upstairs.

Jack, still clutching his briefcase, quietly climbed the carpeted stairs. In the master bedroom was a sight that stunned him and his unexpected presence stunned them, the culprits. Linda, clad only in bra and panties, was sitting on the bed propped by pillows, a joint cavalierly dangling from two fingers. J.W. was across the room sitting on the floor with his back against a dresser. His joint was somewhat elegantly brandished as though he were showing it off rather than smoking it.

"What the hell is going on?"

J.W. was euphorically incapable of reacting quickly and simply stared at his father. Linda, however, immediately moved towards the bathroom, calm in her movements, belying a rage she felt. She stood swaying slightly in the bathroom doorway as she struggled to keep her balance and turned to face Jack.

"We were discussing literature."

She disappeared into the bathroom.

By now, J.W. was on his feet. Unsteady, but upright. He had mashed out the joint in an ashtray that stayed on the floor.

"We thought you were coming home tomorrow."

"Yeah, I can tell. Go get dressed and don't leave the house until we've talked."

J.W. wanted to say something defiantly to his father, but couldn't quite think what it was and said nothing and went to his bedroom. Linda came out of the bathroom with a robe on and without the joint.

"Well, well, the morality police, ready to condemn and to criticize."

Jack and Linda argued for over an hour, one of those husband and wife disagreements where nothing gets accomplished and only piled up acrimony results. Meanwhile, J.W. left the house and Jack did not see him for more than two weeks. Jack's business and J.W.'s appearances in the household caused the gap before Jack could talk to him about using drugs. And it was no use, only Jack did not know it at the time. He thought he had rationally convinced his son of the evils of drug use and how they could ruin his life.

Linda's reaction to being caught in the act of smoking dope with her son led to self-destruction. The recrimination was unbearable and she slipped irrevocably into extended drug use and persistent drunkenness. All of this behavior outside the realm Jack was aware of, knew about, or recognized.

Secret stash, secret bottles, and the secret sessions of being stoned. As far as Jack knew, J.W. and his mother never again toked up together. That wasn't true; there were several more meetings to show the miserable bastard who judged them that they could do this if they wanted to.

Jack's next meaningful conversation with J.W. was several months after the dope smoking exposé. It was about what J.W. would pursue in college.

"I'm going to study computer programming. What do you think, Dad?"

Jack wasn't sure J.W. really wanted an answer. He figured it was more a rhetorical query, offhand in the way it was posed, congenial as one would offer a nebulous question about the weather. But Jack gave it a try.

"I don't think that's the right track for you. I think…"

"Why?"

"Well, you're not the computer programming type…in my opinion."

"Why not…?"

"You're not the pocket-protector type; you're too verbal, too social, too…"

"You mean I couldn't cut it with the course work."

"No that's not what I mean…"

"Yeah, I know, I know….not smart enough with the math…"

"Look, you asked for my opinion, so I gave it…"

It was over, J.W. had moved on and he started at the University in computer programming and failed and dropped out of school and got comfortable with drugs and drug buddies and time slid by and J.W. went from one menial job to another in his focus on getting stoned and being separated from reality.

At one point during this foggy period, J.W. talked to Jack by phone. It was after the divorce and the emotional pressure points for both of them were exhausting.

"I'm probably good at something," J.W. had said, "I just don't know what it is."

"My guess is you'd be good in sales," Jack offered.

"Oh shit, you've said that before."

"I think it could be a fit for you…"

"Yeah, right. I'll talk to you, Dad."

And he hung up.

There were few choices for J.W. to earn a meaningful living and he enlisted in the Navy. He scored well in his testing and more than qualified for his chosen request to be a translator for Naval Intelligence. He was selected to attend the Naval Foreign Language School in Monterrey, California, but he never made it there. Somewhere along the line in an interview he answered a crucial question honestly. Have you ever used drugs?

Instead, he ended up as a radar technician at a variety of bases from Okinawa to San Diego. After four years he mustered out and returned to Columbus.

In the meantime, Linda had slipped hopelessly into alcoholism. J.W. lived with her for a few weeks after he got out of the Navy, but he could not take the drunken stupors and moved on.

J.W. got past the drugs. He was very good in sales. He was cruelly murdered. There was all of this without J.W. ever reconciling his feelings, his life, or his identity with Jack. J.W.'s regrets? Who knows, but Jack carried his share.

18.

Jack stood in Elaine's kitchen staring at her refrigerator. He guessed he'd have a beer. In the background he could hear the voices from her answering machine. She came into the kitchen before he could get the beer.

"Anything important?" he asked.

"Sort of. The stuff from Fred we already knew about, liaison from the Task Force asking me again to keep you on a leash, and a call from my Mom."

"Oh, oh, those mom calls can be tough. One of those?"

"Yeah."

He waited for her to say more, to give some kind of explanation, but Elaine only shrugged slightly and turned away. Jack didn't pry and her response was to change the subject.

"Believe it or not, I've got some steaks we can grill later. Does that sound like something that appeals to you?"

For a brief moment he thought about his own mother. If she were alive, what would she think of his being with Elaine? Probably not approve. He let it go.

"Sure does and I can handle the grilling part."

"Why don't you call Beverly and set up a meeting with her," Elaine suggested, "and I'll get those steaks out of the freezer?"

He nodded and pulled out his cell phone. He turned the phone over in his hand, his reluctance to make the call obvious.

Elaine went to the small area off the living room where she had a desk and computer and returned to the kitchen with her police notebook.

"Here it is."

Jack punched in the numbers as she read them off and hesitated for moment before he hit send. As he made the send command he walked away from her and into the living room. After several rings a young woman's voice answered.

Elaine retrieved the steaks from the freezer and could hear Jack talking, then silent. She put the steak packages on the counter. Jack was speaking again. She peered through the doorway and could see Jack in the living room pacing, phone to his ear, frowning. He spoke again, closed the phone, and walked back to the kitchen. She waited for him to report.

"Tomorrow morning…eight…at the Marriott."

"Good."

Elaine stepped close and put her arms around him. She hugged him tightly and kissed his cheek.

"It'll all work out," she said, "you'll see."

"Maybe, maybe not, but we'll give it a shot."

Now, she kissed him on the lips, gently, sensuously, lovingly, and with a lingering tenderness that made Jack think about what he had said in the car. What was he going to do about Elaine?

She might have guessed what he was thinking because she made a quick change of pace by asking him if he wanted a beer. She didn't want to answer his question right now.

"Yeah, I was just going for one when you came back from the answering machine."

Elaine reached into the refrigerator and brought out two beers and Jack fetched the opener and popped off the caps.

"How would you hide a ton of drug money?" Jack asked as they went into the living room and flopped onto the sofa.

Before she answered, Elaine kicked off her shoes and hiked her legs onto Jack's lap, and took a sip of her beer.

"You couldn't keep it even if you found out where it is…"

"I don't want it, I just want to…"

"Besides, the Drug Task Force is already working on that and the DEA would probably take possession…"

"I wasn't looking for it because I wanted it…"

"Why do you care?"

"Curious. There could be hundreds of thousands of dollars. It was suggested maybe millions. Where do you put it so you don't tip your hand. It's a dilemma for any drug dealer and maybe French or Crawford knew. When Hamner kills Crawford it might never get found. That is, unless it's written down someplace."

"Forget it Jack, the Task Force will be on it."

"How about it being part of the motive for killing J.W.?"

"That's another angle. But French said the murder was because Crawford was upset with being ditched…"

"Yeah, but money is a stronger motive than the emotion you're talking about."

"Oh, I don't know about that, but it's an angle and Fred and I will work on it starting tomorrow."

"Thanks."

"Why wouldn't J.W.'s wife make arrangements for his body?"

Jack shook his head indicating he didn't know.

"Did she hate him that much?"

"Maybe she did," Jack said, "and maybe she was just so upset that it became an afterthought that got away from her. I think she already is back in Italy. I can do it; I don't mind doing it, actually."

They continued talking for awhile and then something Jack said prompted Elaine to stroke his thigh. This gesture led to more touching and soon they were making love there in the living room. The late afternoon sun streaming in created a fractured spotlight to their pleasure.

The next morning, Monday, Jack walked into the lobby of the Marriott shortly before eight. Beverly was sitting, waiting, engrossed in her smartphone. She looked at him over the top of her granny glasses and stood up as he approached. She extended her hand in a limp, but purposeful way of letting him know he did not need to worry about hugging her.

"Bev, you're looking all grown up."

It probably sounded stupid, but that was the first thing that came to mind.

"I am, Dad, all grown up. I'm a big girl now."

The sarcasm reeked, but he ignored it.

"Sit down, sit down."

She did.

"Would you like some coffee…tea…soft drink? Did you want breakfast?"

"I had breakfast and no, I don't want anything to drink."

Jack nodded and looked her over. Fleetingly, he wondered where all the years had gone. Not just in relation to Bev, but as a perspective of his whole life. He was momentarily transported someplace and she stared at him as if he were some strange creature. Perhaps he was. Jack caught himself and came back to the present.

"How do you want to start?" Jack asked quietly.

"Well, Dad, it's been fourteen years..."

"Long time, yeah."

"I want you to know right off, I don't care about closing that gap. I'm here because of Jim's death. I wanted to talk to you to get the story about what happened. I made a few phone calls and found out you were here. I wasn't surprised, really, that you would come here and try to find out what happened to him. I figure you know. Do you? That's what I want, that's why I came."

"From Nashville?"

"No, from LA. I'm working in LA."

"You live there?

She did not answer immediately.

"Does it matter?" she finally said.

"No, just curious. People ask me where you live and I usually say Nashville. I hate to say I don't know, but I can do that."

"What people?"

"People, people I meet who ask about me, about my family, that sort of thing."

"What do you say, divorced, two kids, a son in Columbus and a daughter in Nashville?"

"Something like that, I guess. But as you say, it doesn't matter."

"I didn't say it didn't matter, I asked you if it mattered."

"Right you are."

"Does it matter?"

Pause, one beat, two beats.

"Probably not," Jack said after the pause.

"You can keep telling people I'm in Nashville."

"Okay."

As they had been talking, she had continued to stare at him and now she concentrated on her phone, sliding screen elements around, seemingly engrossed in some bit of information that displayed.

"Tell about Jimmy," she asked without looking up.

"Well, there are three aspects to the story," he began, "and they are connected, and they are difficult for me…"

"Start with number one," she interrupted.

"The report I got said that J.W. was found dead in a city park and the first cause of death was thought to be suicide. It was given to the public that way and I heard about it like that. I came down here to find out what happened because I didn't believe he killed himself. I forced the issue with the police. I told them he would not have killed himself and it was further investigated and determined the first assessment was wrong and that J.W. had, indeed, been murdered. I've been chasing around Atlanta and Columbus, here in Georgia, trying to find out who killed him."

She did not like the fact her father called her brother J.W., but made no comment about that issue. It had been hashed out with him before and now, for her, in a sense it didn't matter so she let it go.

"And getting laid."

"Is that your assumption?"

"Well, hell, you spent the weekend with some lady cop; I hope you weren't just holding hands."

Jack nodded.

"Yeah, Elaine Moss. She's the detective working J.W.'s case, along with her partner."

"And you're working the case, also."

"Yes. And I found out who killed J.W. and why. He's killed again and is on the run. Cops think he has left town, but I know he's around and going to kill again. That's where we are right now."

"What's number two?"

Again, Jack hesitated as he thought about what he wanted to say.

"J.W. was a big-time drug dealer…along with some others…"

"No kidding?"

"No kidding. He found out that he could make a bundle of money moving drugs…"

"Distributing…"

"Yes, distributing, but at the high end…wholesaling, not at the street level. Someone else he knew took care of that."

"I thought Jimmy was doing real well in sales…"

"He was. Doing very well, but the drug business gave him a lot more money than his sales job. And it was part of the reason he was killed."

"Number three?"

"Number three is also the other part of why he was murdered."

Jack did not continue.

"Well, what is it?"

"I learned that…that J.W. was a homosexual. I couldn't…"

"Our Jimmy was gay? Our Jimmy…? Oh, my God."

"That's right, that's what I found out…"

"Who, how, what? He had a lover?"

"Two lovers, actually, that's what got him killed…"

"Damn..."

"Warren Crawford was lover number one. He's a guy who designs custom interiors...a customer of J.W.'s. Crawford had a connection to a man named Bill Shay in Columbus, Georgia, who has a cabinet company where the drugs came in. A guy who works for Shay, named Ryan Coleridge was the mastermind for the drug operation and the supplier contact from somewhere. I assume Mexico, but I don't know. All of this stuff is under investigation by the DEA and a couple of different drug task forces, including one here in the Atlanta area. J.W. and Crawford got the drugs from Shay to sell here in Atlanta..."

"You found out all of this?"

"Not quite. I'm assuming some of this, but it fits, I think..."

"How did this get Jimmy killed?"

"I'm not through with the story. It gets complicated..."

"Go on..."

"Before J.W. and Crawford became lovers, Crawford and an architect named Collier French were lovers. It seems that French then decided to... How can I put it...court J.W.? In any case, J.W. took up with French and took the drug action with him away from Crawford..."

"Jealous lovers, my, my."

Beverly laughed and put her smartphone up to her face as if to hide embarrassment.

"That's right. Needless to say, Crawford was jacked and sent his man Dixie Hamner on assignment to get J.W. He shot J.W. in his hotel room and then took him to Piedmont Park and tried to make it look like a suicide. And he might have made that work..."

"If you hadn't come along."

"Yeah. As I said some of this is conjecture on my part, filling in the gaps, but I don't think the real story is much different."

She continued her stare, adjusting her granny glasses.

"Hamner killed French last Saturday and also killed or had someone kill Spencer Colby, a *Constitution* reporter who was working with me to find out what had happened. Colby found out too much and got too close, I believe. Hamner is on the run. Cops think he blew town, I think he's around and aiming to kill Crawford."

"I can see why he would kill Jim and French, but why would he kill Crawford when they were working together?"

"I think that he thinks Crawford gave him up to the cops. Word gets around fast. And Crawford did, by the way."

"Jimmy got caught in a mess, didn't he?"

"Yes, he did. When I came down here last Wednesday, I didn't think it would get this convoluted and complex. And there's even another aspect to deal with."

She waited for him to continue and played with her glasses again.

"Angelina refused or forgot to deal with what would be done with J.W.'s body once it got released by the Medical Examiner."

"That bitch. How could she do that?"

Jack didn't answer. He looked away across the lobby and leaned back.

"I told Ms. Moss I would take care of it. She's going to notify the ME's office this morning. She'll call me when I can go over there and sign the papers."

"What will you do with him?"

"Ship him back to Columbus. I'll have my partner Byron Adams contact a funeral director he knows. They make all the arrangements."

"And then what?"

"What do you mean?"

"Are you going to have a funeral, bury him, cremate him…?"

"I hadn't thought that far ahead yet."

At that moment Detective Moss walked toward where Jack and Beverly were sitting. When she reached them, she extended her hand to Beverly.

"Hi, I'm Elaine Moss, Atlanta police detective; I'm working your brother's case. At least I assume you're Beverly. You talked to me Saturday."

"Yeah, I'm the sister."

There was a surly tone to Beverly's voice that Jack caught and Elaine seemed to disregard.

"I'm picking up your Father to take him over to the medical examiner's office. I…uh…"

"She knows," Jack said, "I told her that nothing had been done to take care of J.W.'s body."

"Okay…good."

Nothing was said for a moment and the silence was stifling.

"Look, Bev, I need to go with Ms. Moss and get this done. Are you interested in coming along?"

Beverly hesitated as she seemed to concentrate on her phone, pushing the screen around, almost as if she were arranging her thoughts.

"Yes, I am."

Elaine had parked her unmarked police cruiser right outside the Marriott in a no parking zone and in a matter of minutes she had taken them the short distance to the ME's building. She parked in a restricted area that cop cars use. Once inside, Elaine ushered them to the office of an assistant, Brad Compton, who would handle the paperwork.

"Can she see the body?" Jack asked before they sat down.

"She is…?" Compton asked.

"This is the deceased's sister, Brad," Elaine explained. "She just got in town Saturday."

"Well…" Compton started to say, wanting to resist the request.

"Bev, do you want to see the body?" Jack asked.

Beverly did not respond immediately as Jack and Elaine stared at her, and Compton twirled a pen around in his fingers. She held the phone in front of her with both hands as if it were a devining rod which would locate an answer. She brought it up to her pursed lips in a manner that looked as if she was kissing the edge. And perhaps she was. She nodded her head slowly.

"Yes, I think so"

Compton got up and directed Beverly to follow him.

"Are you coming?" she asked Jack.

"No, you go ahead."

Beverly followed Compton out of the office and they went down the corridor.

"I didn't know whether she would want to see the body," Jack said when Compton and Beverly were out of sight. "But I thought she should have the chance if she wanted to take it."

"That was thoughtful of you, Jack."

"Thanks."

"It's times like these that I wish I had a drink," Elaine said. "A nice martini to sip on would be real good right now."

Jack smiled. He wondered how Bev would deal with the sight of her brother, stone cold dead, inert in the sterile morgue storage. What would she think, what kind of reflection on life and death would she have? The realization came to him that he had no idea who this young woman was – his daughter - and the impact of that realization startled him somewhat. Once she was his daughter, now some stranger, Bev was an unknown figure who would never be known by him. Over the years of their estrangement, he had carefully, deliberately deconstructed the parent connection he had once had with Bev. It was disassociation by lack of association and he had been satisfied how well that process had freed him of the emotional potential that could have reigned, could have pestered his thoughts. That process was now surely complete.

Nearly ten minutes passed before Compton and Beverly returned. Compton motioned Beverly to a chair as he got seated behind his desk. It was obvious that Beverly had been crying, but had regained her composure.

"Very well then, Mr. Phillips, I need you to sign here and here and here, and initial here."

Jack began signing.

"Who will be receiving the body…what funeral director?"

"I don't know yet. I have to call my office."

"Let me know as soon as you can, please. Here's my card. Just call this number, it's my direct dial."

"I will; thank you. Thank you very much."

Compton smiled slightly and nodded.

Elaine, Beverly, and Jack went outside and stood in the lot by the police cruiser. Tears filled Beverly's eyes.

"I hated to see Jimmy like that," she said, her words somewhat muffled by the phone held to her mouth, "but I had to do it. I just had to. I'll never see him again; never talk to him again…"

Her voice trailed away and she began to cry with deep sobs and Jack stood there stiffly, resisting his inclination to hold and comfort her, and Beverly shook convulsively from emotion. Elaine stepped to her, wrapped her arms around, and held Beverly firmly at first and then rubbed her back slowly, softly, maternally. Beverly rested her head on Elaine's shoulder and quietly continued to weep.

"I know this nice little place where we can go and get a cup of coffee," Elaine said, "come on, get in and we'll be there in a few minutes."

Little was said by Jack or Beverly during the drive. Elaine carried the conversation by herself with herself and Jack was just as glad that she did. It dawned on him suddenly that he should call By and make some arrangements. He punched By's number into his cell phone.

"Byron, I'm glad I caught you. How are things going? I know, don't worry about me, I'm fine. How's Janet? Good, that's good. Hey listen, I need you to do something for me. I've taken on the responsibility for my son's body. No, no, his wife did not do it. Anyway, I know you had dealings with a funeral director there when your Dad died. Would you get hold of him and have him call the Medical Examiner's office here in Atlanta? I need him to take care of this. Get the body back to Columbus, the whole deal. Okay, thanks, By, that's great, I appreciate it."

Jack read the number from Compton's card, gave him Compton's name, and agreed to talk with Byron later. He closed the phone and looked at Elaine who was watching him with side glances as she drove.

"He'll have him call. My partner…that's who that was."

Elaine smiled, reached over, and patted his hand. Just then they reached the coffee shop and Elaine pulled to the curb. They went inside and sat at a table near the front window.

"Three coffees, Larry," Elaine called to the black man standing near the serving counter in the rear. "There's cream and sugar on the table," she said to Jack and Beverly.

She pointed to the sugar shaker and small stainless steel dispenser in the center of the table. Larry delivered the cups to their table almost before the three of them could say much of anything. Then there was more silence until Elaine decided the silence was making her itch.

"What's your plan, Bev?"

"Go back to Nashville. I came to see what had happened, to see about Jimmy, and I found out. Found out more than I wanted to know, I suppose, but it's a pretty clear picture thanks to my Dad. By the way, Dad, I didn't get a chance to ask you how you felt about Jimmy being gay. How do you feel? What do you think?"

Bev was the first person to ask the question that he had been asking himself. What were his feelings? He had not yet worked it out and only in the last couple of days had he truly thought about how he felt and he still did not have a concrete answer for himself.

"I don't know, I haven't gotten that far with my feelings. I'm not anti-gay. I never thought about what I would think about if J.W. were gay; it never crossed my mind."

"Never?"

I don't know about never."

"I did. I thought about Jimmy being gay…"

"Why?"

"I don't know. Some something, some woman's intuition thing. So it doesn't come as a surprise. And it's okay to me."

Tears came to her eyes again and she caught herself with the phone. She pushed at her granny glasses and turned to stare blindly out the window.

"I think you're going to be all right," Elaine encouraged, "and you're probably right about heading back home. Nothing more to do here. I'm going to suggest the same to Papa Detective here to do the same thing."

"Have you been fucking my Dad?" Beverly asked.

The question was a clap of thunder that neither Elaine nor Jack saw coming, but Elaine was used to jolting surprises and responded without missing a beat.

"That's none of you business, Bev, and not a question you should be asking."

"I figured you were…"

"Forget it."

"Dad, were you at all concerned that we would have to talk about some kind of reconciliation, some way of getting together again?"

Jack also didn't hesitate.

"No way; it's not in the cards."

"That's good, because I wouldn't have wanted it."

"Let me tell you this; talking to one's adult children can be difficult enough about certain things, but it's even more so when there has been a large amount of time go by without any contact. You have issues with me that go way back, that haven't been resolved, and that you harbor. But I want to tell you some things right now. We are all a matter of circumstance. None of us chose our parents and few of us as parents get to chose our children. In both cases, we take what we get without choice. I don't have any big answers about your issues with me, but I do know I won't be whipsawed about the crap in the life of my adult offspring. Whatever your beef is with life or with me, I can't fix that now. And you're right when you say, "it doesn't matter," because there's no reconciliation between us. I can't help the fact that your Mother was nuts and a drunk. I couldn't change that back when, and I can't change that now. It's all circumstance and we are victims without control of much of anything."

"Nice speech. You probably have worked on that for awhile to get it perfected. Oh, yeah, you're right, my Mother was a drunk and crazy…and you were a jerk."

Beverly got up and walked out of the coffee shop and headed up the street before Jack or Elaine could say anything.

"What's she doing? Where the hell is she going?" a visibly surprised and shocked Elaine asked.

"That young woman has been difficult all of her life. You got a chance to see my daughter on display."

"She's coming back," Elaine said sharply as her cell phone sounded.

Beverly charged through the door into the coffee shop and threw herself onto the chair she had just vacated. Some of her hair had flopped into her face and she blew at it in order to push it aside. She finally pushed it aside with her hand after several blowing snorts failed to remove the wild strands. Elaine was on her cell phone.

"I want you to know," Beverly said, "that if you have a service for Jimmy, I'll be there. Just let me know. You have my cell phone number."

"Okay," Jack said. "Is there anything else?"

"Yes. You never answered my question about Jimmy being gay…how you felt."

"Like you said, "it doesn't matter." What I think or feel about his sexual orientation is immaterial; he's dead."

"Bullshit."

Beverly again stomped out of the coffee shop. This time she did not return.

"That was Fred. They're still looking for Hamner's car. No luck with that yet. He says something big is coming down, but he doesn't know what it is. He's guessing a bust by the Task Force. Maybe they know where Hamner is and are keeping quiet on it."

"They don't know where he is. He's out there and he'll get Crawford. Get hold of someone who can order protection for him or we'll lose him as a witness."

"God, you sound like a cop."

Before Elaine could message out, her phone sounded again. It was Brad Compton.

"Hi, Brad. Sure enough, he's right here."

She handed the phone to Jack.

"Mr. Phillips, everything is all set. We have been contacted by a funeral director in Columbus, Ohio, and he is making all arrangements and your son will be sent home."

"Thanks, Brad, really appreciate your help."

Jack closed the phone and handed it back to Elaine.

"That's one of the more unusual father-daughter meetings I've ever witnessed," Elaine said solemnly. "I can't imagine the emotional upset that might cause. I know I'd be upset. What are you feeling right about now? Or can't you say?"

"I said it to Bev. I won't be yanked around by my adult kid. A lot of time has gone by, I've moved on in my life without her, and there is no way to recapture that lost time even if Bev wanted to do so, which she doesn't. And that's fine with me. My life is now. Anyway, I've gotten used to relationships with the women in my life falling apart. From my ex-wife until last Friday with Meg, and all those others in between. Poof, something happens and they go bust. I guess what I'm saying is that I'm not upset and emotionally I feel quite steady. Maybe I'm kidding myself, but I don't think so."

Jack stared at her. He wanted to say something more, but waited to get her response.

"I know what you are thinking," Elaine said.

"Do you?"

"Yes, you're all tense trying to figure out about you and me. How we might fit together, how this would work out, that sort of stuff…"

"Yeah, that's part of it. The logistics; with me living in Ohio, you here in Atlanta…"

"God, you're such a romantic and so practical and organized and systematic and righteous. It's amazing. It's not part of your thought process to factor in that this past weekend was a casual fling.

Jack frowned at her, didn't say anything, and she went on.

"Maybe in terms you might like better, we could call it an unencumbered sexual interlude. Men do that sort of thing all the time, why can't a woman? Besides, we just met a few days ago; you don't even know me. You're on the rebound from Meg and, certainly, you take sex very seriously."

"I thought I did take sex very seriously, but I was sure a pushover for you. I fell right into that action without even thinking about it. Not something I would normally do. I guess right now I'm sort of embarrassed at my lack of restraint. Also, I'm embarrassed at my schoolboy assumption that there might be something that really happened between us."

She laughed.

"Don't be embarrassed, you're a terrific lover. Like I told you, I knew you were a passionate man."

"Is that the way you usually spend your weekends?"

"That's not a very nice question. And don't get petulant, it doesn't become you. No, that's not how I usually spend my weekends. Usually I work weekends to give some of the married people in our department a break. But now and then a guy comes along that I fancy and, bingo, we get away to Lake Lanier and I have some fun and enjoy sex. And I like the booze and good wine and great food. It makes for a nice weekend and a getaway from the blood and filth I deal with on a regular basis. I'd like to do that more often, but it's tough finding the right guy more than once in awhile. You came along at the perfect time for me; I was pretty horny."

"I got it," Jack said.

"Good. Now, I think you should pack your things and head back to Ohio. There's nothing more to be done here in Atlanta. You need to be home to take care of your son's body and make arrangements for a service of some kind. We'll get Hamner and everything will play out. The Task Force will get Crawford and he'll go to jail."

"You think so?"

"Yes, I do. Come on, I'll drive you back to the Marriott.

Elaine ignored the doorman who rushed over when she pulled her police cruiser into the turnaround at the Marriott. She kept the windows up and put the car in Park.

"I'd like to know; did you enjoy the sex?"

He opened the door before he spoke and then turned to her.

"Yes, it was great. And I appreciated you as a person. Excuse me as the romantic schoolboy that I am, but I could care for you. I know that."

She was going to say something else, but Jack had already gotten out of the cruiser, closed the door, and was headed into the hotel.

19.

When Dixie Hamner left Daryl Binser's house on Saturday he was fairly certain Daryl bought his plan for Texas. He believed he could trust Daryl in that regard. That stupid girlfriend, Lilly, was another matter. She would be a problem, which for Hamner meant he had to move fast to become difficult to spot and near impossible to find.

He drove from Daryl's directly to the Lenox Square Mall near Buckhead, not far from the condo he had just vacated, and the same mall where Rodney's car was parked. He pulled the Mercedes into a parking slot as far out in the lot and away from Bloomingdale's as he could. From the trunk, he retrieved a mid-size athletic bag with a Nike logo and a very large piece of luggage which had wheels so that it could be pulled. Hamner yanked up the handle of the luggage, looped the tote straps of the athletic bag over the handle so that the bag rested on the luggage, and closed the trunk lid. He made sure the car was locked, grabbed the luggage handle, and walked away.

After he was out of the mall parking lot and had walked several blocks, Hamner's shirt was soaked through with sweat. And he was breathing heavily, his face red from exertion, and his knees aching from the strain they weren't used to enduring. He kept going, ignoring the heat and discomfort until he reached the MARTA Buckhead Station. His wait wasn't more than a few minutes before the next train pulled alongside the platform. He boarded the Red Line train headed south and rode it to the MARTA Arts Center Station where he got off.

Hamner headed away from the station, pulling the large luggage and athletic bag, and was, by now, sweat-soaked into his trousers and suit coat. Straining, huffing and puffing, he walked the half mile to the self-storage garage on 14th Street.

Once he reached the nearly new silver-gray Cadillac sedan he sought, he took a deep breath, and started to relax a bit. But only a bit, because the press of time was still with him and he could not shake that feeling. He opened the trunk of the Cadillac, pulled the athletic bag off the luggage, and hefted the luggage piece inside the trunk. He put the athletic bag in the car on the front seat next to him and patted it, almost fondly. Inside the athletic bag was three hundred and fifty thousand dollars in twenty, fifty, and one hundred dollar bills. The large piece of luggage in the trunk contained all of the clothes he had kept when he left his condo. He unzipped the athletic bag and took out a wallet that rested on top of the money and replaced it with the wallet he had been carrying. He was now Lester Reed.

Hamner had carefully created Lester Reed over the last year and a half just in case the sweet little Atlanta drug deal went to hell. After all, he knew he was working with a bunch of queers who could screw up the deal at any time. And sure enough, they did. He had applied for and received a legit Florida drivers license using a fake Social Security ID and then bought a condo in Naples as Lester Reed; a financier and investor, he told the owner. He knew that he could alter his looks when need be and had considered several options for doing so, but he had figured that could wait.

He had used the name Arnold Friend when he rented the space for the Cadillac and had shown the rental agent a fake Alabama drivers license. The Cadillac carried Alabama plates and was purchased at the downtown Birmingham Cadillac dealership. The address of a house Ryan Coleridge owned in Eufaula, Alabama, was his place of residence for the registration and the fake license. A buddy of Coleridge's in Phenix City was in the business of making all kinds of fake documents. Lester Reed had also registered the Cadillac in Florida, with the documentation that showed Arthur

Friend had transferred the title to Lester Reed, and that plate rested in its trunk.

On the surface, Dixie Hamner seemed to be a man of limited intellect. After all, he had never completed high school, didn't read much, if ever, and he even disregarded a newspaper. However, he was not dull of brain power and possessed a certain cunning that allowed him to plan and organize, and execute his plan. He was deeply motivated by his own insecurity and paranoia, which had been cultivated and reinforced over time. This is why he had been so diligent in trying to make sure his future movements and whereabouts would be as difficult as possible for the cops to trace. He believed that he had done a pretty good job of it. He figured that once he had put a couple of hollow-point nine millimeter slugs in Warren Crawford and gotten out of Atlanta, he would be home free.

Hamner slowly, carefully backed the Cadillac out of its parking space and drove out of the garage. He felt comfortable in knowing he would not be spotted by the police he knew would soon be looking for the Mercedes. Using the I-75 freeway, he drove to Marietta and reached the apartment building where he had rented a unit as Arnold Friend, a businessman from Birmingham, and used the phony Alabama license for identification.

The modest, one-bedroom apartment served another purpose other than being part of a different identity. Hamner felt its location not far from French and Crawford made it easier keeping close tabs on them without having to drive back and forth to the Buckhead area. He had seen their scheme unraveling as Crawford and French and Phillips fouled their personal relationships which jeopardized the entire drug operation. When Crawford asked him to ex Jim Phillips, he knew it would soon be over and the time had come to move on, although he never expected Crawford to finger him for the killing.

Hamner left the luggage in the trunk, but took the athletic bag with him to the apartment. He stripped off his clothes, showered, and dressed in a warm-up suit that hung in the bedroom closet. He spread out the wet clothes in the kitchen so they could dry. And he would wait. He figured the cops had him leaving the Atlanta area, but would still cover Crawford's house and business. So, if he ran right to Crawford the cops would be there and he would not have his chance. Let a day go by and when he didn't show, the guard would be relaxed. On Monday he would strike.

He muddled through the weekend; watching television for awhile, pacing at intervals, and looking out the window from behind the drapes. He scanned the side streets in view to determine if anyone was watching the apartment building. No one was and he felt secure. He had stocked the refrigerator freezer with prepared dinners, made sure there were a couple of six-packs of beer, and plenty of bagged and packaged snacks. There was no reason he had to leave the apartment until Monday.

Hamner watched several television news reports on Saturday and Sunday which covered the horrific parking lot crash at an Atlanta super market which killed a long-time, respected investigative reporter from the *Constitution*. There was also a review of Spence Colby's career. This included the important stories he covered and highlighted his involvement with the current unsolved murder of a successful Ohio salesmen, James Phillips. It seemed to authorities that the crash was deliberate, but the driver of the van that hit Colby's car left the scene and his identity was unknown. The TV newsreaders in each report closed their stories by saying that the police had few leads on Phillips' murder and no leads for the death of Colby. The news stories gave no indication that authorities believed the deaths of Phillips and Colby were related.

Hamner stared at the walls, checked outside, and drank beer. He finally decided to wipe down and check his two hand guns. His cleaning kit was packed away in the boxes he put in the carriage house behind Daryl's, so he used a wash cloth from the bathroom. He unloaded, wiped, loaded, and wiped the pistols several times. Eventually, he lay on the bed and tried to think if he had forgotten anything. He spent most of the rest of the weekend sleeping and shaking in his sleep like someone's old dog that has run too much.

Sunday night, once it was dark, Hamner went out to the Cadillac, opened the trunk, took a screwdriver from a small tool kit, and removed the Alabama plates. He then fastened the Florida plate to the rear plate holder, dropped the Alabama plates and screwdriver into the trunk, and went back inside the apartment.

Monday morning, Hamner arose about seven, shaved and showered, and still in his boxer shorts and tee-shirt made a cup of instant coffee. He slurped the coffee as he checked his suit. The suit was dry, but ragged looking and did not pass his inspection. From the bedroom closet he took out an almost identical suit still in the plastic sheath from the dry cleaners. With a clean white shirt from the closet and a brand new tie he had never worn, he dressed, and, checking the bathroom mirror, satisfied himself that he could meet the day. He removed his jacket and slipped into the shoulder holster harness he carried on his left side. He clipped another holster to his belt at the small of his back. He then put his two pistols into the holsters and donned the jacket again. He approved of the mirror image which did not show he was carrying.

There was plenty of time; time to make breakfast. Again, he took off the suit jacket and laid it neatly on the bed. Back in the kitchen, he poked about in the freezer compartment until he found a beef dinner that looked decent to him. At least the photo on the box made it seem appealing. He followed the microwave instructions, standing expectantly in front of the buzzing unit until its bell rang. He sat at the kitchen table and slowly ate the beef dinner from its container. He was somewhat satisfied without thinking much about whether it were good or bad food. All he knew was that he was no longer hungry and time had passed and now, he could move on to Crawford's place.

He was Lester Reed at this point and figured he could move about with some degree of safety. If he were stopped for some unlikely reason, his drivers' license and registration would show him as Lester Reed and a police check with Florida would verify who he was and that the car was properly titled and registered. He drove several blocks to a small café which was full of morning hustle and bustle, and pumped coins into a newspaper machine. Hamner lingered over a coffee, pretended to read the paper, and wondered to himself why time seemed to drag so. The Colby death story was not on the front page, but he noticed an update on page six. Police still had no information as to who the driver of the van was that crashed into Colby's car.

It was nine-thirty. Hamner knew Crawford's business opened at ten, but that the man himself would be there by now, working in his office. As he drove the short distance to Design Interiors, Hamner wondered what protection the man would have. Those thoughts evaporated as he turned the corner a short block from the strip mall that housed Crawford's business and saw several Marietta police cars and other unmarked cars that had to be the law. He stopped in the middle of the block, pulled to the curb, and got out of the car. He stood on the sidewalk for several minutes watching the scene around Crawford's business. He was confused at first. What had happened? Maybe Crawford had killed himself or maybe one of Shay's or Coleridge's guys had gotten to him. He walked toward the next intersection where he could see the yellow crime scene tape. He could hear the squawk of the two-way radios and hear the murmur of the large crowd which had gathered at the corner. He stood at the rear of the crowd and watched as SWAT cops got back in their cars and SUVs and drove away.

After a few moments watching, Hamner asked the young Hispanic woman next to him what was going on.

"They take him away," she said, "before ten o'clock, a few minutes ago, I guess. Got him in handcuffs behind his back. Pushed him into the police car."

"Who was it?"

"I dunno. One lady over there say it the Crawford guy who own the studio. That's who it looked like to me, but I not sure. I work next door, but I not know him good."

Hamner nodded, moved slowly back away from the mass of onlookers, and walked to his car in a casual manner that would not draw attention. He carefully turned around his car and drove to the Marietta police headquarters.

At the opposite end of the strip mall, on the far side of the intersection, and outside of the growing mass of the curious, Jack Phillips pushed by the crowd until he was against the yellow crime scene tape.

"Hey, officer," Jack yelled at one of the Marietta policeman working to maintain control of the viewers, "Jack Phillips, I work with Elaine Moss, Atlanta detective and your guy Larry Davis…"

The officer moved toward him as Jack held up his wallet showing his Ohio drivers license.

"…on my son's murder and also worked with Spence Colby of the *Constitution* who was murdered last Saturday. What's going on?"

The cop looked at Jack's license before he spoke.

"Drug Task Force picked up a guy named Crawford a few minutes ago. Took him to Headquarters for booking. That's all I know. We just have to keep everybody away from the building."

"Marietta headquarters or Atlanta?" Jack asked.

"Ours, Marietta."

"Thanks," Jack flipped over his shoulder. He was already headed for his car with a quick-paced walk.

Jack wondered about Hamner because he believed the man was surely around here someplace. He shook slightly, involuntarily, in reaction to his sense of things as he strode to his car. Realizing that J.W.'s killer might be so close caused Jack to react to a wave of anticipation and a dose of fear. Hamner was very dangerous, he knew, and he also knew he did not have the experience, the real street smarts of a guy like Hamner or of a cop like Elaine who could go after Hamner.

He slid his hand to his waist to feel the firm comfort of the Glock. He was almost certain that Hamner had not left town as Elaine believed and that Hamner would come after Crawford. It was the justice of revenge and Hamner would be the executioner. Maybe Hamner was in this crowd somewhere lurking about, watching, and complaining to himself he was too late to nail Crawford. But he's close by; Jack didn't doubt it.

Jack headed for Marietta police headquarters. It was important to know what they will do with Crawford. Will he get bail? Held without bail? He had to find out. Jack knew that Hamner would also be trying to learn where Crawford was going to be.

Jack parked in the first spot he could find two blocks from the police headquarters building. The area was swarming with marked and unmarked police vehicles, and the trucks and cars from news media. He quickly walked the short distance, stopped across the street from the headquarters building, and looked around. He scanned up and down the block to see if he could spot Hamner. He was looking for the Mercedes he had last seen Hamner drive away from the tea room. He's here someplace, Jack thought again. He's nearby.

He pushed through the crowd which milled about and went into the police building.

The Drug Task Force had arrested sixteen others besides Crawford that morning in a coordinated sweep of Marietta. These were known street dealers who were involved in the French-Crawford-Phillips drug scheme in a loose organization developed and managed by Dixie Hamner. This federation of drug criminals, and yes, they all had criminal records, were followed to police headquarters by a clacking throng of wives, girl friends, mistresses, buddies, customers, attorneys, bail bondsmen, creditors, loan shark operatives, and other hangers on. Such was the noisy mess that greeted Jack when he got inside headquarters.

Jack's cellphone rang just as he stepped toward the Sergeant who was trying to keep control of things. He pulled out the phone and backed away to a quieter spot at the wall near the entryway.

"Yes…?"

He could see that it was Elaine.

"I assume you're in your car on the way back to Ohio."

"No, I'm not…"

"Why? Where are you?"

"I…I'm in the reception area of the Marietta police headquarters. It's pandemonium here and I can hardly hear you…"

"What the hell are you doing there?"

"They arrested Warren Crawford this morning and he's in custody right now. I don't know what the rest of this nonsense is that I see going on, but there are lots of folks here who don't look very reputable. My guess is that there's been a drug bust."

"You were going to head for home…"

I didn't say that, that's what you wanted."

"Yeah…"

"Look, I told you Hamner was not going to leave town until he killed Crawford. I came here to Marietta to warn Crawford that Hamner was still around and he would come and shoot him. Never got to Crawford; cops got him arrested and in here first."

"Give it up, Jack. With Crawford in custody there's nothing more for you to do. Head for home."

"There's Hamner…"

"Oh, I suppose you're going to try to arrest him? The cops can't do it?"

"They haven't."

"They will."

"Hey, Miz Moss, what would you do if you were Hamner, maybe change wheels?"

She was silent.

"What happened to Elaine?"

"I left her earlier this morning."

Again, she was silent.

"I realize I've been looking out for the wrong car. He's changed cars, that's why I haven't spotted him."

"Please quit trying to be a detective and go home."

"Naw, I don't think so. I think I'll find Hamner, after I talk to Larry Davis."

"Jack…"

"What?"

"Don't do anything stupid…"

"Like what?"

"Like confronting Hamner if you spot him."

Now he was silent.

"And stay in touch with me. Please."

Jack closed the phone and headed back to the Sergeant.

"Hey, get word to Larry Davis that Jack Phillips is here and wants to talk to him."

"Who the hell are you," the cop shot back.

"I said Jack Phillips. He knows me."

"So what?"

"So, I have some information he can use."

The Sergeant shrugged, picked up his phone, punched in a number, and then relayed Jack's message. In a few moments, a red-faced Davis approached Jack.

"Listen, Mister Phillips…"

"He's here. Nearby, and he's changed cars."

"Who he…?"

"Hamner, and he wants to kill Crawford."

"How do you know?"

"Well, I…"

"Hey, okay, come on in my office and get out of this crap. Too noisy."

Jack followed Davis to his office.

"Now, how do you know this…what do you know?"

"It's my…my sense about it; I can feel it. I know he's not going to run away yet."

"Your women's intuition, I suppose?"

Jack didn't answer and just looked at Davis.

"Sit down."

Davis pointed to a chair near his desk.

"Look, Mr. Phillips, I know you were upset about your son, I understand that, but you've been a real pain in the ass as far as this investigation goes. We're getting this thing taken care of..."

"Yeah, tell that to Collier French's friends and relatives. You guys think Hamner has headed out..."

"Doesn't matter, the net has already been thrown for him. Going, staying, it doesn't matter, we'll get him..."

"What are you looking for, what car?"

Davis picked up a sheet from his desk and read the car's description and Georgia license number.

"He's in another car."

"How do you know?"

"He's not a dope. He knows that if he hangs around long enough to kill Crawford he has to be in another car, a car that is hard to trace. He didn't count on you guys picking up Crawford this morning. By the way, what's Crawford's status, bail or held without bail?"

"The big boys are working on that. Jurisdiction argument. The state of Georgia wants him and so do the Feds. Either way I don't think he'll make bail. They're trying to figure out who is going to arraign him. It may take awhile, but my money is on the Feds."

Jack's cellphone rang. It was Elaine.

"I'll get out of here with this," Jack said, before he answered the call.

"Great, I'd appreciate that."

Jack moved to the hallway which ran to the reception area and stopped. It would be quieter here.

"Elaine, what's going on?"

"I'm glad it's Elaine and not Miss Moss. Anyway, we found Hamner's car in the parking lot at the Lenox Square Mall. You were right."

"There's no prize…we still don't know what he is driving, now."

"Don't say we. You are not a detective, you're an advertising guy from Ohio. Go back there and do advertising and let us do our job. And anyway, I realize we don't know what he's driving. We're checking taxi cabs to see if one picked him up and Fred is checking with MARTA to determine if their security cameras caught Hamner. There's a MARTA station not far from the spot where he left the car. Where are you now?"

"Still here at Marietta police headquarters. Just talked to Davis. He says there's a tug of war between the locals and the Justice Department over who gets to prosecute Crawford."

"You should leave Larry alone. He has enough to do without dealing with you."

"Yeah, he's let me know that."

"Can I convince you to just get in your car and head for Columbus, Ohio?"

"No, not right now. I'm going to hang around here and see what happens to Crawford and maybe then we find out what kind of move Hamner wants to make. I don't think he's going to give up right away. When he finds out that Crawford is going to be held without bail, then maybe he moves on, but not before that."

"Crawford not getting bail?"

"Davis doesn't think he will."

"An expensive lawyer like he'll get will have him out, trust me. Hey, I've got to go. I'll call you when I know more. Stay out of trouble and go home."

"Yeah, yeah." He closed the phone.

Frustrated, Jack went down the hallway, through the reception area with its noise and confusion, and pushed his way outside. There was no consolation for him being right about Hamner changing cars; that was a simple matter of deduction. Jack didn't wear frustration well. He was a doer, a man who figured things out, and acted accordingly. He wanted to catch Hamner, but could he when he didn't know what kind of car the man was now driving?

He stood on the steps, again scanning up and down the street. No recognition, no sense of Hamner and a car. Now, wait a minute. Jack caught himself. When Hamner ditches his Mercedes, what kind of car does he move to? Of course, he would switch to another luxury car. But what make? Jack adjusted his notion of what he was looking for and stared down the block. What he was seeing were the modest vehicles used by the Marietta police, the DEA, the Justice Department, and the other governmental agencies both local and federal. And then he spotted the silver-gray Cadillac near the far corner, just across the intersection. There he is, Jack guessed, that has to be Hamner. Who else would be driving a nearly new Cadillac around here? Maybe one of the attorneys or hustlers clamoring inside, but chances are its Hamner. Worth checking out, anyway. He leaned back against the building so as to not tip his hand that he had spotted Hamner. When a clutch of lawyers huddled nearby blocked his view of Hamner, Jack took advantage of the screen and ducked back inside the building.

Jack went straight to the Sergeant in charge.

"Hey, can I get out the back? A bunch of reporters are going to hound me if I go out front."

"You the one saw Davis?"

"Yes, I am and I don't think Larry would want me to get wrapped up with those news guys right now."

"Hey, Mooney," the Sergeant called to one of the other officers. "Take this guy to the back. He needs to escape from some of the reporters we got around here."

"Sure thing," Mooney said, and motioned Jack to follow him.

"Thanks, Sarge, you're a big help."

"No problem."

Jack tagged along with Officer Mooney through a labyrinth of hallways until they were at a door in the rear of the building.

"Here you go." Officer Mooney threw open the door for Jack.

"Thanks, Officer."

"Okay."

Jack walked through the police parking lot and angled his way to the street that ran towards where the man he thought was Hamner was parked. He headed up the street and soon could see the Cadillac. He stopped and then moved sideways so he could not be seen. There was a man sitting in the Cadillac. He wasn't positive, but the man looked like Hamner. He realized that if he approached the car on foot, Hamner would simply pull away and be lost again. Jack doubled back to the street running behind the police building, walked the two blocks toward where he had parked, and then cut back to the street on which Hamner and his car was parked.

Jack decided to circle around several blocks and approach Hamner's car from behind. He would park and see what happened. He turned his car around and made the circuit of blocks until he was slowly coming down the street towards the Cadillac. There was a parking spot more than half a block from Hamner's position. He pulled to the curb. He would wait.

A man with a briefcase, probably a lawyer, walked from police headquarters past where Hamner was parked. He stopped and it was obvious the man was talking to whoever was in the Cadillac. It had to be Hamner, but he wasn't sure. It had to be. Now, the man was gesturing and pointing back at the headquarters building. He listened for a moment, shrugged his shoulders, and walked away past where Jack was parked to his car still farther away from the police building.

After a few minutes, the Cadillac slowly pulled out from its parking spot, paused for the STOP sign at the corner, and made a right turn.

Dixie Hamner had seen Jack enter police headquarters and later had seen him come back out onto the steps and look around. Hamner knew Jack did not know what he was looking for. A small crowd gathered and Jack had disappeared. Most likely gone back inside, Hamner figured. Then the lawyer-looking guy came by and Hamner asked if Crawford made bail. The man told him that Crawford had not yet made bail and rumor had it than in all likelihood he and all of the others arrested would not be released. At least not today. The lawyer said he couldn't wait around for the authorities to make up their minds who was in charge and if anyone would walk.

Hamner was so confident in being another fictitious person that he disregarded the idea that anyone would follow him. He was functioning now as Lester Reed, a man unknown in Atlanta, a man who could move about with little fear police would get to him.

But Jack Phillips had homed in on Hamner's Cadillac and now was gingerly following at a safe distance. Driving as though one would tip-toe behind a suspect, Jack trailed the short drive to the apartment building where Hamner parked the Cadillac and walked inside.

Jack knew he was operating from instinct; after all, his motivation coming to Atlanta in the first place was based on instinct. Jack could not know that the man he saw emerge from the Cadillac was functioning in another identity, he only knew he was viewing Dixie Hamner parade away to the building as one with impunity, a man safe from the press of the law and authorities.

He drove past the apartment building as he saw Hamner pull open the vestibule door. There he is, Jack thought, acting as if he were a free spirit, acting as if he thought no one could touch him. Why? How could he be so casual in his behavior?

Jack drove around the block and parked on the street that ran alongside the apartment building, but where he could view the front entrance. He could see the Cadillac, he could see the front door. Now, what? Jack wondered why there seemed to be nothing furtive in Hamner's actions. He must feel secure, that he was safe. He had changed vehicles; he had what…changed identity in some way?

Jack wished he had binoculars. The license plate on the Cadillac did not look like a Georgia plate. That's it. He has another car and another state's license on it. Where he would be headed after he killed Crawford. So simply, so easy. The cops are running around looking for him in the Mercedes with Georgia plates and he has made the change.

Jack pulled out his cell phone. Who to call first? He didn't have Larry Davis' number with him, so punched in Elaine's. It rang several times before she answered. It was her artificial voice as she asked him to leave a message. He told her message base where he was and what was going on. He said as emphatically as he could that he could not, would not wait forever for her to respond. So there, he had reported.

He waited thirty minutes or so and decided he would check out the lobby and the tenant list. He slid out of his car and walked to the apartment building front door as casually as he could. He took note of the license on Hamner's car and memorized it. He got to the building and entered. The lobby smelled strange to him, but he could not identify what the smell was. Perhaps it was the lingering scent of a woman's perfume. He read the names on the tenant registry not expecting to see Dixie Hamner, but wondering what alias was being used. The name Arthur Friend, of course, meant nothing to him.

Jack tried the inner door on the chance it was not locked, but it was. There was no point in pulling the old ruse of buzzing one of the tenants to enter because none of the tenant names were meaningful. Jack was about to head back to his car with the intention of going back to police headquarters to alert Davis, when he saw Dixie Hamner staring at him through the lobby's glass partition. He tried to squeeze himself against the wall to stay out of the man's sight, but it was not possible.

Hamner saw Jack in the lobby pulling back and away to the wall behind him. Hamner pulled his gun immediately and thus began those frozen frames of action that etch memory and define outcomes. For Jack it became all reaction; nothing intellectual about it, mere stuff of survival, the necessary moves to not get killed. He knew this man would kill him if he could.

Hamner's first shot hit the wooden door jamb that splintered and drove shattered pieces into the lobby. His second shot hit the wall above Jack's head and plaster flew about.

Jack had pulled his Glock and dropped to his knee and fired three quick rounds at Hamner as Hamner fired four more rounds at him. And it was over that quickly. Hamner was gone, Jack could not feel the pain, yet knew he had been shot, and knew he would need help. He saw the blood on his jacket and he winced. He had been knocked back onto his butt and had slumped sideways onto the floor.

20.

Talking, dialog, conversation, whatever you want to call it, even face-to-face, is sometimes not enough to bridge the gap that is needed to repair a relationship. When that gap is between a parent and a child the challenge can be even more monumental.

Now, as Jack thought about his dead son, what resonated with him was their last face-to-face conversation. Jack remembered that he and J.W. met several years back in Cincinnati while both were on business trips and they drank beers and had some laughs. It seemed a pleasant enough occasion at the time, but now Jack wondered what really had happened then. They had scheduled that meeting in advance as they had done numerous times before. It was just before the estrangement had become apparent and a certain well-maintained amiableness still graced their conversation. In Jack's memory there was an overriding feeling that this meeting had been different somehow. They had spent the time reminiscing about their favorite toys when they were young.

"Slot cars were a real trip," J.W. said, "I could not get them out of my system for a long time. I just got such a kick out of speeding them along the track we had in the basement."

And he went on about the cars, their colors, their speed characteristics, his own sense of attachment to the best ones, and the meaning of involvement with their action. It was almost as if he were talking about some kind of living thing, as if they were alive, and that if only some magic pixie dust could be sprinkled on them they could respond to his adulation. As if they could talk back to him and tell J.W. how they appreciated his care for them and how much they respected the fact that he had packaged them so carefully and kept them all these years and had stored them near him, near to his heart. All in memory, all in childish fantasy, all in some uneasy connection to the past; childhood long gone, always waiting to be retrieved in the idealized yearnings of the unfulfilled.

"Every time I bought another car or every time you gave me one, Dad, I was thrilled."

J.W.'s acknowledgement of being thrilled about receiving a slot car sounded superficial and glib to Jack, almost patronizing in its tone as the words were spoken. He had worked within himself to shrug off the negative feelings about the emotional revelation his son had experienced. It sounded too pat, too phony to him. But that response he also shrugged off and sipped at his beer.

"What was your favorite toy?"

Jack though a moment before he answered.

"I guess it was the microscope set I got one Christmas. Pretty good one, too. Not top of the line, of course, because my folks couldn't afford the most expensive one…"

"How did you know there was a more expensive one?"

"Good question. I don't know, but I did. Maybe saw the more extravagant one in a store. I'm not sure. All I knew then was it was great and I didn't think much about there being one that was more elaborate, more expensive."

"Did you use it all the time?"

"No, you know, I didn't. I saved it for special times. When I was bored or there wasn't anything else to do. So I saved it. Then I would pull it out and go to work. I remember looking at a hair I pulled from my head. Flat and thin and almost colorless under the lenses. I made specimens on slides and looked at all kinds of things. Nothing held my interest very long and then I would move on to something else."

"Wow, must have given Grandma fits."

"No, not at all. She seemed to understand my short attention span and merely directed me to another activity or told me a story or gave me a chore to do. Anyway, she wasn't bothered by me, fortunately. By my lack of long-term concentration; which I still don't have."

Jack realized that J.W. was puzzled by what his Father had said. There was the quizzical look, the frown, and the looking away. There are those times when a parent is talking with a child that the dialog is nonsense, even when that child is an adult. This must be one of those times, Jack had thought.

The estrangement between them had become a fact several months after the Cincinnati meeting. The next time Jack actually saw J.W. was at the medical examiner's office in Atlanta. He saw the lifeless being who could not respond. Oh, yes, there had been several phone conversations in the intervening years, but no more getting together where facial expressions and body language could be read. The language which characterizes true communication theory comprises more than the sending and receiving of words, it encompasses an environment of visual signals between the communicators.

Those phone conversations had opened a window for Jack into the nature and complexity of the estrangement with his son. One element was the crushing emotional impact his divorce from Linda had on his son. He should have been able to weather the storm better at his age, but as a late-bloomer J.W. didn't have the emotional maturity to cope as well as he might have. On the other hand, divorce can be emotionally devastating no matter how it is rationalized. And, as Jack had long surmised, it became apparent that Linda had worked against him behind his back with both J.W. and Beverly. That effort of hers had been manifested in his lack of a relationship with each of his children.

A second element was the impact the neurotic behavior of Angelina had on J.W. She had made it clear she did not like

Jack, didn't want Jack in their home or to be around their children. A double whammy for J.W.; his anger and Angelina's anger all wrapped up in the rejection of Jack.

The last time Jack and J.W. spoke to each other on the phone it was a long discussion which made almost no sense to Jack. Actually, Jack reckoned, it was less a discussion and more a lecture from J.W. It happened about two years ago. Jack had called J.W. to see how he was doing and the result was confusing to say the least. In fact, Jack started writing down notes as J.W. spoke as if that would help him discover some meaning in his son's words. The diatribe went from the search for a moral compass to finding the meaning of life to the multiple and important reasons for being a Methodist, and much criticism and condemnation of Jack in between. But nothing in J.W.'s long, rambling discourse was mentioned about his sexual orientation. Jack now reasoned that the subject of homosexuality could have been at the very core of what J.W. was trying to convey. Perhaps that was the key.

In any case, no resolution of their relationship was reached and then J.W. was dead. Maybe the resolution for Jack would be that he knew he could accept his son under any circumstances.

21.

The sounds of the gunfire died away, but the concussion of the shots still pounded in Jack's head. There was that odd memory of the echo of shell casings bouncing off the tile floor, of feeling bits of wood and grains and small shards of glass hitting his face and neck and chest, and the sound of slugs smacking into the wall behind him.

And then there were the unpleasant, penetrating smells that Jack recognized. The primary dose that he remembered was the spray of gunpowder, so unmistakably present, so pungent in close proximity, so terrifying in its residual effect. There was the odor of blood, his own blood oozing from him that Jack could identify. He wondered how bad the wound was and whether he would die. He wondered if there was time for help to get to him, even if someone had sent for help. Had someone heard? Had they called for help? Surely it was all taking place, surely he would be saved.

What he had not felt or even sensed was being hit by a bullet from Hamner's gun.

Jack eased himself into a sitting position against the vestibule wall, inching his shoulder and hip and ankle in an undulation much like a caterpillar. This was before he felt the pain. The sensation of pain had been suspended through the shock mechanism that protects the body. That suspension was quickly over and the pain took Jack in a vise grip and held him motionless. He wanted to reach for his cell phone, but he could not make the action, could not control the movement. He was frozen, inert, helpless, and yet aware that he was sitting on the vestibule floor. He could see that Dixie Hamner had retreated, no longer in view, and he hoped against hope that somewhere back there, somewhere out of his sight, Dixie Hamner had dropped as he had, and too, was bleeding, perhaps fatally.

Jack struggled to regain control of his own body, to be able to move his arms, to feel for his gun, to reach for the wound he knew was in his shoulder, and he worked within himself to find the strength. Through sheer force of will he reached for his shoulder where the wound pumped precious blood out and into his shirt and jacket. He pressed at the wound as best he could to stop the blood flow and that made the wound hurt worse. He had some sense that he was losing blood rapidly and knew he needed help quickly and wondered what would happen and thought he heard someone talking to him, asking him something, and then there was blackness.

One of the apartment building residents called 911 almost as soon as the gunshots were fired, someone with quick wit and presence of mind. Police and emergency medical were on their way within a minute or so of the shooting. The EMT van got to the apartment building first, which was a blessing for Jack. The man and woman techs found Jack in the vestibule and immediately began a regimen to keep him from bleeding to death. This was not an extraordinary medical circumstance, but still critical in Jack's case. It was not one of their more difficult situations to deal with and render care. Jack would be all right.

He had dropped unconscious from blood loss and shock, but awoke as the emergency technicians worked on him.

"Stopping the blood loss," the man said to his partner.

"Good." The woman was checking his vital signs. "Pulse a little fast, but okay."

"Who shot you?" A police face poked into Jack's view.

Jack thought about the question without answering as if there were some disconnect between hearing the words and the spot in his brain where he should be forming an answer. He moved his lips, but didn't say anything.

"He's lost a lot of blood and…" the man started to explain.

"I know, I know, but we need to find out who shot him…"

"He's in shock."

"Can you hear me?" the police officer asked Jack.

Jack nodded slightly.

"Who are we after? The shooter?"

The police officer picked up Jack's gun.

"This yours?"

Jack nodded.

"We need to get him moved," the man tech said.

"Did you shoot?"

"Yeah," Jack answered.

Jack could speak and the dryness in his throat was not as bad as it had been.

"You think you hit him?"

"I sure as hell hope so."

The technicians with the help of the police officers eased Jack on to the stretcher the techs had brought with them into the vestibule. Jack looked up into the face of Larry Davis.

"I told you to leave the police business to us. This is why. You get yourself shot just like this."

"No kidding…"

"No kidding, he says, well, shit. Was it Hamner?"

"Yes, he…"

Jack stopped, counting in his head.

"He what?"

"He fired six times…"

"How many shots did you get off?"

"Three…"

"Do you think you hit him?"

"Yeah, I think so."

Just then, one of the uniformed officers came into the vestibule from the building lobby.

"There's blood on the floor back there, Detective, our victim here must have made good with one of his shots."

Jack's eyes closed. The pain was terrible and he was having difficulty staying conscious.

"Let's get him out of here," the man tech said.

Detective Davis took Jack's gun from the uniformed officer and shook his head in frustration as he watched them wheel Jack to the EMT van.

"Get this crime scene taped off and secure for the lab guys. I'll see if I can find any witnesses."

When Jack regained a dulled form of consciousness he was in a hospital bed throwing off the effects of anesthesia. He had undergone surgery to repair the damage from his gunshot wound. He was groggy and it was difficult to focus his eyes.

"I…I need my glasses."

It was Elaine who handed them to him.

"Hi," she said quietly.

"Hi."

Jack held the glasses in his right hand and awkwardly tried to push the glasses onto his head.

"I usually use two hands to put my glasses on."

"Here, let me help."

Elaine took the glasses and slid them over his ears and centered them on his nose.

"How's that?"

"Good."

He saw Detective Davis sitting in a chair nearby.

"I need to get your story," Davis said, still seated.

"I imagine."

Jack didn't really mean it to sound sarcastic, but somehow it came out that way. Davis rose and came to the foot of the bed.

"You could be dead…"

"You want the story or do you want to lecture…"

"Both, god damn it. You could be dead. Dead because you would not listen to good advice. This whole thing is messy enough without you getting yourself killed. Things didn't go as fast as you wanted, but we were never sitting still. Never, not once. You couldn't accept that fact, not realizing that we've been working on this group for over a year and we knew we were going to get all of them, including Hamner."

"We'll get Hamner," Elaine said.

"He isn't Hamner, he's someone else."

"Let's back up," Davis said as he pulled his note pad from an inside pocket. "Start at the beginning, after you left my office."

Jack took a deep breath and sighed.

"I left the building and stood on the top of the steps to look over the parked cars up and down the street. I knew that he had ditched the Mercedes thanks to Ms. Moss and figured he would be in some luxury brand. I spotted this silver Cadillac at the corner of the next block and thought that might be a good prospect. I went out the back of your building and up the side street so that I got close enough to ID the driver. It was Hamner. I got back to my car, circled around and parked behind him down the block.

"He didn't see you?"

"Saw my car probably, but wouldn't have known it was mine. Anyway, after awhile some guy came by his car and Hamner stopped him and they talked. After the man walked away, Hamner pulled away and I followed."

"To the apartment building?"

"Yes. I didn't get too close and he didn't realize I was on him. He parked outside the building and went in. I waited for awhile and then decided…"

"Decided you would become a detective again like you did down in Columbus, where you also almost got yourself killed."

Davis was angry.

"Go on."

"Yeah, I guess. Sitting and waiting for a long time is not one of my strengths. I went in the vestibule and checked the resident's names. No Hamner. Then I saw him in the lobby and he saw me and pulled his gun and fired. Before I could get my gun out two shots went by me and then I had my gun out as I went into a kneeled position. I squeezed off three shots before I…"

"Before you were hit?" Elaine asked.

"Yeah."

"Anything else?"

Davis had flipped his note pad closed.

"That's about it."

"Okay. Now let me tell you that you're done with this business. You are going back home…"

"Ohio," Elaine interjected.

"Back to Ohio and let us do our job. We will get Hamner. If you don't leave and go home, I'll have you arrested for interfering with police business. Understand?"

Jack did not respond and closed his eyes. He did not see Davis leave the room.

"Where am I?"

"Kennestone Hospital."

Jack opened his eyes and looked at Elaine standing next to the bed.

"Thanks for coming."

"We didn't part on such good circumstances. This made it even worse. I had to come…I…I had to come."

"I'm glad you did."

"You missed me already, didn't you?"

Jack laughed and it hurt. He coughed and snorted and closed his eyes again. He was uncomfortable and immobile and hated both. He opened his eyes again and looked at Elaine with an intensity that caught her by surprise.

"There's a lot of emotion in that look. More than I might have imagined."

"You're the one so casual. You're the one who could kiss me off as your weekend screw."

"I know. I know that I kissed you off pretty easily. My style, my technique. It's for my own protection, my emotional fortification."

"Your routine?"

"I suppose."

There was more in her than that simple answer and Jack knew there was more and he waited and the silence came and he watched her face hold steady, her eyes stolid, her demeanor the result of being unwilling to reveal herself. She turned and pushed the nearby chair next to the bed. She kicked at it a bit to get it positioned the way she wanted and sat down.

"I was vulnerable," Jack said, "I could care. It meant something to me…at a bad time."

He coughed again and the pain made his face tighten.

"I know…"

She patted his arm.

"When I heard you had been shot…Larry called me…my mind flipped back to us and the weekend and our time together and the easy way we…"

Jack's eyes were closed, but he was listening.

"…we clicked. I think we clicked and it…"

"Scared you?"

"Yes. You were, all of a sudden, very valuable to me…"

"Valuable? That's an interesting way to put it."

His eyes were still closed.

"I couldn't think of another word for it."

"Important?"

"Yes, I guess, important. Our time together became, as I was seeing it, something I had not experienced in a long time. I was beginning to feel something for you beyond the banter and the sex and the shared time. It felt good and it felt bad and I was willing to step away from that and as you said, kiss you off."

"I was happy with my good fortune. I got dumped by a woman I thought was a heavy-duty part of my life and low and behold, here was another woman who could replace the emptiness I temporarily felt. Boom, boom, just like that, the genie grants my wish and there she is. It's you and, yeah, we clicked."

"Yes, we did…"

"You wanted to unclick it…"

"I did, yes…"

"Now? You're here unclicked. Is it official duty to protect the Atlanta Police Department, pity for this worthless wretch, or to reclick? Second thoughts?"

Elaine smiled and took his hand and pulled it to her face and kissed it gently and held it to her cheek. He opened his eyes and stared at her.

"Click is like locked. I didn't want to be locked…"

"You had a hard time having sex with me and disassociating the passion, didn't you?" Jack posed.

"I don't know…" Elaine responded softly.

"It meant something you couldn't figure."

"Maybe, maybe I was taken with the moment. I hadn't had sex for awhile. It felt so good and I had missed that."

Jack closed his eyes and smiled.

"I'll move to Atlanta. I'll open a branch office here. I don't want you to be deprived of my consort service. I can get…"

"You need to get some rest and not worry about me. Besides, you're going home tomorrow. The future is you recovering from the gunshot wound, getting back to your agency, and coming back to testify against Hamner and the guys in Columbus."

"You'll have a hell of time getting him…"

"We will get him and it won't take that long, believe me."

"Longer than you think. But I will come back for that."

She smiled again and again patted his hand.

"I'd come back for you."

"I called your office," Elaine said quietly, "and told them what had happened. Your partner is coming to get you and take you back to Ohio. All of the press wants your time, but I have kept them at bay. At least for now."

"Who...?"

"Mr. Adams. He is flying down tomorrow. He'll drive you home in your car. You'll be okay to travel the docs told me."

"Would you think about coming to Columbus?"

"Yes, I would."

"We clicked didn't we?"

"Yes, I admitted that already. We clicked. I..."

"You what...?"

"I wanted more of you and I didn't want to fess up to that."

"Why?"

"Threatened my set world, I guess. I was ready and willing to have everything go on just as it was and you came along and my world got out of whack..."

"We clicked."

"We clicked. What the hell does that mean, anyhow?"

"Easy. It means the something happened between us. The indefinable magic that makes two people simpatico. That's a Spanish word, incidentally, that can't be translated directly into English..."

"I know. And I know what it means. In English it means that when you and I make love it really feels good and sure and solid. More than just sensuality, more than just pleasure, more than a temporary release of passion; it means a link up of the psyche."

Jack laughed and coughed and reached for his shoulder where the aggravated wound hurt and throbbed.

"I'll send that to Wikipedia and the dictionary guys."

"I mean it…"

"Yeah, I know you do. Will you come to Ohio?"

"For a visit?"

"For a visit, look things over, meet my cat, see where I work, see where I live, and have sex with me again."

The door to Jack's room opened and Byron Adams pushed his way into their interchange.

"By," Jack said with a look of admiration and respect.

"Hey."

He came straightaway to the bedside, next to Elaine, ignored Elaine, and grasped Jack's hand.

"I booked onto a fractional jet and got here faster. Screwing around with commercial and it'd be noon tomorrow before I could get here."

"I'm Elaine Moss, I called you."

Elaine stood and reached her hand toward him and wondered what kind of man he was.

"Right, yeah, Ms. Moss. Thank you for calling me. We'll get this guy home tomorrow. Glad you took charge, Ms. Moss, Jack would not have called me. He's too tough for that."

"I could…" Jack began.

"Hold it right there. You aren't in charge, Ms. Moss is and she says you head for Ohio tomorrow and I'm here to make sure that happens."

"Thanks, but…"

"Go with the flow, buddy, it's been determined."

"Where are you staying? I can get…"

"I'm using your room, partner. I've already got the key to your room. You get a good rest and tomorrow I get you back to Columbus."

"Sit down," Jack directed, albeit weakly, "there's a lot of day left."

Bryon placed Jack's hand on his chest and sat on the edge of the bed.

"I knew you liked guns, I just didn't know you carried one around with you."

"No point in having a gun," Jack said, softly, "unless you're ready, willing, and able to use it."

"You carried a pistol down here?"

"Yeah, it's why I drove. I could bring my Glock with me and not have a problem."

"For what reason? Your son committed suicide."

"Yeah, they said that, but I never believed that for one minute. I came down here thinking that I was going to go after his killer. I knew my son didn't kill himself; he had to have been murdered. If I got to the murderer, I would kill him."

"That conscious of it; that predetermined?"

"I don't think so."

"You're lucky to be alive…"

"I shot his killer, I know I hit him…Hamner. I know I got him. Right now he's looking for someone to fix his wound or wounds. I fired three rounds at him. He made a big target and I don't think I could miss at that range. I was close; he was close to me."

"Well, cowboy, you're going home…without the trophy. You're alive, that's the best you can do right now…"

"We'll get Hamner," Elaine said softly, "it really won't take that long."

Jack's eyes were closed and Elaine motioned Byron towards the door. He dutifully moved from the bed and followed her into the hallway.

"He might not be ready to leave tomorrow," she said.

"I'm prepared for that. We'll head north when he's ready."

22.

As Dixie Hamner had walked into the lobby he saw Jack standing in the vestibule trying to figure out what to do next. He thought of it later, but he should have stopped and retreated. He would have avoided what happened next. But instead, his reflexes took over. He pulled his gun and fired six times at close range. This was a target form he could not miss and would not miss. Glass splattered like flakes of silver paint, wood chips blew away and against the outer wall, and Hamner was certain that Jack Phillips was going to be dead.

There was this sure thought Hamner had that he had killed Jack – the Phillips guy – and he could move on and things would be okay. When three shots came back at him he was stunned. His surprise was as much from Phillips' ability to return fire as from the two bullets that tore through him. He was turned sideways by their impact and sagged against the wall. His knees buckled, but he refused to let himself fall down and staggered back, sliding on the wall, grabbing at his left arm, and pushing his head against the wall as a brake.

Dixie Hamner, aka Lester Reed, aka Arnold Friend, wondered what the hell had happened. Why wasn't Phillips dead? He should be dead; he was close enough to be dead from blasts of a shooter who was very good at shooting.

Hamner stumbled back to his apartment and with some difficulty got his key in the door lock and let himself inside. Once inside the apartment, he went to the bathroom to find out what damage had been done to his body. He pulled off his suit coat and laid it on the toilet. The red stain of blood on his upper left arm caught his eye first. He unbuttoned his shirt as quickly as he could and pulled it off and threw it in the bathtub. The bullet had gone through the inside, fleshy part of his arm near his body. He looked at himself in the mirror and saw that where the bullet struck was at the same level as his heart. A few inches over and he would be dead.

He had no first-aid materials, so he tore a strip from his shirt and bound his arm. It seemed to stop the flow of blood. The second bullet had gone through the waistline fat handle on his right side. It was bleeding, but not like the arm had been. He took another long strip from the shirt and tied that around his waist. It would have to do for now. He slipped on his suit coat and looked in the mirror. He saw the white face, the bleary eyes, and felt the pain. Got to move on.

Hamner grabbed the athletic bag with the cash and stopped by the apartment door. He realized he needed medical care and went back to the bedroom and picked up Doc Colburn's card from the dresser. He'd give the Doc a call. There wasn't much time before the cops would be swarming all over this place and he quickly left the apartment, and went out the rear door of the building. He had thought about going back to the lobby and making sure Phillips was dead, but he had to get moving. Anyway, even if the Phillips guy fired back he figured he still must have hit him and he assumed Phillips would probably be dead by now.

Hamner took a cell phone from the athletic bag and threw the bag in the trunk. He eased behind the wheel and pulled away from the curb. The EMT unit was just pulling up as he left and the sound of sirens in the distance told him that he had moved along in time. He drove for several blocks until he saw a Circle K gas station and convenience-store and pulled through by the pumps. He buzzed down his window and tossed his Arnold Friend and Dixie Hamner cell phones in the trash container and headed for Atlanta.

With the Lester Reed cell phone he had stashed in the cash bag, purchased in Naples, Florida, he reached Doc Colburn.

"Doc, I need your help."

"Daryl not doing well?"

"Naw, me, not Daryl. Not doing so good at all. Couple of spots for you to patch up. Couple of nicks."

"Bullet nicks?"

Hamner didn't answer right away.

"Yeah, like that."

"Come on. Got my address?"

"Yeah, your card. I know where you are anyway."

It took Hamner more than forty minutes to get to Doc's in East Point and the pain had intensified considerably. Hamner had difficulty keeping his head up as he pulled into the driveway and stopped. He struggled to get the car door open and bobbed and weaved to the side door. Most of the house and yard were hidden behind trees and shrubs and he figured he wasn't being watched.

"Didn't think a guy like you would get hisself shot once, let alone getting hit twice."

Hamner winced as Doc probed.

"What'd you figure?"

"Too smart to get shot; too clever to let someone pull on you," Doc said.

"Things happen you don't expect, always."

"True, very true."

Colburn worked on the arm first, cauterized both the entry and exit wounds, and then dressed them. He gave Hamner a shot of something and the pain quickly subsided.

"A little pain medicine to help you."

"Thanks."

"How's Daryl doing?"

"I don't know. Been too busy getting organized to move to Texas. Daryl's coming down there when he gets a little better. I think he'll be okay."

"I think so."

With both wounds dressed and shot with lidocaine, Doc pulled out a cigar, slowly, deliberately clipped the end, and lighted it with an obvious sense of pleasure. He puffed and sent light gray smoke towards the ceiling before he spoke again. Hamner still sat on the kitchen table where Doc had performed his ministrations.

"Sorry about the accommodations. It's what happens when they take your license away. Hospital privileges are not available."

"You did great, Doc, don't worry about it. Thanks."

"Come on. Sit over here on the sofa. Get comfortable for awhile. I don't want you taking off too soon. Just relax. Have a whiskey with me."

Doc turned to the cupboard and pulled out two glasses, then fetched a bottle of Jack Daniels from a sideboard. He poured two inches in each of the glasses. He brought one of the glasses to Hamner.

"Here's to Texas," Doc saluted.

"Here's to Texas," Hamner echoed.

Hamner's drive to Naples, Florida, was a brutal challenge to stay awake and suffer through the pain. Hamner now was Lester Reed, with proper drivers license, auto registration, and deed for a condo. The lidocaine had worn off and his arm and side hurt unmercifully. He could not get in a position that would let him feel comfortable no matter how he situated himself. Doc gave him some pills to ease the pain, but warned they would make him drowsy. He had to stay awake because he wanted to drive all the way through to the condo. Then he could rest, and then he could take the pills.

Mile after mile he looked at the scenery he passed without really seeing what it was. Night came and he concentrated on the road ahead. He made the usual stops, got gas, used the gas station restrooms, and grabbed a snack. Straight from Doc's house to his condo in Naples; almost eleven hours of torture and his frozen grimace showed the strain. He arrived around four in the morning, parked the Cadillac, and hauled the athletic bag inside to his condo unit. He would get the luggage later. He already had a full wardrobe of Florida clothes in the condo. He was exhausted and ached. Once inside, he took one of Doc's pills and fell on the bed. He did not bother to undress and went sound asleep.

Hamner awoke mid-afternoon feeling somewhat better, although his wounds throbbed. He took another of Doc's pills, undressed, showered and shaved, and dressed in slacks and polo shirt. He looked out the bedroom window to a view of palms, a pool, and bright sun. He figured he was home free. A little hair dye, some plastic surgery, and he thought he would not be identified. He did not realize that the Marietta and Atlanta police were already on his trail.

That morning while Hamner was still fully clothed and unconscious on his bed, Elaine and her partner Fred White were with Jack handling their end of the investigation for Larry Davis.

"Hi, you look like you're doing pretty well…"

"I am, Miss Moss, I am…"

"Anyway, you remember Fred White, my partner?"

"Yes, I do indeed."

"We need to ask you some questions. You weren't in such good shape yesterday to answer questions so I waited until this morning. You up to it? You look like you are."

"Yeah, I am."

"You told Larry Davis it was Hamner who shot you, that right?" White began.

"Yes, it was Hamner. I saw the look on his face before he shot. He was shocked to see me, but he reacted damn fast."

"And you reacted damn fast also. Got off how many shots?"

"Three. I think I hit him. I had crouched down and squeezed. One of his got me after that. The first couple missed. He moved back, I could see him, but I was not in shooting position and I was…sort of struggling with my wound."

"You followed him there?" Elaine asked.

"Yeah. I spotted him near police headquarters in Marietta. I was pretty sure he didn't see me."

"You followed his car?" White asked.

"Yeah, the Cadillac. I figured he had switched cars and assumed he would have something like a Cadillac or a Lincoln. I spotted the Cadillac."

"Did you get a plate number?"

It was White again.

"Yes, I did. I memorized it, but figured I might forget it, so I wrote it on a note pad. That way if I lost him and caught up I would be sure to have the right car without trusting my memory."

"You wrote it down?"

"Yeah, it's in my car wherever that is. Probably still by the apartment building."

Elaine's cell phone rang. It was dispatch; there was a lead of sorts. A woman had called in saying that her boyfriend was dying and she knew about Dixie Hamner and the killing of Spencer Colby. Elaine made notes as dispatch reported, asked for uniformed backup be sent to the address of the call, and snapped her phone shut.

"We need to move on this," she said to White, "it might get us somewhere."

"What?"

"Some woman called in about the Colby thing and talked about Hamner. Said her boyfriend was dying, said he had been in some kind of wreck that killed Colby."

"We need to get that license number to Davis," White reminded her.

"Right. Jack where are your car keys? With your belongings here?"

"I guess. I think in that drawer."

Elaine went to the rolling chest near his bed and opened the top drawer. There was Jack's watch, wallet, keys, some loose change, a pen, and his glasses. She pulled out the keys and dropped them on top of the chest.

"We'll talk to you later, Jack. At least I will. Before you leave."

She looked at White and he nodded.

On the drive from Kennestone Hospital in Marietta to Daryl's house in Atlanta, Elaine called Detective Davis.

"Have one of your guys get over to Phillips' room in the hospital and get his car keys. He has the license number for Hamner's Cadillac written down and in the car. It's a Florida plate. I think that's about all he can help us with right now."

"That might be enough."

Davis thanked her and asked her to stay in touch.

Lilly opened the front door almost as soon as Fred White had rapped his knuckles on it. Two Atlanta uniformed were already there in the hallway when White and Elaine entered.

"Come on in. He's dying, look at him, look…"

"Calm down, ma'am, we'll get him to a hospital as soon as we can," White said as he nodded to the two officers.

White stood talking to Lilly in the hallway, getting her name and other information as Elaine went to Daryl on the sofa.

"Hurting bad?"

"I'm dying, I'm going to die. My ribs…I think ribs are broke. I can hardly breath, my lungs are for shit, they're not working right…it's bad. Doc was here but…"

Daryl's eyes rolled back in his head and Elaine thought for a moment that he had died. Then the eyes rolled down and he stared straight ahead.

"Get an ambulance here," Elaine directed to one of the officers.

"Tell her," Lilly yelled from the archway, "tell her what you did. Tell her it was an accident…"

"I didn't mean for him to die…"

"Colby?" White asked.

"We was just supposed to scare him…"

"Hamner got you to do that?" Elaine questioned.

"We was just supposed to scare him."

"Really?" White didn't believe him.

"It was an accident. I wasn't going fast, just enough to give him a good smack…"

"I'll say," White said, "good enough smack to kill him."

"No, it wasn't like that…"

"What did Hamner say?" Elaine leaned in towards Daryl who was breathing heavily.

"He said we should hit his car in the parking lot to give him a warning. Ohhh, ahhh, I think I'm dying, honest."

"Where is Hamner going in Florida?" Elaine pressed.

"Florida…?" Daryl looked puzzled.

"Yeah, he's headed for Florida."

"No, Texas. I'm supposed to meet him in Texas. He has a ranch in Texas, near Waco."

"He has Florida plates on his Cadillac, so, yeah, Florida."

"Cadillac…?"

"Yes, he's driving a Cadillac…"

"No, no, Dixie's got a Mercedes, a…"

"Not now he hasn't…"

The EMT crew pushed their way into the room.

"Take it easy," one of the techs said to Daryl, "we'll have you to the hospital in no time. Where does it hurt?"

The techs listened to a short version of what had happened to Daryl, where he was in pain, and how he was feeling. They then quickly had him onto the stretcher, into the EMT van, and they were gone.

Something Daryl had said stuck with Elaine. A reference to a doctor, a quick mention, but it had registered. A doctor treated Daryl, a doctor known to Daryl and perhaps Hamner. Jack said he was sure he had hit Hamner which would mean that Hamner would need medical care. A medical guy these bozos all knew. Probably illegal, maybe an ex-con, but regardless, someone they trusted to help them.

"Miss…"

Lilly was moving through the hall towards the front door.

"I'm going with Daryl…"

"Hold her officer…"

Before Lilly could get to the front door and before an officer could stop her, Fred White was to her and took her arm and pulled her around to face Elaine.

"Couple of questions and then one of these officers can take you to the hospital."

"What do you want?"

"Daryl said something about a doctor. Who is that?"

"Doc Colburn. He come here and worked on Daryl."

"What's your name, by the way?" Elaine asked.

White still had Lilly by the arm.

"Lilly, Lilly Martin…"

"Tell me, Lilly, where does this Colburn guy have an office?"

"He don't have an office. Uses his house. He used to have an office, but he got busted. Did time, lost his license. Still a damn good doctor, though."

"Where does he live?"

"I don't know…"

"Telephone number…?"

"In my phone book, in the dining room."

Lilly pulled and White went with her, still with a firm grip on her arm. She flipped open the book and called out the numbers as Elaine wrote them down.

"Very good, Lilly, thanks."

"Officers, take Miss Martin downtown and book her for accessory to murder…"

"You said I could go with Daryl."

"I lied. Get her out of here."

Elaine looked around and then got on her cell phone to Headquarters. While she waited for someone to pickup, she directed White.

"Fred, get dispatch to get an officer to the hospital to keep an eye on Daryl and some uniforms here to tape off this place as a crime scene. We also need a crime scene team to check this place out for prints and any other evidence."

White nodded and punched his cell phone.

"Harry," Elaine spoke into the phone, "need your help…"

Elaine gave the man the number Lilly had dictated to her and asked for a check of what address was connected to that number. She clicked off her phone and waited. In a few minutes he was back to her with the address.

Elaine and Fred waited for officers to arrive and secure Daryl's house and then headed for Colburn's.

"This address is in East Point," White said.

"I know."

Elaine was driving.

"We should let them know about this."

"I know."

"Should I call them?"

"No. If we need to get them involved at some point we will. Let's wait. See what doctor Colburn has to say. He knows they're bad guys, but he probably doesn't know much about why Daryl was hurting. I want to know if he treated Hamner…"

"Thanks, I figured that was on your mind."

Colburn answered the door when White knocked. Elaine and Fred showed their badges and backed Colburn into his small living room. He said nothing and viewed them with an impassive look.

"About what?" Colburn asked.

"You are?" White asked.

"Ned Colburn…"

"You're a doctor?"

Elaine stood very close to him as White looked around to make sure no one else was there.

"Yes. I don't currently have a medical license, but you're always a doctor. Always ready to provide medical care."

"For a guy named Daryl?"

"Yes, Daryl Binser. Had a rib injury, minor difficulty."

"He says he's dying," White said.

Colburn looked at White.

"He was going to be fine when I saw him."

"You treated a man who is a felon and you did so without being licensed. That's not good."

White had come back close to Colburn.

"We want to know about your treating Dixie Hamner," Elaine said, "that's why we're here."

Colburn was shaken. He put his hand to his face and his body sagged.

"I'd like a drink."

"What's your usual, doctor; gin, scotch, or bourbon?" Elaine asked.

"Bourbon. In the kitchen."

"Fred, take care of doctor Colburn while I fetch him some bourbon."

Elaine walked to the kitchen, found a glass in the cupboard, and poured from the bottle on the kitchen table.

"Here's your medicine, doctor," Elaine said as she came back to the living room. "Now tell us about Hamner."

Colburn took the glass from Elaine and downed nearly half of the bourbon before he answered.

"He was here yesterday. Two wounds, arm and side, neither one serious, but needed to be treated. Untreated, he could have some problems. I had him rest for awhile and then he left. Said he was headed for Texas and we had a drink on it."

"Did you see his car?" White asked.

"Yes…well, not really. I mean I saw it for a moment or so, but I don't know what kind it was…"

"Color?" Elaine asked.

"Silver, I think…"

"License plates?" White asked.

"I don't know. Probably Georgia, that didn't register with me. I saw him drive away through the window and wasn't paying that much attention. I was just glad he was gone."

Elaine said nothing as she made some notes and White merely stared at Colburn.

"Are you going to report this? I mean Hamner is dangerous, you have to do what he says."

"Right. It would have helped your cause if you had called authorities as soon as he left, but you didn't, so you're screwed."

Elaine flipped her notepad closed.

"Are you going to arrest me?"

"No, but you'll be hearing from us. Don't leave town."

Elaine and White let themselves out as Colburn sat with his bourbon. Elaine's cellphone rang as they walked to their car.

"Moss…"

It was Detective Larry Davis.

"Yeah, Elaine; it's Davis. We got the Florida license plate number Phillips wrote down. And Phillips was right, Hamner is someone else. He's now operating as Lester Reed. That's who the Cadillac is registered to in Naples. The address on the registration is a condo also owned by Lester Reed.

"So much for Hamner going to Texas," Elaine said. "Just a smokescreen."

"You bet it was. We've notified the Naples police and they're on it. They should have Hamner shortly. I'll keep you posted."

"Thanks. You know Hamner probably thinks we're not on to him this quickly…"

"Right, I told the Naples guys that. They could keep him under surveillance and grab him when he leaves his place rather than going after him with a SWAT team. They said they'd take that under advisement. The DEA and FBI boys are also involved so who knows what will happen."

The Naples, Florida, office of the FBI, acting on the basis of a Federal fugitive warrant, coordinated the effort to arrest Walter "Dixie" Hamner, aka Lester Reed. Special Agent in Charge Cameron Willis ordered a team of his Agents to serve the warrant at Hamner's condo. They were backed up by Naples police and three agents from the DEA Naples Task Force.

When the FBI agents rang his bell and knocked on his door announcing they had a warrant for his arrest, Hamner was too stunned to react. He had taken some of the pills Doc had given him and was in a half-stupor. His mind whirled, he had difficulty even imagining the law could be on him so fast. How? How did they get here like this? He had only been here a few hours; he wasn't even rested. What was going on? It was all a jumble in his mind.

The FBI did not wait for Hamner to sort it out or to respond. They battered the door open and had him restrained and cuffed before he could make the decision to get to his pistol.

"How did you know I was here?" Hamner asked, his speech slurred somewhat.

The agents ignored his question as one of them intoned his Miranda rights.

23.

Jack dressed in the clean clothes Byron brought to the hospital. He dressed slowly, contemplatively, deliberately, and with a certain air of derision for his circumstance. Each button was a matter of concentration, each motion a more elaborate movement than normal from underwear to sport shirt, from pants to shoes. Slowly, systematically Jack got himself ready to check out. He wanted no help and grimaced every so often as he went through the motions.

"Hurts, I imagine," Byron said. "Probably want to keep your arm in that sling."

Jack did not respond, but continued his effort.

"I took the liberty of packing the rest of your clothes. They're in the car."

"Thanks."

Jack was finished dressing and moved from the bed to a nearby chair. They were waiting for the paperwork to sign and the mandatory wheelchair. Byron brought the sling to Jack who reluctantly allowed the sling to be slipped over his head. He put his arm in the loop and sat back.

"Elaine is on her way…"

Jack smiled at Byron.

"…she called me."

Jack nodded. There was an uncomfortable silence for a moment.

"I took care of the Marriott…"

Jack smiled again.

"…tipped the concierge…"

Jack laughed.

"Thanks, By, I really appreciate your coming down here and…and taking care of things. I've got to get out of town. It's great you'll drive me back."

"You know, it's okay, Jack…"

Elaine slipped into the room like a fresh breeze and went right to Jack. She bent and kissed him before he could stand. When he did stand, she hugged him tightly without pressing on the wounded shoulder and kissed him again. She did not let go of him, her left side squeezed against his right side.

"Good morning," Jack said.

"Good morning. You look a lot better. How you feel?"

"I hurt a bit, but I'm fine."

"Hey," Byron said, "I'm going to check in with the nurse's station and see where their wheelchair is."

He left the room quickly.

"I miss you already…"

"So you're not unclicked."

"No, I'm connected and somehow we can't…"

She paused and kissed his cheek.

"We can't end. We need to continue. What do you think?"

"Yeah, that's what I think. I don't know how, but that's what I think."

Elaine released her hold on Jack and touched his good shoulder.

"Relax until they get here to release you."

He went back down into the chair and she leaned her hip against the foot of the bed.

"You'll be pleased to know that the FBI and Naples police got Hamner yesterday. Thanks to you for having the presence of mind to write down his plate number, we were able to trace him to Florida. I say we, I mean Davis and his guys in Marietta did. Hamner should be back in Atlanta in a couple of days. He'll stand trial, you will have to testify, and so you will have to be back in town. But I hope sooner than when that business comes up."

"I think that's for sure, but maybe you'll come and see me even sooner than that."

She laughed and turned her hips full on the bed and leaned back and shook her head. She could not imagine herself in this situation with this man. Good God, how could it have come about? Where will it lead? She wondered where these emotions and circumstances would take her. She figured it was a ride she could survive.

"Why," Jack asked, "were you so sure you would get Hamner so quickly?"

"Because guys like Hamner always think they are so smart, that they can confuse the trail to them, that they can get away and hide and no stupid cop can find them. It's the arrogance and the cocksureness that gets them in trouble and gets them caught. He never figured his Florida license number would get fingered. Because of you, it was."

"Well, I guess you were right."

Byron escorted a nurse's aide back into the room. She was pushing a wheelchair with a clipboard of paperwork on the seat.

"Hi, Mr. Phillips, I'm Bonita and I'm going to take you downstairs. But first, I need you to sign and initial some of these papers."

When the papers were taken care of, Bonita sort of helped Jack into the wheelchair. He did not really need much assistance to stand, pivot, and plunk down.

"Let's get rolling," Jack said.

Byron and Elaine followed as Bonita pushed Jack to the elevator and negotiated him to the first floor lobby and out the door. A stretch Lincoln limousine was parked at the curb.

"Where's the car?" Jack asked.

The limo driver jumped out, came around the car, and opened the rear door. He said good morning and gave a wimpy kind of salute.

"Here's the deal, Jack," Byron said, "we're not driving back to Columbus, we're flying. I have a chartered plane waiting for us, and we're going to Columbus the easy, fast way."

"My clothes…"

"In the trunk. Don't worry about a thing. It's all arranged. You deserve it, Jack, you've been through a lot…"

Bonita hovered over Jack as he stood from the wheelchair and slid into the back seat of the limo. Elaine got in beside him. Byron walked around and got in the other door and sat next to Jack. It all happened so swiftly Jack hardly had time to protest or question. Doors closed, driver in, and they were on their way from the hospital.

"You knew about this?" Jack asked, looking at Elaine.

"Yes, Byron told me what he was going to do. It made sense…"

"Quite the extravagance, By…"

"I know, but easier."

They were now moving quickly through traffic, covering the relatively short distance to Dekalb Peachtree Airport, a general aviation facility in northeast Atlanta.

"Thanks for seeing me off," Jack said and reached for Elaine's hand, "this gives us more time together."

"You're so romantic…"

"Yeah, right…"

"The limo will take Elaine back downtown to police headquarters, so you don't have to worry about that…"

"I wondered. Hey, what about my car. We're leaving my car here…"

"Yes, we are," Byron said, "and it is no longer your car. I sold it."

"Sold it…?"

"Yes, to the night auditor of the Marriott. He was thrilled."

"You probably gave it away…"

"Not really. He paid a reasonable price for it. We'll get you a new car when we get back to Columbus. You needed a new car, anyway."

"I hit town a week ago today," Jack said, "a week tomorrow since we met."

"Seems longer than that," Elaine sighed.

"Yeah, it does. A few things have happened…"

"Time flies when you're…"

"Right, don't say it…"

"It's true. Didn't you have some fun?"

Byron laughed and Jack shook his head.

"I don't think I'll comment on that."

They were quiet the rest of the drive. At the airport, the luggage was stowed aboard as Jack, Elaine, and Byron waited in the lounge. Elaine lightly rubbed Jack's left arm which dangled in the sling and held him to her with her other arm. Jack didn't seem to mind the attention.

The call came to board and Jack and Elaine embraced and kissed and Elaine buried her face in his neck. She realized she wanted to cry, but she didn't.

"I don't know how to say good-bye," Jack breathed into her ear, "I guess because I don't want to say good-bye…I don't want to leave."

"Then don't say good-bye," she whispered, "just get on the plane, get home, get well, and call me."

The chartered jet shot up to cruising altitude and Jack eased his seat belt. Byron sat across the cabin from him. They were alone except for the crew. It was truly a private jet ride. They did not speak to each other for almost ten minutes before Byron spoke.

"You were right. Lots happened in a week. I'm sure you never had a stretch of days like this."

"No, and unlikely that I ever will again."

"Shot at and shot. I doubt if that would have happened if you weren't carrying a gun."

"Listen, anti-gun guy, I'd be dead if I weren't carrying a gun…in both situations."

"Maybe…"

Maybe, nothing."

There was more silence between them for a considerable amount of time. Jack started to nod off, lulled by the sound of the engines. His shoulder throbbed, but he ignored that and closed his eyes. Byron was already snoring.

"Through all this bullshit I've really been remiss. Even starting back in the office last week…"

Jack started awake as Byron spoke.

"I haven't told you how sorry I am about your son. I am sorry, Jack, Connie and I both feel for you. It has to be difficult and I haven't expressed that and I wanted you to know how we felt. We're sorry; you have our sympathy and our condolences."

Jack had come wide awake.

"Thanks, By."

"How can I help?"

"Just understand. Be patient. I'll eventually get back in the swing of things, but it might take awhile. I've got to sort everything out. J.W.'s murder, getting dumped by Meg, getting connected to Elaine, meeting with my daughter, Beverly…"

"Dumped by Meg…?"

"Yeah, she called, said it was over."

"Why?"

"I'm not a Negro…"

"What?"

"Let's not even get into it. It's over."

"Okay, you can tell me later."

"Thanks…

"You forgot getting shot…"

Yeah, that, too."

"That's a lot to deal with…in one week."

Byron chuckled.

"And I learned that J.W. was a homosexual…"

Byron stared at Jack, eyebrows raised.

"Yeah, a fag. And, worse than that, he was a criminal. A drug dealer, big time. Yeah, all of that stuff."

"How do you feel…?"

"How do I feel about it? About J.W. being a homosexual? I haven't even processed that. I haven't processed his death yet. There's this sadness that should be in me that isn't there, that hasn't arrived. Send me an email, By, tell me my son was a homosexual, a drug dealer criminal, and he was murdered. Maybe then it will become real. Right now, none of that is real; it hasn't sunken in, hasn't penetrated my…"

Byron waited for Jack to continue.

"I can intellectualize my regret that we never got reconciled. It's a thought process; a stunningly sober thought process without any emotion. All intellectualized and codified and categorized so that there is no emotional pain. I've got to work on feeling the pain, By. Somehow, I need to feel the pain, experience it, and let it go. That's what I have to do."

Byron made no response.

"So, how do I feel about my son being homosexual? That's the real answer you want, that's the answer everyone will want. Death they know about, Meg they can explain, Elaine they say will be a blessing, my wound will heal, and Beverly is a difficult situation and has been for some time. But what is the answer to the big question that cannot be answered. Not by me, at least. As far as I'm concerned, being a homosexual is not a choice, it's who someone is. Buried in the DNA curl is some chromosomic anomaly that makes it so. That's what I believe. I just wish that I had known about it with J.W. a long time ago."

"Would it have made a difference?" Byron asked.

"I honestly don't know, but it might have. Anyway, I regret we never got reconciled. Maybe sometime I'll really be able to feel that and not just intellectualize it."

"Jack, you've always been able to deal with tough stuff. It's one of the reasons I'm glad we're working together in a tough business. And it's one of the reasons Janet and I wanted you to head the agency. You never collapse under pressure. Even the emotional crap that comes along, you just seem to be able to…I don't know…rise above it somehow. Maybe it's your way. The way you deal with an issue like…"

"Like my son's death?"

"Yes, and the rest of it."

"Yeah, the rest of it. What's your take, By, on homosexuality?"

Byron did not answer right away and Jack waited as the question hung out there, unanswered.

"Well," Byron said, finally, "about the subject generally I really had never formed some solid idea like you have. All I know is that we, you and I, have worked with gays all of our careers. Something I've accepted without thinking too much about it. When I was younger, it kind of bothered me, but I got over that and that was it."

"And about J.W.?"

"I wouldn't have figured it. It never ever crossed my mind that he was gay. So it comes as a surprise. And like you, I feel worse finding out that he was a damn drug dealer…"

"Big time criminal with a big time criminal enterprise."

"I'm sorry Jack…"

"I am too."

They were quiet the rest of the flight and didn't speak until they were on the glide path to Bolton Field in Columbus. Jack dozed and Bryon ran through a new client proposal. The order came from the cockpit to fasten seat belts.

"I have a limo for you here, also. One for me, too. You're on your own; I don't think I need to see you home."

"By, you've been great. I really appreciate it. And, yeah, I can get myself home."

They shook hands and hugged and held on to each other longer than one might have guessed, but the emotion was intense and neither man wanted to break down and reveal the depth of his sensitivity. Byron helped Jack into his limo and he waved slightly as they drove away.

The limo driver carried Jack's luggage to his condo and into the living room.

"That's good right there, thanks. It'll be fine."

Jack handed the driver a twenty, but the man demurred.

"It's all taken care of. Mr. Adams took care of everything."

"I guess he did. Thanks."

Jack walked down to Mrs. Brady's. She knew he was coming, she knew from Byron Adams when he would be getting home.

"I should offer you tea, which I would usually do, but I've made you a Manhattan. The bourbon is very good. I know it's very good because Carl, Mr. Brady, used to drink it exclusively. I hadn't had any in the house since he died, but I got some this week. I wanted to be prepared when you came back. I've followed everything on the news. I told you to be careful and you didn't listen to me, Mr. Gunslinger. You're lucky to be alive."

"Well, I'm not so sure…"

"No, you are."

"I don't think it's that dramatic.

"Sit down here. I have your drink ready. Mr. Adams alerted me. How's your shoulder?"

"It's okay, going to be fine. Not much pain, but I'm aware it's there…the wound. Where's Millie?"

"She's asleep on my bed and couldn't care less that you're back. But I care. Sit, sit, and relax."

Jack sat at the table in the warm, pleasant breakfast nook of Mrs. Brady's kitchen and wondered about this woman he had so taken for granted. He suddenly realized she was much more than the simple, silly old lady who readily took care of his cat. She placed the Manhattan in front of him. He realized for the first time that she was attractive, that she had certainly been a beauty when she was younger, and there was this calm, earthy quality about her he had never noticed.

"In honor of Carl, whose birthday it will be in eleven days and in respect for your loss and in celebration of your return, I am having a drink with you. It's the first one I've had in some time; since New Year's Eve, I guess. It too is a Manhattan, but watered down some from the one I made for you. For yours, I used Carl's recipe."

Jack held his glass up and extended it towards Mrs. Brady. The glasses clinked and some bourbon was spilled and ignored.

"Thank you. Your gesture means a great deal to me. Cheers."

"Why should it?" she asked.

It was a shocking response, but Jack did not flinch.

"Because, Mrs. Brady, this whole episode changes things, brings things into perspective…"

"That may be, but I'm sure you never thought about me once since you left…"

"Not true. I thought about you today on the flight home…"

She chuckled.

"What do you think of your drink?"

Jack sipped his drink a second time.

"Good, very good."

"Thank Carl."

"I do."

Mrs. Brady took a long, steady swig from her drink, didn't swallow, and placed the glass onto the table. She tilted her head back and then let the fluid slide into her throat.

"You had quite an adventure…"

"I did, yes…"

"Never pictured you with a gun. I thought of you as Mr. Advertising Man…and a ladies man."

"It really didn't occur to me to tell you about it."

"You were pretty silly to do what you did, don't you know."

"I guess."

"I'm glad you made it through everything okay."

"Thanks, I am, too."

Neither of them said anything for a few minutes as they sipped their drinks.

"These are special Manhattan cherries."

Jack nodded and pulled at his drink.

"Hasn't caught up with you yet has it?"

She asked the question in the nicest way, soft, caring, and fully appreciative of his mood and circumstance.

"No."

"You're one of those all-in-his-head guys, I figure."

Jack smiled.

"Yeah, I live in my head. It's the way I do business, it's the way I create, and it's the way I deal with life's bullshit."

"Totally Teflon."

She looked out the window and took another big swig of her drink and this time finished it.

"Carl was Teflon, that's how I recognized it in you. No remorse, no panic, no worries."

"I'm not totally emotionless as your reference might imply. I went to Atlanta because I cared; it was an emotional reaction."

Millie sauntered into the kitchen, stopped to stretch, and sat looking at Jack. He called her and she came to him and rubbed and meowed and cocked her head to be scratched.

"Did you miss your cat?" Mrs. Brady asked.

Jack rubbed Millie some more before he answered.

"I don't think so, but I am glad to see her."

"You were busy," she said.

"I was."

Mrs. Brady rose, took Jack's nearly empty glass, and went to the counter where the bourbon bottle sat. She mixed another Manhattan and put it in front of him.

"Thanks."

"I'm already drunk," she said, "and I've had two sips."

"Your glass is almost empty."

She looked at it and nodded.

"Then I deserve to be drunk."

"I guess so. Look, I've got to…"

Jack's cell phone rang.

"Who is it?" Mrs. Brady asked.

Jack looked at the phone.

"My lady friend in Atlanta."

"Don't answer it."

He started to press the receive button, but she placed her hand over his.

"Don't answer it. Talk to her later."

Jack put the phone back in his pocket.

Mrs. Brady stood, came around the table, put her arms around Jack's shoulders, and pressed her cheek to his. She gently kissed the side of his face and nuzzled to him.

"It's okay to cry, Jack; your secret will be safe with Millie and me. We won't tell."

He bent his head forward and his shoulders sagged.

"I know, I know."

He began to sob and he shook slightly and she held him and Mrs. Brady cried with him.

Printed by Libri Plureos GmbH in Hamburg, Germany